THE CALAMITIES

BRUCE DUNDORE

authorHOUSE®

AuthorHouse™
1663 Liberty Drive
Bloomington, IN 47403
www.authorhouse.com
Phone: 1-800-839-8640

Published by AuthorHouse 06/18/2014

ISBN: 978-1-4969-1525-2 (sc)
ISBN: 978-1-4969-1524-5 (e)

ENTRY 1

ERECTILE DYSFUNCTION AND THE USE OF MECHANICAL DEVICES TO ENCOURAGE FUNCTIONAL ERECTIONS.

The male population in the area of study no longer suffers from erectile dysfunction. The progress of both pharmaceutical and mechanical therapies has rendered this condition completely treatable, and now just a minor nuisance along the lines of Restless Leg Syndrome and Autism, afflictions of note in the first ten years of the century. However, The Institute decided that the treatment of Subject's erectile dysfunction was to be mechanical, as the chemicals in the pharmaceutical treatments might have unknown side effects due to the Subject's biology, and the questionable safety standards at the state-controlled pharmaceuticals. A complication to the treatment of ED is that great numbers of the female population in the researched area – perhaps as a result of The Calamities – were no longer interested in having anything to do with the manipulation *of* and penetration *by* the penis. It was imperative that The Institute find a female with the traditional sexual desire found in pre-Calamities. The Institute's research generally found the numbers of such females greater among lapsed Catholics. It was imperative that we have a verbal and mental record of the use of the device by the Subject and the attitude to the device by his new partner, and so, via hidden sound and visual recording devices and other advanced technologies, we are able to make a day-by-day record of the Subject's experiences. These, his real-time musings and observations of attitudes of the population he moves

1

around in, will provide a candid, non-research environment to help inform the data. These entries will be culled and edited into what will be the BOOK OF JOHN, one of several books in a larger collection of observational treatises that The Institute will use to advise regarding either the evacuation from or the continued habitation of the planet.

—Thanks to my GOBOYGO Ultra-Lite Penis Pump, I'm in full salute.

Marsha flips the HARD switch from the ON to the OFF position. She pulls the plexi-shaft off my newly rigid cock, drops the contraption to the bedroom floor, straddles me and directs my manhood, my horn of pleasure, my mechanically manipulated magnificence, into her vagina, which is lubricated with the patented GOGIRLGO mint-scented imitation petroleum jelly with ORGASMA-TINGLE.

Marsha has two minutes to achieve orgasm. That's the time it takes the vessels of my penis to lose blood and return to the limp condition, and me to restful sleep, which I need, which we all need, especially if you've been in a coma.

My name is John Smith. I'm semi-fresh from a coma I came out of five months ago. I don't remember much about my life before the coma, so I can't say my penis ever functioned like I've been told it's supposed to function. I can't remember normal. Not anymore.

My Docs say I was quite the ladies' man. Good to know there's a legacy of cocksmanship. Probably ran in my family if I knew who they were, which I don't, which is another result of the coma and The Calamities.

Back to the matter at hand:

I've read *Erections for Dummies*. Not appropriate to my condition. Machinery is an important part of my sexual behavior now, like hot rods were for teenagers sometime in the Age of Black and White.

My Docs refuse to prescribe any of the penis drugs as I might experience all the contraindications these drugs and pomades warn about – sweating, shortness of breath, constipation, restless leg syndrome, oily discharge, rash, heart palpitations, adult-onset diabetes, tumors, or a six-hour erection – and who the fuck in their right minds needs that litany of shit.

I have my machine. Marsha's gotten used to it. *Girls love guys with machines* is what I say.

I met Marsha as soon as I came out of the coma. She said she liked my confidence. She also says I'm distant.

I don't know if I'm capable of love. If I was capable of love before the coma, maybe it's the coma that makes it hard for me to feel what Marsha says she feels for me.

Recently, Marsha likes to pump the GOBOYGO herself. Since she can't get me up wearing lingerie or talking dirty, manning the pump is the closest she gets to seducing me. She says it's fun because a man's junk is different from a woman's and the pump turns my dick into a shape she can use. She says it's like playing with dolls. Women love dolls. And machines. That's what she tells me.

She gets upset that I can't achieve orgasm, but that's also a result of the coma. I have watched some of the CRL-sponsored pornographic digi's with Marsha – man/woman, woman/woman, man/man, man/woman/man, woman/man/woman, man/pig, woman/horse, woman alone, horse alone – in her attempts to get me hard, and have seen many scenes of voluminous ejaculations, but they don't do anything for me. That'll change. When I get better, it'll be like I spent a year at a yogurt farm.

*****

About five months ago, my eyes slammed shut and I drove off the road in the middle of the night somewhere out in Bakersfield, California. I was driving a 4-Chin – an Asian automotive rattletrap – and it smashed into a huge solar station. My doctors said they had to cut away the doors and roof to pry me out.

I have no one except Marsha. My family was incinerated at a shopping mall in the last attack by the Ottawan Separatists over ten years ago, so there is no one to tell me about me or show me pictures of me before the coma.

Once a week, Marsha fills in my historical cavity as it relates to The Calamities. A top ten hits history lesson. It hurts her to tell those stories. She's sweet to try, but she lost her whole family in the firebombing of Sacramento, and lost her best friend when she was struck by an errant piece of satellite that had descended to Earth while she was taking a bath. A fucking fluke. Imagine, soaking in the tub, getting all wrinkly and sleepy, and the next thing you know, you hear a deafening crash and then that's it. Over. Cut to black. Life is a bitch and a half and you better like what you have now. You better appreciate it. Better not sit around and mope 'cause it's not perfect. 'Cause it's never perfect. Nothing is anymore, if it ever was.

Marsha orgasms. And cries. With tears. I love the taste of them. Salty. Briny. Makes me warm. Gives me energy. Thank god for the little things in life.

"Do you love me, John?" she asks as she rocks back and forth on my newly hard penis. "Cause I fucking love you. I love getting your cock hard and fucking it."

She calls my penis "cock." She likes how it sounds. I like how she says it. It does sound harder than penis. Consonant rich at both ends, it sounds like it comes with its own exclamation point even when spoken softly. "Dick" is another word that sounds harder than penis. "Cock" and "Dick" are the nastier, brawling, big brothers of "Penis," always ready to spit in your eye and get into a tussle. If you got a small one, you call it a cock and it instantly sounds bigger.

Two minutes. Orgasm achieved. Right on schedule. Marsha catches her breath. She's clammy from sweat. She leans forward and I lick the parts of her that are the saltiest. She's got very active sweat glands. I think she senses when I want salt and can sweat it out at will. She tells me it's strange I lick her like I do. But I love the salt in the sweat.

Marsha wipes herself and tries to fool herself into thinking her wetness is me. But it's not. She sits on the edge of the bed and looks at me with eyes that stare right through me, like I wasn't there. It's as if when my penis returns to its limp state, I start to fade away. Sometimes a man is just a dick, in the eyes of a woman.

She complains to me that I don't let her in, that I'm closed off and cold. She also says I'm crude sometimes. I can't help that. I'm not hoity-toity, so what? I'm street. Real. A mensch. A regular guy. With a machine to make his dick hard.

Fuck it. I feel fine. I'm happy. My girlfriend tastes like salt.

ENTRY 2

THE CALAMITIES AND THE RAPID DETERIORATION OF THE PLANET.

B eginning in the early part of the 21st century, there was the attack called 9/11 – which was essentially the calendar day the attack happened and it happened in three different places so the existing media couldn't call it The World Trade Center Attack or The Pentagon Attack – which were just two of the places it happened. The World Trade Center Pentagon and Shanksville, Pennsylvania, Attacks had no resonance, so the media just called it by the date that it happened. The Institute believes it was on this date that the media became less imaginative, as they might have given the disaster a much catchier name – like Plane Death Day or Run-Away-Run-Away Day. The Institute has tested these names and found them to be 33% more memorable. After the 9/11 incident, the Empire of the United States suffered what can only be deemed a national psychosis, and so unsettled the rest of the world that there were, in rapid succession, the Economic Collapse of 2008, the disasters of 4/14 in France, 6/17 in Stockholm, and 1/21 in Shanghai. Each of these was also named by the media and politicians of the Empire of the United States. Over one hundred fifty-two thousand people died in those events. These were followed by the Months of Rioting worldwide that resulted in over fifty thousand more deaths and about forty billion dollars in property damage. Then came the nuclear attack on Seattle and the Northwest, the plague in New York, and the series of natural disasters of earthquakes, hurricanes and tornadoes, drought, sandstorms, flooding, and the great asteroid storm of 2028, which destroyed wide swaths of both the West Coast of North America and parts of the southern tip of South America. A huge hole in the ozone made most of Canada uninhabitable, and three quarters of what was called Greenland melted. When the oceans flooded every coastal city on the planet in the space of one year, the naysayers and lesser educated finally gave up their resistance to the concept of a changing climate. In this forty-year time span, approximately thirty million people died from either the multiple wars, natural disasters, radiation, food poisoning, terrorism, murder, or suicide. The situations continue to cause death, further deterioration of the atmosphere, and tremendous psychological strain on the inhabitants of the planet. It is, in the words of one noted historian at an online technical university, "Some serious shit."

—My coma has pretty much wiped the shelves of my memory clean as concerns The Calamities. I have some vague idea, random images in my head, made dull and blurry by the coma, like my memories were sitting in a jar of warm skim milk. You know something is floating around, but you really can't tell what it is.

Marsha has done her best to bring me up to date, but I don't feel her horror, her loss, her anxiety about what happened in the past or what might happen in the future. She wants me to be more aware, so when she talks about them, I can join in and we can have a conversation. Right now, I just nod and smile. Honestly, that's what I thought women wanted you to do when they talked about something painful. Just listen. I read that somewhere, or saw it in a digi, as there isn't all that much worth reading anymore. I want someone to listen to me too.

That's why I have a dog. Her name is Lassie.

Marsha puts her robe on and steps on Lassie's paw.

"Damn it! Stupid dog!" she screams.

Lassie doesn't acknowledge her paw getting stepped on. She just calmly shifts her body out of Marsha's path.

Lassie is a Fru-Fru, which is a breed of dog no bigger than a dowager's purse. They were bred to keep in small apartments, and to only eat the pellets they shit. It was known as a "sustainable" breed. The only thing about with them is that, generally, their breath stinks, but that can be overcome with several drops a day of eucalyptus oil.

Marsha thinks it's funny I named her Lassie. I didn't name her. My Docs did. The dog came pre-named. She was a gift to me by my Docs after the coma. My mood Doc, Doc Manning, told me she would be a comfort to me psychologically, and my medical Doc, Doc Peeples, said that a dog would help keep my brain active with routine. They said it would be good for me to engage the dog in my thinking, to talk to it about my thoughts and observations, as that would aid in jogging my memory, and turning the experiences and observations I have into memories. I'm good with that. I listen to Marsha. Lassie listens to me.

"Collies are named Lassie," she said. "Timmy? Lassie? Lassie Come Home? It's a documentary, John! We studied it in lower school," she says and I have no fucking idea what she is talking about.

Lassie is a watcher. Not a watchdog. A serious watcher. She watches every interaction I have with people we have at the apartment, or when we go out. She especially watches Marsha, particularly when we have sex. At first, Marsha would put the dog out of the bedroom, but Lassie knew how to open the door.

I never knew how a dog that small could reach the door knob, but Doc Manning says it's because before they got her, she was a circus dog in Ecuador and learned how to do all sorts of nifty tricks. She can roll over and play dead, sure, but what I've seen her do that really made an impression was balancing a ball on her nose while she was watching a digi about seals. She did it better than a seal. In fact, I caught her a couple times imitating shit she saw on the digi's. Like the one time she was watching some cop and robber show, and a robber was hugging the wall, creeping along it so he wouldn't be seen by a helicopter above. Lassie got on her hind legs and crept along the hallway wall, just like the robber. Impressive. I could've sold tickets to that.

Marsha would lock her out of the bedroom. But Lassie would howl and that would piss Marsha off. With the sound of the penis pump and the dog howling on the other side of the bedroom door, you can imagine it wasn't the sexiest atmosphere no matter how many candles I lit. So she gave up on Lassie not being able to watch, and then, after a while, she started making something out of it. She'd take her clothes off, like at the strip clubs that used to be all over the place at the turn of the century, and dance around in front of the dog. She stopped when Lassie actually did a better lap dance move than she did.

Lassie would watch us fuck, like she was on a grant to observe creatures in the wild, like she was grading us, taking notes to bring back to her fellow circus dogs to incorporate into the act should the clowns go on strike.

"It's time for my morning run," I say to both Marsha and Lassie.

"Stay in this morning. Just this once," Marsha pleads, "I'll make you an omelet with some "I Can't Believe It's Not Bacon.""

I like phony bacon as much as the next guy, but Lassie has my sneakers in her mouth and waits by the door. Gotta run.

Feet blur beneath me. Lassie does her short-legged trot by my side. We cross Sunset Boulevard, into the foothills of Hollywood, where the air is fresher and the cars are fewer and so it's safer. It's just after sunrise. The sky's bright red. I can hear the sound of distant morning ambulances busy taking the previous night's suicides, accidents, and death by natural causes to the crematoriums. The night is filled with unlucky shit.

My doctors said the running and talking out loud to Lassie would be good. I figure the running keeps the blood moving and so feeds the brain and so feeds my memory. I tell Lassie all the things Marsha told me about this fucked-up world. Sometimes repeating the stories made them weirder, like how did we get ourselves in this shit storm, then I remember that a lot of it had to do with actual shit storms. I think the dog really understands what I say, as occasionally, on some really strange piece of history, she would turn her head and give me a look that said, "Really?" but in a Dog way. Circus dogs might be the best kind to have.

"Let's review, OK Lassie?" I say between breaths. "We have the water wars with Canada, the Swiss underground and their suicide bombers, the Christian Wars in the south and west, the Nationalist Militias in the north, and the battle against Islam, now going into its sixtieth year, and the Digi-Devices are doing a story on the new game of full-contact chess on Sunday."

Suddenly, I realize I am alone.

I stop, and see Lassie at the bottom of the hill checking out some homeless soul passed out on the sidewalk. She is staring right at him. He comes to and waves her away. She doesn't move, and just sniffs the refuse and vomit around the man.

She'll catch up. She's interested in the world and what I have to say about it.

There's a pack of coyotes up ahead. Canyon mutts. Canine cannibals.

They've grown twice their size due to the chemicals and hormones in the food scraps and medications people threw away. We have drugs for everything and people piss so much out it makes a strange brew of the water supply.

They surround me. They yelp, growl, foam at the mouth. They circle me, their red-yellow eyes like small, angry laser beams. I fucking hate coyotes. But I'm a confident man, a real cocksman, and they will sense a superior creature. Unless they are all hopped up on steroids, which are being consumed like candy by the elderly, those with bad bladders, who piss steroidal urine into the water supply, which gets lapped up by coyotes. Serious muscle milk.

"Lassie," I call, "C'mere, girl!" If she shows up, maybe they'll attack her and I can get away or run to a house. I can get another dog. Maybe one that hadn't worked in the circus. Maybe one not from South America. But a dog nonetheless. One Marsha might like.

I feel a tug at my hand. It's the first brave coyote, trying to show the others what it's like to approach a full-grown man.

"Shit!" My index finger's a bloody nub, sheared clear off, right through the bone. Surgical. Precise. I feel a sudden warmth in the hand. No pain. It's like someone put a hot towel around my finger. Yeah, I got a pack of dumb shit coyotes on the juice. Worst kind. They've been taking kids and medium-sized dogs recently. Pulling them right out of their strollers and back yards. Now they want me. Fuck 'em.

The pack fight over the finger, two of them locking their teeth on it and pulling it in two at the knuckle.

The smell of my flesh and blood makes the others forget I'm a man of some size. I'm just meat now. They race around me, yelping that horrible sound, and they nip at my snacked-from hand. They bite at the wrist, and then three of them sink their teeth in my bicep and shoulder. I kick. "MOTHERFUCKERS!" I spin around, swing them off, and the others corral me, circling, yelping, eyes and tongues on my blood. I fall. They come at me, barks, growls, snorts, and snarls. I can hear flesh tearing away from me. "MOTHERFUCKERS!" I scream again.

I can see a tendon stretch from their mouths to my shoulder. I see the leader of the pack run up the street with my arm in his mouth as the others escort him as if they were his security detail.

Then…Lassie. She leaps over me and runs at them. They turn and know they are about to get some great Latin food. Circus dog! Yum.

Then she lets out a howl I have never heard from a dog before. It's a high-pitched siren. A scream like a little girl's with tremendous pipes alerting the authorities to an assault by her minister, or something I remember from an ancient digi about alien body-snatching with people screaming this weird sound every time they sensed someone not transformed to their own. Strange image in my head. Maybe from loss of blood. Gotta keep my shit together. I am a confident man.

The coyotes shake their heads and blood sprays from their ears and noses. The leader drops my arm, and staggers around like a drunk on a bender. The others are in a state of complete disorientation. They fall, get up, fall again, their legs turned to putty. They cower and crawl on their bellies toward Lassie, begging for forgiveness, or like they were approaching a god, their tongues lapping the blood that pours from their noses.

The god Lassie continues her shriek. Then she stops, abruptly, and the absence of her howl is replaced by the whimpering of the coyotes. They sound like a litter of kittens. They sneeze the blood out of their noses. Then they run up the hill and disappear. Lassie takes my arm into her mouth, turns to me, and I know she is telling me to follow her.

*****

Goddamn it. My fucking arm is in my dog's mouth.

I'm up. I fall. Up again, but my left side, the one with an arm, takes me in its direction. I stagger to the left, pulled by the weight of it. My right side is empty. It's got no say in this. I have no counterbalance on that side of my body. I fall.

I'm up. I veer to the left again.

I'm off-kilter. Fuck. I fall, slow head-over-sneakers tumble. A tree stops me. Something in my stomach. I open my mouth and a boatload of thick liquid pours out. Mucus and blood and maybe some "I Can't Believe They're Not Tacos" from last night. I don't feel good. Not good. Not good at all. Never felt worse. Wish I were in a coma. Blood drips out of the mass of ripped flesh where my right arm was pulled out and I can feel it descend across my chest and down to the elastic on the waist of my jogging shorts. It's wonderfully warm. The colors of the sky are beautiful. The sounds of the city are gone. I look at my sneakers. My sneakers are pretty.

I hear myself breathing. It sounds good. Air going into the lungs and then coming out the mouth or nose, carrying with it a tad of saliva and my snot, and I feel my lungs struggle to breathe, and blood seeps out of my nose. I wipe it with the back of the hand they didn't take.

Follow Lassie. Follow the dog. Do this!

The dog stands at the corner, my arm in her mouth. I have to find a way to balance myself. Marsha is a good seamstress, always patching and fixing things. She will sew my arm back on. Maybe tape it back in place. But I must get home. Too much bleeding. That can get nasty.

I open my mouth again and more thick blood chokes out.

I sweat. My blood smells like cotton candy.

I lean to the right so I can fight the drift to my armed side. No good. I fall, catch myself with my left hand.

Idea: I will do this sideways, like a crab. Turn my left side to the direction I'm going and fall all the way home. But it'll be in the right direction. This makes sense. This is good. I'm a smart fucker, a real problem solver, even in difficult times.

Here we go. Up. Lean. Good. I stumble toward Lassie. She trots ahead. Now I'm jogging sideways, following my left arm. I think I can complete my run this way. Put in that mile. I feel OK. Numb, a little woozy. Maybe I can complete my workout at home. I'll do deep knee bends for leg strength. I'll do pushups for my upper body. I'll pump and fuck Marsha and eat a dessert, apple cobbler, with nuts, or just some ice cream, or maybe a slice of "I Don't Believe Your Mother Baked This Cake."

But the blood fills my mouth. Dammit, if it weren't for the blood in my mouth, I could finish the mile.

My front door. Lassie drops my arm on the welcome mat and barks.

I'm sure she wants to show Marsha what she brought home. Other dogs in the neighborhood bring home squirrels or rats and dump them on the doorstep, seeking approval from their master for a handful of kibble. Lassie was never interested in other dogs. Never bothered to sniff their asses. And they never bothered to sniff hers. In fact, they always ran from her.

I think South American circus dogs might have a very superior attitude to other non-circus dogs. I understand Argentinians are very narcissistic. Maybe Lassie was originally from Argentina before she joined the circus in Ecuador.

The door opens. Marsha opens her mouth, and it looks like she's screaming, her eyes going from arm to dog to me and back again, but no sound comes out.

"Get the pump!" is what I scream, but I can't hear myself either.

ENTRY 3

INCIDENT TO SUBJECT JOHN AND A PROFILE OF THE COUNCIL OF RULES AND LAWS.

P RE-ENTRY: *The Institute has assessed the situation to Subject John and is awaiting further developments. This was an unplanned event, so there is no contingency as regards the project. But Doctors Manning and Peeples feel it will not impact the successful execution of the research and, in fact, might add another dimension. Let us return to the cultural and societal overviews to help inform the reader on the Subject's observations.*

ENTRY: The central agency regulating all interactions among the citizenry since the second collapse of the Empire's government calls itself The Council of Rules and Laws (CRL). It is responsible for – with other "lesser" agencies – roads, medical care, education, the network, all communications, safety, food quality, travel and transportation, garbage pick-up, water, air quality, defense, offense, weapons development, and energy. The Council is comprised of seven men and two women. They meet six days a year to ensure efficiencies of decision making. The shorter the meetings, with a quota of five decisions per meeting, the more effective they believe they are. There is very little debate. In fact, The Institute has it on good authority that most decisions are made by drawing pieces of paper marked Yes or No from an opaque box. The Institute has come to the conclusion via objective study and analysis that they are not very effective due to their lack of meeting more often and the length of each meeting. The Institute has found they would be more effective if they met just three more days a year. The CRL has informed The Institute they would take its findings under consideration, once they find the time. The Institute receives payment from the Council for these findings, which it uses to pay the Subject and as cash flow for its research. The female members of the CRL generally serve coffee.

—"John?"

It's Doc Peebles – medical – in my dream.

I see his face looking at me. He smiles.

"John?"

It's Doc Manning – mood – joining in. They both look at me and smile. Then I hear Marsha sob. Her sobs are real. They end the dream. And then, of course, it's not a dream. Never was. This is real. I'm in The Institute hospital.

It's calm. Smells nice. I feel fine. The coyote incident was the dream. This is real. I must have passed out. Marsha must have pumped too hard. I had a massive decrease in blood flow to my big head due to blood flow to my littler one.

I'm having a feeling like the feeling I had when emerged from the coma, only here, I can remember things, like my dream about the coyotes ripping the shit out of my arm. Fuck! That was scary.

Was I hit by a car? Did I have a heart attack while running? Heart attacks are common. I remember Lassie and her high-pitched sound, and the coyotes, red-eyed, bloody snouts. A very interesting dream. Never had a dream as vivid as that.

Time to get up and treat my guests like a proper host and find out why Marsha is crying. I need to find out why I'm in the hospital, and what time is lunch because I am very hungry.

Elbows on mattress, push up. Let's go. Okay that's not happening. My arm must be asleep. Again…

Elbows on mattress, push up. What the fuck? My cerebellum should have automatically clicked on this and made it happen. My left elbow pushes me up and rolls me over to my right side. Nothing on my right side bolsters me. Somehow, I am not communicating effectively to my right arm. I have to focus now.

I struggle to get my right elbow in place to push up, but I can't feel it. It must have fallen asleep. I will have to massage it awake.

"Stay calm, John," Doc Manning says.

"You're safe here, John," Doc Peebles says.

"John, it was horrible," Marsha says.

My Docs look at Marsha and make a face like she just stole a bunch of rare cookies from the rare cookie jar. She is way over the top, face soaked in tears, and that just makes me horny to lick them off. It's a salt fest on her face, streaming down in rivulets, dripping off her chin, shiny, wet satisfying salt. A banquet, her face is all wet from tears. It would be an orgy for my tongue.

"Marsha, come here," and she does and I lick her face like a dog licks his nuts and she pulls away from me and now stands in the corner of the room under a digi-screen. She cries even louder. The picture on the screen, sound off, is of a fire at sea. So with her crying and people getting burned alive on a boat, jumping off into oily waters, creating even bigger fires, there is a lot of tension in the room.

"What the hell is wrong with you?" She points to my right arm, like there is something on it, like a bug or something and I should brush it off. So I try to brush whatever it is that is bothering her off my right arm and for some reason, I can't find my right arm. Of course, my hospital gown is white and the sheets are white and the room is white so it must be under the sheets and I can't see it because there is so much white around me.

I pull the sheet off, but the sheet isn't covering my arm. There isn't an arm. There is nothing but the end of my shoulder. White bandages cover it, and a yellow, milky substance stains the bandages. This sucks. This sucks big time. This was not in the plans. This was not part of the journey.

"Just a little medicine for the wound, John," says Dr. Peebles.

"Apparently, you were attacked by coyotes," says Dr. Manning.

"That was a dream," I tell them, and Marsha howls with tears again, like she is having the biggest orgasm she ever had. Which would make me happy.

"John, you were attacked by a band of hormonally enhanced coyotes and they tore your arm out at the shoulder," Dr. Peebles explained, "Lassie tried to bring the arm for a reattachment, but it was very damaged, very torn up, the nerves and blood vessels frayed and many of them completely destroyed. The arm itself had lost a lot of blood and was dying. It just became an impossible situation. Do you concur, Dr. Manning?"

"Absolutely," Dr. Manning concurs.

Marsha is silent, her eyes like little steamed dumplings we get at the restaurant around the corner.

"Will you be serving dumplings for lunch?" I ask Dr. Peebles.

"If that is what you'd like, John. We can order in."

Good. I'm hungry. Lose an arm, gain an appetite. Life goes on.

ENTRY 4

FOCUS GROUPS AND INFORMATION GATHERING FOR A BETTER AND BRIGHTER FUTURE.

The Institute employs Subject to moderate its weekly focus groups. This method of information gathering was adopted by The Institute to learn more in face-to-face settings with members of the populace about coping mechanisms and survival strategies for the future. It is a time-honored technique that many corporations have used in the past to test strategies for communications and product development. The Institute reports its findings once a month to the CRL on CRL-sponsored projects towards informing them should they want to fund programs or agencies to aid in the well-being of the general population. On other days, we test new flavors of butter and syrups. We also test the efficacies of CRL-formulated diversionary desserts. There is a direct corollary between the responses received and the quality of snacks offered the participants. The Institute will often re-test participants, this time offering them richer, sweeter, and saltier snacks, and find their positive responses increase seven percentage points. The Institute is curious, in the case of Subject, to his reactions and data to his adaptation to his new post-coma and erectile dysfunctional world. Now that he is absent an arm, The Institute is interested in seeing peer reaction to the double blind of no erection, no appendage. At this point in his journey, The Institute hasn't resolved how to expose Subject's erectile dysfunction to the groups. The arm they will see. We're not sure Subject should show them his penis.

—"You have strong healing tendencies," says Doc Peebles. I think that Doc Peebles and Manning are two of the smartest people I know. Sharp these guys are. Mental giants. Odd at times, due to their visible curiosity to everything they encounter every day; like it was the first time each time they did something. Pouring coffee, they seem to marvel at how the coffee pours. Watching someone comb their hair mesmerizes them. Shaking someone's hand seems to give them great pleasure.

I work for them. I work in a focus group research company. Doc Peebles is not just my medical doctor, he is also my dentist. Doc Manning handles any personal issues I might have psychologically. He also repairs my car.

It's wonderful to have every aspect of your life attached to the place you work. One stop and you get all your stuff taken care of. Marsha thinks it's strange. I think she's jealous. I tried to get her a job at The Institute, but she didn't pass the personality profile. Too high strung. But that's probably what makes her taste so salty.

*****

"You'll need therapy, John," says Marsha. "I know a good therapist."

"Doc Manning takes care of me," I tell her. "This is no big deal."

"It's my friend's therapist," she continues. "His father had his leg amputated after he got injured in The San Francisco Riots," she says as she picks at the skin in the palm of her hand. She does that when she is nervous. Picks the skin clear off. It gives her hands a rough feel. Not so good on my cock. That may have contributed to her not being able to get me hard with her hands.

I can tell Docs Peebles and Manning make Marsha nervous. They treat her like a little girl. But they are doctors, and doctors are superior to other citizens, right? Otherwise, why would we listen to them?

"We can handle John's needs right here…" Manning says and drifts off because he can't remember her name.

"Marsha," I say, and he picks up on it.

"Yes, Marsha. John is in good hands with us."

"He might have some phantom pain," Marsha says and I could tell it was something she just learned off her InfoDevice.

Doc Peebles gives Manning a knowing smile and throws a dismissive one Marsha's way and says, "We don't believe in the concept of phantom pain at The Institute."

"Well, you better 'cause it's a fact," Marsha snaps. "John, get some real help. I can ask around." I wish she didn't snap at them like that. These are my bosses and doctors. You don't snap at doctors. They could royally fuck you up, you snap at them. "Marsha! I'll be OK here. The arm will grow back."

*****

Honestly, I don't know what I said that set her off, but she went over the top with that, like if I had just killed her goldfish or kitten or one of the types of animals that people get very upset about when they die or you kill them.

"That's crazy! You need help!" Marsha screams between catching her breath and sobbing frantically.

"We'll take care of him, Marsha. It's best you rest, John," says Manning in his velvet voice, almost monotone, certainly calming.

"What the hell's the matter, Marsha?" I ask. "Things grow back. Plants, mold, leaves, lizards. Lights go out and you replace them. Things don't just stop and not grow back or not get fixed and made better and we go on. How stupid would that be? You've heard the doctors. I have strong healing abilities. So my arm will grow back, good as new, might be even stronger. Christ, everybody knows that!"

I meant that little speech to calm her down, but instead, she ran out of the room, then came back and flopped down in a chair and covered her face. I think she's all dried out, no more tears, as she got real quiet, then sat up straight, and just stared at the wall opposite her.

Doc Peebles takes my temperature with the temperature rod. He checks under my throat for swelling in my glands and then looks into my eyes with a light scope.

"What day is it?" I ask.

"What day do you think it is, John?" Doc Manning asks.

"I don't know, really. I have no idea."

"Sunday. You've been medicated for two days with a mild pain killer and tranquilizer," Dr. Peebles informs me.

"Well," I say as I run the calendar through my head. "I have work tomorrow."

This sets Marsha off again. "Work! Fuck work!"

"Then how do we pay the rent and food bills, not to mention heat and electricity," I say to set her straight. Money doesn't grow on trees anymore!

That's an expression I'm fond of but don't really understand. I can only conclude that sometime in the past, before The Calamities, trees grew money, maybe in Marsha's back yard, which is why she has no respect for the need to work.

"We're subsidized, John! No one has paid those things in the past six years! That's why we pay taxes to MOM," she says through her red swollen eyes. MOM is the Ministry of Money. We don't like them much, but they're hard to hate with that name, unless you hate your Mom. I think that was part of the plan. Genius, in retrospect.

Marsha's right. Since the great collapse and the rise of the robotic work force, the CRL, via MOM, takes care of most things, except for liquor, recreational drugs, private cars, and our Devices. But you have to pay into the system. So I have to work to pay into the system. But it's a wash. You don't pay in what you get back. I think it's done to make sure people continue to have a sense of worth. Good on them.

"John, it will be OK to take tomorrow off, if you like," Doc Manning says.

"Fuck tomorrow! He lost his fucking arm! He takes as many days as he wants!" Marsha screams.

"How long until the arm grows back, Doc Peebles?" I ask and on that note Marsha says something about insanity and leaves.

"It's best you rest now, John," says Peebles. "There will be plenty of time to answer questions."

"She is dealing with an entirely new situation. And she will have to get accustomed to your recuperation," Manning adds.

An orderly enters the room with a large box.

"Someone order dumplings?" he asks, scanning the room.

ENTRY 5

THE EVOLUTION OF THE SPORTING EVENT AND MASS ENTERTAINMENT.

According to Institute research, sporting events in the 20th and earlier part of the 21st century were very big business. As rules and regulations changed, and the players demanded more payment for their talents on the teams, the corporations that owned the teams had to raise the price of tickets to compensate the athletes. In addition, broadcasting rights to games were sold at ever more exorbitant prices, requiring the broadcasters to interrupt the games more often and longer to run advertisements to recoup the costs of the rights. This changed the events, as between each pitch in a baseball game, there was a commercial inserted, not to mention between batters, after a hit or strikeout, and eventually, as soon as the ball left the bat. The broadcast audience was informed as to the success of the hit when the commercial ended. All told, if sporting events lasted approximately two hours of actual play, they were disrupted by three hours of commercial time. This angered viewers so much they refused to watch the games or buy tickets. This led to increasing the thrills inside the non-commercial time by allowing a baseball pitcher one shot at a batter's head an inning, and allowing the batter to take the bat with him to first base to take a mandatory random one-handed swing at the first baseman. Two hands on the bat were a penalty, usually a fine on the player in the thousands, which went back to the broadcasters. This level of random violence kept people glued to their television sets. In football, the players became far more lethal with the

advances in equipment. When concussions and paralysis became the norm, the leagues made contact rules stricter, which angered paying customers, collapsing the ratings. So, the leagues took most of the equipment away, thinking the athlete would adapt. But by this time, the athlete was accustomed to hitting others with his well-cushioned head, and more players were knocked into unconsciousness per game, with an occasional, but not unusual, death. The ratings went up, and cost per telecast was recouped. This is what they call a "win-win" in sports parlance.

—I have a tremendous amount of energy this morning, if, in fact, it is morning. My eyes are open but the blinds are shut. The room is dark, but the hallway is lit. There is no sound out there and I'm feeling spry but lonely. I feel light on my feet, probably because I am one arm lighter. I could pump myself and take Marsha against the wall, I'm feeling so peppy.

I trust my doctors. A lot of people complain about doctors, but I trust Manning and Peeples. Like I said, everything is contained at The Institute: job, medical, dental, and they feed you whenever you're hungry. In fact, I could walk out of this clinic right now and just walk down the hall and be at my place of work. But Marsha told me she would pick me up, and I'd like to go home and have a shower in my own bathroom.

Marsha brought me a fresh shirt and pants, underwear and socks. She had to throw away all the other stuff as it was so covered in blood. I reach for them, and I realize once again the limitations of reaching for something with your right arm when you don't in fact have a right arm.

I thought I'd have the arm back when I woke up. How long can it take for the arm to return, really? A week? A couple of days, at most? How long does a working arm need to grow back? It's not like it's got any internal organs. C'mon, *limbs is simple,* is what I say.

I sit on the edge of the bed and capture my left foot in my left pant leg, then step into the right pant leg. I stand, pulling my pants up with my left hand. I move the left hand around the waist of the pants to make sure it covers my waist evenly. There's a belt in the loops of the waist, and that's a bit of a trick. But I can do this. I'm a confident man.

"How're you doing?" It's Marsha, standing by the door, watching me thread one end of the belt through the buckle.

"Fine," I say, "I'm going to have to learn to do this until my arm grows back. It's interesting," and I pick up the shirt with my left hand and hold it up by the collar so I can put my left arm through the sleeve and now I am caught in a paradox. I cannot achieve this, cannot put my hand through the armhole when the hand is holding the shirt.

I am frozen as to what to do next. My breathing is faster now. My mind whirs at finding a solution. I throw the shirt in the air and try to stab the armhole with my left hand and the shirt falls to the floor. I stick my hand in what looks like my left armhole and all I do is push the shirt across the linoleum floor. I step on the shirt so it won't slide and now I feel my heart pound as this isn't working at all. The simplest task and it's way beyond me. I'm not feeling so peppy. Air. I need air. Marsha watches me. She's concerned. She doesn't know what to do.

I try to catch my breath and suddenly, and this was the very first time in my life I can remember since the coma, I'm crying. Like a baby. Like a sissy. Like a little girl. Or like I have seen babies cry. Tears roll into my mouth. I tongue them in. They are not salty like Marsha's. My tears are like water. My blood is like oil. I'm nothing like her. I'm a freak.

Marsha holds my head in her arms. She comforts me. Earth mother. Very nice. She smells good. She smells like milk from her morning bowl of "I Can't Believe It's Not Cereal."

"Shhhhh…" she says. "Shhhh…it's gonna be OK. We'll figure it out and I'll be there to help…shhh…"

"Until the arm grows back," I tell her. "Then you'll leave me. Then you'll have enough of me. What do I give you? Nothing. I have nothing to give you."

Oh, shut the fuck up, John. You fucking crybaby! I'm embarrassing myself now. I can't stand me. I can only hope that I will love my new arm, 'cause the rest of me sucks right now. Maybe I need a new body part to renew faith in me.

Faith. Did I say faith? Jesus!

Jesus? Did I say Jesus?

Shut the fuck up, John!

"Shhh…shhh…" Marsha keeps saying, making a sound that helps drown out my crying and my dumb-as-dog-shit thoughts. It also helps her not hear me, as she keeps that sound going like she's losing air.

Now, slowly, she helps me get my shirt on.

*****

Marsha pushes my wheelchair down the hospital hallway. It's flooded with two sports teams, bruised and bleeding, green jerseys on one group and red jerseys on the other. Their jerseys are festooned with every sort of corporate or organizational name and logo. The men are huge – football players likely, a sport I have no love for.

I see bleeding foreheads and faces. The only sound is moans and swearing through the moaning. I see limbs going in directions not humanly possible and occasionally the sharp end of a bone protrudes through the skin of an arm or leg. One player holds his ear in his hand, another a nose, and yet another a tongue.

Through their moans they insult each other, forever competitive, and would no doubt rise from their gurneys and do battle again if they were paid for it or there were a crowd nearby to cheer them on. They are savage to the core, but savvy enough not to go at it physically without remuneration or acclaim.

Marsha wheels me out, with my fresh new clothes, my hair combed, and my right shoulder ending in yellowed gauze bandages, and they stop their taunts of each other and whatever each team stands for that is so diametrically opposed to the other. The clinic hallway has become the stadium and it goes silent. I am now like the teams on the field. The players are the spectators watching me, as if there is a tragedy unfolding. A player down, spine mangled, never to walk again, or a player down, skull cracked, never to think again. The tragedy is me. They watch me. All the gladiators. They look at my shoulder and their eyes travel down my armless side and stop at the empty arm of the wheelchair where my hand, if I had one, should be resting. They watch my eyes. And my eyes hold their stare. I am the freak. I am the injured one.

I am different now.

ENTRY 6

THE TICKETISTS AND REVENUE COLLECTIONS FOR INFRASTRUCTURE IMPROVEMENT AND CROWD CONTROL.

In their six-day-a-year wisdom, the CRL created the Union of Sanctioned Ticketists (UST), which was a trained militia armed with the TicketTaker 1000 ticket-issuing and citation machines. Ticketists, the prime revenue-raising arm of the CRL, also offered a source of behavior control. They write tickets and citations on every infraction or mode of conduct including: illegal parking, jaywalking, smoking, public intoxication, spitting, chewing gum, raising your voice in a quiet zone, suspicious running, carrying an unloaded weapon, making idle threats, eating with your mouth open, denigrating the Council of Rules and Laws, having sex with a minor, having unprotected sex, not finishing what you order in a restaurant, restaurant reservation neglect, ostentatious wearing of wealth, and not having made a significant purchase in the past three months as the recovery is still weak, which is what three series of governments had been saying for the past thirty years. The Institute, through its astute research, found them to have largely aggressive profiles, and this was vital to their success as not only did they issue the tickets for what was an unpredictable and continually expanding laundry list of minor and major infractions, but they also functioned as collection agency for unpaid tickets. They were not afraid of physically assaulting the debtor, or demanding sexual favors from either the male or female, depending on their appetites. So, the Ticketists engendered a low current of fear among the population. There had been some complaints about them, and one small demonstration against them, but the CRL meets only six days a year, so complaints are slow to be addressed. In the meantime, they provide the CRL with about a third of its operating revenue, which goes to keep roads somewhat usable, and food and water somewhat safe.

—Lassie sits at the end of my bed watching me.

I pet her head. She takes my hand in her mouth, very softly, and holds it there. When I try to remove it, she tightens her jaws around it, not letting go. I feel she holds my hand like she is taking my pulse. She is very thoughtful looking with my hand in her mouth. Her eyes go left and right. Her pupils dilate and shrink. She is sensing something. I bet she senses the cells in my body joining and morphing into my new arm. I bet it excites her canine instincts, sensing human growth. This is a very talented dog, I think. There is a great deal animals can learn in the circus.

After a period of time, she lets it go. My hand isn't wet from her mouth. It's dry. And it's warm. It feels good. I almost want to give her my hand again.

"You've been asleep for a week," Marsha says as she carries some little laundry stacks – dark shirts in one stack, white shirts in another. "I called your doctors and they said it was OK. That it was normal that you sleep. I called my doctor and he told me I should call an ambulance. I think your doctors are strange. Where did they go to medical school?"

"I'm awake, right?" I tell her, "Nothing wrong with me. So which advice is best?" She kept folding and refolding the laundry, and placing it in the closets and drawers, keeping herself busy. Occasionally, she would look over to me, then to the nub of my right shoulder and then look away, like my nub was some terrible secret to be avoided. Or like I'm in bed violating a child and she is disgusted but it's just what I do so she is in a state of reluctant acceptance. Maybe that's a little dramatic. I just think her turning away from me like she saw a turd is a little insulting.

"Your half of the bed is untouched," I say. "Where have you been sleeping?"

"On the couch," she says as she folds and arranges T-shirts and socks and other items in the one drawer she allows me to have as my own, even though it was she who moved in with me. I wonder if all women mark their territory by putting clothes in drawers and closets.

"Why?" I ask her.

"Let it go."

"No. Why?" because I'm not going to let it go. I know a long time ago, in the Age of Black and White, men and women slept in the same room in separate beds. But that changed in the Age of Color. A lot of things did.

She spins around, holding one of my freshly folded T-shirts in her hand and starts twisting it into what starts to resemble rope.

"Because, when you rolled over on your side, your right side, your right armless side, it's was like you were sinking into the bed and it freaked me out! You were like one half of a person. OK? Good enough for you? Happy with that?"

"Jesus, Marsha. You're a helluva treat to wake up to after a week's worth of sleep. Maybe you should just throw a pie in my face. You gotta get over this. Right now, I'm missing an arm. Big deal. It'll grow back!"

"For God's sake, John! Stop it!"

"Why does saying that upset you? Is there something you know that I don't? Did my doctors tell you anything? Or did your expert doctor, who would have had me go to the emergency room to sleep, say anything?" She's stacking and folding faster now, all nerves and avoidance and organizational therapy.

"Fine, John! You're right!" she barks, "It will grow back. Maybe you'll grow two arms. Maybe each hand will have ten fingers, and you can play concert piano, or become a handball virtuoso, or maybe with three arms and twenty-five fingers in total, you could do really sophisticated shadow puppets. Whole crowd scenes, maybe reenact The San Francisco Riots!" she says as she finishes the folding and sorting and stands there waiting for my reaction to the wealth of employment and performance opportunities she just presented me with, not to mention the reinterpretation of historical events with shadow puppets. Which, frankly, is not a bad idea. I can see the entertainment in that. I could sell some tickets, especially with the backstory of me having lost an arm. I could market it as a real phoenix rising sort of thing. Everybody likes a comeback.

"I just woke up," I tell her, "I am not ready for a confrontation about you not believing the simplest of premises: my arm will grow back."

"Oh hell!" she says and stomps out of the room. She really is a good person. I think all this change has unsettled her. She'll come around.

I'm unsteady. I push off the bed and make what seems to be an endless amount of small moves to get my feet flat on the floor. My legs suffer a lack of muscle tone. I stiff-joint my way to the bathroom and stop in front of the mirror.

I stare at the bandages on my shoulder. The ooze that was so wet in the hospital has dried and crusted on the gauze. The wound itches like crazy. I scratch the gauze, take one of Marsha's combs and scrape it over the bandages. But the itch spreads from one spot to another and I chase the itch across the bandage, tearing it up as I go. I'm a cat with fleas, scratching and trying to bite the spot, but without a cat's flexibility.

I can't reach the tormented spot and now the comb doesn't work as I've broken off its teeth. I rub my nub against the grout on the tiled wall, up and down, humping the bathroom wall with my shoulder. I am powerless to stop what I know is pretty fucking bizarre behavior. I want to stop. I can't. I am under the power of the nub.

I pull the bandages off. They get wetter and wetter as I get closer to the ooze. They fray and disintegrate in my fingertips. The fleshy sludge of the wound collects under my fingernails, and now the bandages are off and blood pours down my side. I grab a towel and stop the flow and sit on the toilet. I try to catch my breath, and I think that if I could cry I would feel better. I try to push the tears out, but this does not come easy to me now. I must've used up the only batch I had at the hospital.

There is something in tears. A toxin, perhaps. A misery toxin that the body wants to expel. It cries out the toxic tears and voilà, it feels better. I wish I could do it right now. Enough! Get up. Let's get going here. This growing back of arms is making me dwell on myself to an obnoxious extent. This is not the way of a confident man.

The towel is sopped through with blood and the fluid of the wound. Marsha calls into the bathroom. I tell her I'm on the toilet. She doesn't mind when I come into the bathroom when she is on the toilet, and I wouldn't do that if she didn't say "Come in" when I knock on the door. I don't like it when she barges in on me. I feel the evacuation of body poisons should be private. Once, I went to see a game of Basket Slam and when I went to the bathroom, there was a line of men peeing into a trough almost forty feet long. Strong streams fueled by beer and soda and energy drinks.

Unlike other men, my piss evaporates the minute it meets the air. When I pee standing up, I have to watch out which way the wind is blowing or if there are drafts, as I – or the wall – tend to get covered in a yellow mist cloud. Not pretty and hard to explain.

At the game, I sent a cloud down the length of the trough. No one noticed it, as they were likely drunk, judging by the dullness of their eyes and the strength of their streams.

Doc Peebles says my misting is because of the drugs I had to take to rebuild my internal organs after the accident. He said it would return to normal soon enough, if I ate a lot of salty foods, like crackers and the complete range of salamis offered at many of the finer food stores. But I hate those meats.

I like dumplings.

I pull the towel off my shoulder. For the first time since the attack, I see the end of my shoulder and the mass of puckered red and scratched-up flesh that forms the healing cap on the wound. It oozes more milky white fluid. I lean into the mirror to get a closer look and run my hand over it. The skin tingles. It feels nice. It's super sensitive. Very alive. Fertile. The perfect flesh farm to grow an arm. The little folds in the skin where they stitched up all the rips and tears to the flesh and muscle seem to breathe. The folds seem to undulate, like they're making something, like an old woman's toothless gums would chew something soft.

*****

Why am I on the bathroom floor?

Marsha looks down at me. I can barely make out her features as she is silhouetted against the bathroom light.

"John, are you all right?"

"What happened?" I ask, "Did I go to sleep for a week again?"

"You passed out."

She grabs my left arm and pulls me up. I notice my wound has a giant gauze bandage over it, loosely attached to my chest with medical tape. She has patched me up, like a flat tire, but the bandage is there more as a cover. It's clear she isn't a nurse. The bandage is like a veil over the wound, obscuring it from her view. She didn't spend much time with it. She changed it like a shitty mother changes her baby's poo diaper. Nose in the air, divert the eyes, get it over fast and so what if the diaper is loose.

"You need to get back to bed," she says as she steadies me out of the bathroom and into the bedroom hallway.

"My skin moves."

"Good, John. Now get back to bed."

"Let me show you," I say as I peel the bandage off the wound.

"Stop it!" She lets me go and I fall to my left side and into the open closet. I tumble deep into it and upend a shoe rack and a hanger full of her scarves and my ties. She backs up and sits on the edge of the bed and covers her face in her hands while I discover a long lost sock. A good one. Extra padding in the heel. I wondered where that sucker went to.

"I don't know how to deal with this," she says.

"You can start by helping me out of the closet," I say as I notice a yellow and black striped tie lying on my stomach that I had been looking for over the past three weeks. I must spend more time in here.

I'm dressed. Wasn't easy. In fact, I know I'll have to map this whole process out mathematically in order to devise a system that is easier and doesn't leave me so frustrated. Marsha could've helped me, but Ezra, the regional Ticketist, came to visit, and she is in the kitchen making him a sandwich.

Making Ezra sandwiches is how she pays off her tickets. She makes twenty of them a week, packages them up, and either he comes to pick them up or she delivers.

Ezra is a bit of a chore.

ENTRY 7

"I CAN'T BELIEVE IT'S NOT BUTTER" AND THE EVOLUTION OF CALAMITY-RESISTANT FOODS.

I n the latter part of the 20th century, the now defunct food and chemical company Unilever did extensive research and discovered that the public wanted a substitute for butter, which was coming under governmental scrutiny for causing heart disease and obesity. It was later discovered that Unilever had done the research and subsequent publicity against butter because they had discovered a mixture of artificial substances that had the same taste as butter, but could be sold at a much higher profit margin. In tasting groups, 70% of respondents said the same thing upon tasting the butter substitute: "I can't believe it's not butter!" The executives at the time decided there was no better name and introduced it in the market as "I Can't Believe It's Not Butter (ICBINB)." It was an instant success, spawning a series of imitators, each of which did their own research to prove that "ICBINB" was unhealthy. These were: "Butter It's Not!," "Isn't It Butter?", "What? Not Butter?," and "You'd Butter Believe It." None of them had the success of "ICBINB." The product was bought from Unilever in the early part of the 21st century by a group of out-of-work NASA engineers who called their company the "I Can't Corp." They advanced the formula to emulate almost every food substance known to humanity. This was needed as the gradual warming of the planet made successful mass agriculture virtually impossible and so all sorts of food categories were threatened. The scientists and NASA marketers tried a re-naming convention, but nothing worked like the

"I Can't Believe…" nomenclature. All other products were to be in the same naming format as "ICBINB" using doubting phraseology of "I Don't," "I Won't," "I Might Not," "I Shouldn't," and others. I Can't Corp became one of the most successful companies in the world, eclipsing the East India Company of many centuries ago. It also maintains its own army.

—"Hello, Ezra," I say as he sits at the kitchen table cleaning his Ticket-Taker 1000. Marsha spreads "I Can't Believe It's Not Mustard" on his sandwich, puts the roof on it with the second piece of "I Don't Believe It's Not Bread" and puts it into the "I Won't Believe It's a Sandwich Bag."

"Hey, John," Ezra says to me as he flips some switches on the Ticket-Taker 1000 and starts up its menacing ticket-spewing whir.

"Heard about the coyote attack. I ticketed them last week."

"You ticketed coyotes?"

"I have to. They broke the law in attacking you."

"How will they pay?" I ask him, incredulous that he would find the idea of ticketing a wild animal sensible or productive.

"Not my problem. You don't have an arm. You'll have to get a permit for that," he tells me as he grabs his sandwich box, looks inside, counts, then punches the keys on the machine again and hands Marsha a ticket.

"You're one short."

"Damn!" Marsha says as Ezra opens the front door and leaves.

"How much longer will you be making sandwiches for Ezra?" I ask.

"I have six more tickets to pay off…so that's six months of sandwiches."

"Ezra is strange," I tell her.

"You can't achieve erection, never orgasm, have lost an arm and think it's going to grow back, and he's strange?"

Low blow. Marsha has bonded with Ezra. It has taken over two hundred sandwiches, but he is a constant in her life.

I'm late for work.

ENTRY 8

THE FAILURE OF CLONING IN THE CREATION OF A LESS SKILLED AND COMPENSATED WORK FORCE.

Approximately two decades ago, during the height of The Calamities – and with the huge loss of human population – vast depositories of cryogenically frozen ova were injected with sperm from prison donors. The CRL, and the thirty remaining survivors of the disease research community, gave up pursuing stem cell research for the cure of diseases and infirmities and turned their attentions to creating a cloned population to replace the loss of population and replenish the pool of unskilled labor to fill what was termed at the time "crappy jobs." This was influenced also by the failure of the stem cells to cure any of the conditions they were supposed to cure without dire consequences. The Council of Beliefs and Mythologies (CBM) demanded that the ova be seeded, as ultimately the birthrate was so low it threatened the survival of the species and, more importantly, the economic system. The thousands of ova were injected with donator sperm and hatched in incubators. The CBM then sent the babies to orphanages to be socialized. But with The Calamities decreasing the number of qualified teachers and behaviorists, the children, neglected and malnourished, grew up mean. They also grew up faster and stronger than normal toddlers, and at age three or four, could handle weaponry with some accuracy. It was estimated that the average four-year-old male had the strength of an average thirteen-year-old. Soon, they destroyed the orphanages and went on a rampage against the very society that created them and the corporations that funded the program. Given that they had the DNA of a prison population, The Institute believes they had extraordinary organizational skills and a sense of marketing. They banded together in tribal organizations and disguised themselves with facemasks that resembled either the physicist Albert Einstein or the person named Mark Twain. At this time with the information at hand, it is not clear which individual was depicted on the facemasks, nor is it clear who the Twain figure was. According to the accepted data on the Info Device, he was either the 17th president of Toronto, or a writer of books about berries, but the information is sketchy at best. The sole purpose of The Stemmers – as they liked to call themselves –was to destroy all advertisements in the public sector. Their mission was to get back at the system that demanded they be born so they could fill a mundane, yet necessary job, and the most visible representation of the corporation was its advertising, as the five remaining corporations had become so efficient that they were headquartered in condominiums because most of them didn't need any more than ten people to run them. The Ticketists, in an effort to control The Stemmers' behavior, have issued thousands of tickets for public nuisance, making noise in the quiet zone, and expired firearm registration. The tickets are a temporary stop-gap to their obstreperousness, as there is no current law against the destruction of advertising, and it takes the CRL a long time to make a law, as they only work six days a year, and they take the sixth day as a half-day – with an early lunch.

—I drive a Foyota Excess. It gets five miles to the gallon. All the new technologies had ultimately failed and we were all back on oil, natural gas, coal, and methane. They had perfected a process of recycling human excrement that worked for a while, until the food supply was contaminated with calcium and made a lot of people chronically constipated. That started a shortage of excrement, known on the street as the "Shitless Years." A lot of people think the oil companies did it as the methane was chewing into their profits. I think the oil companies get blamed for too much.

The Excess was marketed as a car for the rich. They would buy it to show they could still afford five miles to the gallon, much like I read they gave birth to children in the early part of the 21st century to show they could afford to raise them. Children were better than big wrist watches back then.

The Excess was stripped down to combat the perception that the rich had grown soft. It was an enormously expensive and painful car to drive. I'm surprised their soft butts and spirits could take the jangly ride. The brochure claimed it did zero to sixty in 12.6 seconds but its top speed was only really forty, so that's marketing for you.

My Excess was given to me by the company, after the accident and my emergence from the coma. It's free of charge as it is festooned with advertising for all sorts of wrinkle resisters, household dusters and steamers, and one for The Ultra-Blender, which can turn your oldest leftovers back into tasty, nutritious mulch and, with a change in spinning apparatus, can do small loads of laundry. Very clever.

The Excess is a stick shift. I don't think my Docs counted on me being without the arm. Needless to say, on my first day back to work, driving is more of a chore than usual. My left hand goes from steering wheel to shift.

When my hand leaves the wheel, I steer with my knees, which, in the enormously cramped cabin of the Excess, is a short distance.

The seat doesn't slide back or recline, so I am in a forward crouch when I drive. I can't get it out of second, so I'll drive to work in that gear. It doesn't matter, as it's bumper-to-bumper, with everybody working within five miles of the place they live, and with the speed bumps the Council of Roadways and Sidewalks installed so that the poorer people in faster cars can't go faster than the rich people in slower cars. Not to mention the streets were reduced to one lane either way to allow for the rail system that runs east and west but hasn't operated in years.

*****

I stop at a light. A truck stops on the street perpendicular to mine and two Stemmers jump out and machine-gun a digital billboard promoting "I Can't Believe This is Advertising" that hovers over Sunset Boulevard.

The whole thing smashes to bits and pieces that rain down on my Excess. Then, the Stemmers assault whomever they can. Women, other children, old men, and younger men – bigger than them – the Stemmers have no fear. They ransack pocketbooks and pockets and steal wallets and take candy from the littlest ones. They also kick people in the shins, which, in its way, takes the visual threat away from the Stemmers, as short fucks kicking grown men looks funny. They also wait outside of food dispensaries and take the newly shopped groceries from the populace. It's how they live.

Suddenly, an army of Ticketists arrives on the scene and starts issuing tickets. The strange thing about this is that the Stemmers accept the tickets. Rumor has it that the CRL allows them to redeem the tickets for the last remaining inventories of what is known as candy corn. I've never tasted candy corn, so I don't know what the allure is. I'm thinking it's a calmative and they would be bigger nuisances without it. The CRL is pretty crafty, when you think of it.

One of the Stemmers sees my promotions-covered Excess, runs over and bangs on the hood with a tire iron. That's a huge waste of time and midget muscle. The Excess is made completely out of damage-resistant titanium and wire-meshed windshields, which are hard to see out of but were installed to ensure that the slow-moving rich would be safe in their cars.

The Stemmer just stares at me through his bushy white eyebrows and mustache mask and scowls, "Media Elitist! Promotions Whore! Corporatist!" Though they are mean and grizzled small children, they are big babies nonetheless.

Then, he sees my nub. He sees I am struggling. If I had two hands, I might have shifted to escape. He comes around to the passenger side, and leans into the car. He is no more than eight years old. His arms are tattooed with pictures of candy, cups of soda, and scoops of ice cream.

"What happened to your arm?" he asks, in a child's voice that is not so much changing as changing too fast and his larynx is on overdrive. His voice breaks into soprano on any second syllable that starts with a consonant.

"Coyotes took it," I tell him.

"Don't you fucking hurt the coyotes! They have as much right as we do to live, you corporatist, *bon marché* piece of *merde*." No one knew why the Stemmers sometimes mixed French and English, but they did. The Institute thinks it makes them sound more temperamental. And he's got it all wrong anyway. He thinks I actually bought this car myself.

"I'm not rich and I didn't hurt anyone, you fucking midget!" His head snaps back at the insult, "They bit my arm off. But it's OK, 'cause it will grow back," and with that he looks at me sideways, like he is trying to empty his brain out of his left ear.

"Corporatists think everything regenerates. Voilà! Profits, growth, as long as it's not regulated! But it eats *tout dans la* path. Corporatists die!"

"Stop it with the sophomoric lecture, fa chrissakes, and let me go to my little job that pays me just enough to live," I tell him and I'm not going to take shit from these dwarfs. I'm sorry they're angry, sorry they got the screwed by the corporations or whoever fucked them over, sorry they die young – around fourteen and, usually, crippled – sorry sorry sorry, but I not going to take shit from these dwarfs.

"You *parle* strange," and I've been accused of that by Marsha. She thinks I swear way too much and thinks I talk like one of the bad guys she saw in an old digi when she was a kid.

He looks at my armless shoulder. There is a kindness in his eyes.

"Do you really believe it will grow back, *Monsieur*?" and now this little midget is not so much a Stemmer as a child.

"I have to believe that," I tell him, "Why wouldn't it? Doesn't it all come back over time? Even after the worst of The Calamities, some of the forests grew back, right?" and at that he hangs his head, then looks around at the calamity his own army of Stemmers has caused.

"I have to do this, *pour* appearances, OK?" and he bangs the side of my door with his baseball bat and hops on his scooter and takes off into an alley, missing a ticket for not wearing a helmet by maybe three seconds at most.

Sweet kid. A little confused with the corporatist crap. They need a new cause. They're beginning to embarrass themselves.

In the chaos of their evacuation – and the Stemmers mostly seek to cause chaos – I see a bike rider hit a car, the car roll over him and turn a corner; a homeless man crawl out of a manhole in the middle of the street as another car rolls over his leg as he tries to make his way to the sidewalk to an old blueberry muffin that sits on the curb; a pack of coyotes snatch a toddler from its baby buggy and the mother chases after them; a man stabs another man and steals his Device. The Ticketists then begin issuing tickets to the distraught crowd, ensuring many months of revenue for the CRL.

It's an efficient system, I think.

ENTRY 9

FOCUS ON HUMANITY AND THE BENEFITS OF FOCUSING ON EVERYTHING.

F OCUS ON HUMANITY is a research company, providing governments and the remaining corporations all over the surviving industrialized world with qualitative and quantitative data on human behavior, likes and dislikes, and most importantly, purchase intent. With The Calamities of the past forty or so years, it became necessary for corporations and the Council of Rules and Laws in particular to know more about the emotions and thoughts of the citizenry so that they could create programs and services for them and find ways to control and cauterize their anxieties through spending. Everybody had less money, made less money, and essentially, there was widespread belief that everything that could be made had been made. There were fewer and fewer patents being requested, and the research and development side of companies shut down as sales of virtually everything besides food and Device games ceased after the second asteroid storm destroyed much of the revitalized manufacturing sectors of the Midwest and released a virus that caused about seven million deaths, and a lifelong chronic condition that resembled Crohn's disease. The general population had seen so many tragic events in the past fifteen years that nothing made them feel better. People got more and more depressed because they felt there wasn't anything left to purchase, even though if there were, they didn't have much money to do so. It is the idea of the limitations that bothered them. It was that their dreams and hopes were suddenly finite. FOCUS

ON HUMANITY seeks to research the way out of this predicament. Our motto is Knowledge Is Knowing, If You Know What We Mean.

—Here we are! My home away from home: The Institute. The sign above the parking garage says FOCUS ON HUMANITY. That's my company, my caregiver, where Docs Peebles and Manning await me the first day back after the attack. I've been told that in the old days kids used to look forward to the first day of school, where they got to see all their friends and wear new clothes and maybe the girl you liked last year would like you this year. I've been told that and I have some images in my head of that.

At FOCUS ON HUMANITY, it's my job to ask questions and coordinate the answers and attitudes of the focus group. I'm what's called a Focus Group Moderator and Opinion Coordinator. When I conduct groups, I wear a paralyzer gun for protection. You have to. Never used it, but it's nice to know it's there.

After each group, I summarize the answers and have lengthy discussions of the findings with the Docs. They're smart, but sometimes they're confused by people's responses to certain stimuli. I seem to be able to help them there, as Marsha teaches me a great deal about the way average people think, since she herself is average, and I mean that in a good way. The world could use a lot more average. That was one of its problems; there were really too many above average people, all intellectual spit and polish and abstract thinkers, and the rest were astoundingly moronic. Whole political parties run by the above average were created by the corporations to appeal to the moronic, which in turn gave the corporations more power, which in turn led to several of the avoidable Calamities. Average is very welcome today.

FOCUS ON HUMANITY is maybe the best place I've ever worked. But that's easy to say because with my comatose history, I can't remember where else I've worked.

Right inside the lobby, which is electronically surveyed and totally secure, there's a projection on a white wall from a projector hidden in the ceiling. It's a projection of what The Institute – FOCUS ON HUMANITY – stands for. It used to be a big copper plaque with the letters engraved, but that was stolen for the copper content. They went to aluminum, but aluminum got scarce and was also stolen. They tried plastic, but then there was a plastic shortage due to the oil shortage and that went too. They tried writing it on a chalkboard, but chalk wasn't very dignified. They tried to make the letters out of clay, and though they were cute, they were hard to read. So they settled on an outdated projector that no one would want, hidden in the ceiling, projecting their Mission Statement on a clean white wall. It's fairly impressive. Very professional. Sometimes they run a color through the letters, and when they do, it gives the Mission Statement a whole new meaning:

FOCUS ON HUMANITY investigates fear and hope, happiness and sadness. We seek to discover what makes you hungry, what makes you sick, what makes you angry, and what makes you kill.

We seek to understand why you like cats better than dogs, fish more than worms, women better than men.

We want to know why you say tomaaato while others say tomahhto, and why that matters at all.

We want to know how you feel about old people and death and about babies and life.

We ask you about the news of yesterday, today and what you think will happen tomorrow. We ask you what would be your perfect world and how you feel about the one you're in.

We want to know who you love and who you hate, who you'd kill and who you'd save.

We talk to couples, singles, groups, families, strangers, friends and enemies, pet owners and animal haters, the employed and unemployed, sane and insane.

We seek to know your pleasure and pain. We watch as you have sex with the grotesque and we gauge your arousal or disgust.

We strap electrodes to your genitalia and see if your lover will shock you.

We inject you with euphorics to see if you will forgive them.

We extract blood and urine, feces and semen, and swab your mouth for DNA.

We clamp your nipples, peel back your foreskin, slice open your eyeball, prod your anus, abort your baby, inject you with cancer, extract your teeth, and we pay two hundred Council units an hour.

In short, we Focus on Humanity. Because knowledge is knowing, if you know what we mean.

That's their Mission Statement. I think it could be shorter.

*****

I'm in front of a mirror looking at myself. It's the men's room. I feel odd because the last time I stood in front of this mirror looking at myself, I was looking at a man with two arms. I'm standing in exactly the same spot: middle mirror, middle sink, but the image is off. My memory has two arms. My reality has one.

I draw my right arm on the mirror with some moisturizer. A thick finger painting starting from my nub, running down the mirror reflection of the side of my armless body, then loop-the-looping for pinkie to thumb then all the way back up to where my armpit would be had I an arm that would make a pit. It's a little sloppy, as I would normally draw with my right and am not much of an artist. The hand is a little balloon-like. I try to draw the little wrinkles of the shirt, but all it does is make it look like I have an old fat man's arm.

The attack, like the rest of my life, feels like the morning after a bender. Sketchy, vague, distant, with the requisite "Did that really happen," and "Did I really do that?" No details or backstory. I was running, then I wasn't, then coyotes attacked me, then I had no arm, then I woke up in the hospital. Then I became a freak. That's enough. I get busy wiping my shit little art project off the mirror. The waxy moisturizer spreads itself in a smear, so now my entire reflection is a blur and just how perfectly fucking ironic is that.

The day is starting off a little rough, a little undignified. I have to pull this one out. There's something that's nagging me, no, demanding me to do, a voice in my head that won't be ignored and is screaming at me in a breathy whisper, "Take off the bandages! Look at the nub that is your shoulder! Feel the skin! Feel it, dammit! Run your fingers over it and into the folds! Into the folds. Pull them out and taste the wetness. Taste what you taste like inside," and that kind of sick shit is hard to ignore.

As is the itching. The fucking itching. A crazy buzz saw of an itch. A deep itch, way inside, shooting across my chest. An itch with tentacles. A sadistic itch. It makes my ears prickly. It shoots down to the fingertips of my surviving hand and tingles them. I rub the nub against the tiles on the wall, but that doesn't stop the itch. I scratch it with my fingers. Not enough. I hit it with my fist. Not enough. I rip the bandages off, run my fingernails over the new, pink, healing skin, fast, scratch now, scratch faster, tear into the skin, but it keeps itching, unstoppable and I reveal their brain: the folds.

The folds. Like a landscape of white lava you might see from high in the air. Folds like melted taffy. Folds like a bowl of thick noodles. They undulate to the itch. I stick my finger inside one of the folds. Deeper. Deeper still. My whole finger. I don't want to scratch my insides with my nail. That would be like scratching an intestine. No good can come of that. I pull the finger out, wet, and the itch continues. "Taste it," the voice says again, "Taste what you taste like inside." OK. Sure. It's me, after all, all me. I lick my finger. I taste like nothing. I need some salt.

*****

The itch is a god and it wants worship. I do worship you, Oh God of the Itch Deep Inside My Armless Shoulder. What tribute can I offer? Water? Yes! Water.

I splash cold water on the nub, cup my hand, and feed it water. The itch continues. It wants more. Something more. I rub it against the towel dispenser, against the serrated edge that cuts the paper towel off, against a wire mesh trash basket.

I fill the sink with the hottest water the faucet will give me and I try to drown the itch. My shirt is torn half off, my tie wet, and I dunk the nub of my shoulder into the sink. The hot water stings more than the itch. The god retreats in his demand for worship. I can breathe.

I pull my dripping nub from the water. I grab a paper towel and dab the rivulets of blood that cascade down the folds and threaten to stain my shirt. Used paper towels surround my feet, like someone was preparing to set me on fire, like a witch in the ancient stories of the early part of the world that doesn't matter anymore.

The nub is horrible looking. Freak skin. It's the skin from a diseased baby's ass. And I touch it now, run my hand over it, and I notice a small bubble has emerged from the twisted mess of pink hairless flesh.

A small white bubble, like the nub is shitting out a piece of popcorn. I touch it, and the bubble retracts back into the fold. Then, it comes out again. I touch it, and it disappears again. Hide and seek. Hide and seek with the itch. Is this what the God of the Itch looks like? He is a small god. I should be able to defeat him. No worshiping the small gods.

I wait. Nothing. I pry one of the folds open. Nothing. My visitor is gone.

*****

"Are you OK, John?"

It's Doc Manning. I didn't hear him come in. I was too busy pounding my shoulder against the wall. "Yeah, I'm fine. I think I'm fine," I say, but I can tell he doubts me, and why shouldn't he? My shirt is torn off, I'm drenched in water, my shoulder is red, and the sink and floor of the bathroom are wet and covered in pieces of paper towel. The nub bleeds a bit. The blood blots into my shirt as I try to slide it over the nub.

I look like a fucking criminal, like a guy washing off the evidence of an especially brutal and extremely amateurish murder.

"Can you work today? Are you ready?" I always liked the way Doc Manning talked. Cool like the other side of the pillow. Soothing, measured, even keel, each word approximately a quarter second away from the next, syncopated, melodic. I could learn how to play the piano to it. Not like Marsha's. She is more emotional, more passionate, and that's good in a way, though her voice can unnerve me, or maybe it's what she says with it. I don't know. Perhaps if I had my arm back, things would be clearer.

The people I monitor in the testing situation are shrill or are usually shouting, agitated, weeping, or whimpering, their moods reflected in their voices. When trapped with them in a small room, you can smell their anxiety or their joy. It takes a measured man, a cooler head to be able to listen to what they're saying and not be swayed by how they are saying it. I am that man. I have found that out since I emerged from the coma. I don't remember if I was this way before. But if I wasn't, then the coma gave me something necessary: memory loss that caused a dulling in my emotions. I appreciate the gift. I haven't seen being able to feel as an ability I'd want in this fucked-up world.

"I'm fine. Ready to work. I was just cleaning up," I tell him.

Who the hell do I think I'm fooling?

This man is one of the most brilliant psychologists on the planet, and a terrific accountant. He looks at my nub, then back to me.

"It's growing back," I tell him. "Look, in the folds, a bit of the very beginning of my new arm is pushing through. Like a little bubble, a seedling. I saw it, chased it, but it went back into hibernation. It's not ready yet."

"That's good, John," he says in that voice.

"Feel it," and I aim the nub at him. He looks at it, runs his hand over it, then puts his hand back in his lab coat, where all good doctors keep their hands.

"No wait, it will pop out, the bubble, like one of those games at the arcade."

"Whack-a-Mole?" he asks correctly. "I very much enjoy that game."

And he waits, and, of course, nothing. Nothing to reinforce what I know to be true.

"Are you thinking hard about your life, John?" I'm supposed to think hard about my life. It was one of the key instructions Docs Manning and Peeples gave me when I emerged from the coma: to think about what I see and hear every day; to talk to Lassie about what I see and hear; and to always have feelings, or assessments, of what I see, hear, smell, and feel. All the senses, be conscious, be vigilant, turn them over in my head, be clear about them, orderly in my thoughts, write them down if I wanted, talk to the dog, talk to myself, talk to Marsha about things big and small, but think hard, consciously, overtly, like I am reporting back to some sad cripple locked in a tower who is paying me a lot of money to live vicariously through me, and can hear my thoughts and observations over a digi device. It's a fucking pain in the ass, but if they say it should be done then done it is.

"I am. And I know that my arm is growing back," I tell him. "What do you think about that? Marsha doesn't like me to say it. But what else would it do? Everything grows back. Nails grow back, hair grows back too. The days grow into nights, nights into days... So you see..." and I stop, as Manning has taken out a fresh piece of gauze and is bandaging up my nub.

"Do you believe me?" I ask him.

He reaches into his lab coat pocket and pulls out a little vial of pills. "Take these, John. They will help."

I take the vial and pour a couple into the palm of my hand. They are huge. "What are they?"

"Just some medication. Antibiotics, supplements, anti-inflammatories."

"You know I have a sensitive system right now. Are you sure these are good for me?"

"You don't question your doctor, John. You know that. We didn't go through years of training just to be questioned by the very people we seek to help. You accept, you take the medicine, and you get better. Unclutter your mind. Rid yourself of doubt."

He's right of course. Doctors are like gods, in a way. With better vacations.

"It doesn't matter what I believe," he coos. "It's what you know to be true. Your arm won't grow back just because I or anybody else believes it will. This is something you must access, absorb, and understand. Are you ready to go to work now? We are running late."

ENTRY 10

FOCUS GROUP #775 – PIE IN THE FACE OF DEATH.

The purpose of this test is to discover if images normally associated with appetite reduction are still valid in the post-Calamities mentality. The test involves the presentation of two different flavored pies and the viewing of digi images from past Calamities disasters, of which there was a wealth of material. Pie is a food substance currently in demand due to its comfort-causing properties and portability. It is considered far superior to the Cake, which was arguably the preferred comfort food pre-Calamities. Each respondent is allowed to choose his or her favorite pie to consume after the first digi exposure, but must then choose the other flavor for the second digi. The Institute will record heart rate, skin surfaces, and, of course, the most visual of behaviors: the eating of the pie. We will record the amount of pie on the first forkful, as that is also an important marker to appetite voracity, especially when the first pie is their favorite, or close to favorite, flavor. The Institute has narrowed the most popular pie flavors post Calamities to cherry and lemon meringue. We don't serve ice cream with the pie, as we have found that invalidates the results. Also, Dr. Peeples feels ice cream an insult to his pies. He has become quite proficient in the baking of pies. So much so, he has begun to sell them independently in the FOCUS ON EVERYTHING ELSE store. He calls them Peeples' Pies.

ENTRY 10-B: ADDENDUM – MULTI-PURPOSE BEVERAGES:
The Institute serves the multi-purpose beverage ORLATT in groups.

ORLATT is a weight maintenance drink that also fights wrinkles and aging by reducing the ability of the eye to focus on the user's reflection in mirrors, digi stills or vid. It provides ten hours of time-released energy for those suffering from lack of energy, and the same ingredient that gives energy to the laconic also modulates the hyperactive. It retards joint degeneration and numbs low-level pain by dulling the nerve endings close to the extremities and head. It arrests hair loss and can, in forty percent of the cases, increase hearing. And it is considered refreshing. It comes mainly in lime and is very good with pie. It is very expensive – almost a whole week's worth of salary at CRL minimum wage – so, for many of the respondents, it is a treat, and it positively affects the impressions of The Institute, which causes more participation on the part of the respondents. As a result, The Institute can pay respondents less and ask them to stay longer. We consider this, in the popular Pre-Calamities vernacular, a "win-win."

—I sit alone in the focus group room.

It's a sterile, windowless place, with a long table under fairly bright white lights. There are cameras and sound capture on the ceilings and behind the one-way mirror where Peeples and Manning observe the group in real time, and where Peeples warms his pies, except for the Lemon Meringue, which is served at room temperature. The cameras on the ceiling shoot what the respondents are saying and there are also cameras below the table to see what the respondents are doing with their hands, as the Docs find that interesting. I wonder if it's also because they like looking up women's skirts, but the Docs don't seem to be that interested in women. Or people in general. Not in the way you should be. People to them are curiosities to be studied. I don't think they have many friends. Hell, what am I talking about? Neither do I.

In addition to the sensor attachments, they can gauge anxiety or lying by the amount the respondents wipe their hands on their thighs. Also the crossing and uncrossing of legs, the tapping of feet, or the sliding in and out of loose shoes speaks volumes. I am not sure the wiping of the hands isn't the result of the pie-eating and the restlessness caused by the Orlatt, but I'm not a doctor, so this would be what is known as "speaking out of school," which is an expression the Docs use but that I don't really understand.

Speaking of Orlatt, there's a side table filled with bottles of the stuff, along with water. No one drinks the water. They don't trust it anymore.

Orlatt, a saturated solution of more chemicals than water could ever hold, is considered the healthier choice. Personally, it tastes like shit and makes me sweat.

The sleeve of my right arm dangles empty at my side. Limp, like my penis before Marsha pumps it. I have to do something about it. I'll tie it in a knot, or several knots, to shorten it so it won't dangle, get in my way, make me look stupid.

No. That'll make it look worse.

I'll roll it up like a fireman's hose and tape it to my shoulder. Or I'll fling it over my shoulder, like a scarf. Or I'll fold the cuff over the sleeve and fold the sleeve all the way up to what would be my elbow if my elbow were there. Maybe I'll get a pair of scissors and cut it off, but this is a good shirt and the arm will grow back and then I'm out a fucking shirt. I can't believe these are the big decisions I have to make these days.

I'll stuff the sleeve inside the front of my shirt like that Frenchman Napoleon did in paintings. That's what I do. I don't want to have these types of decisions in my life. I'd like my life to be about contemplating only the larger issues – death, hatred, love, community, relationships, brutality, violence, birth, survival – and you can't do that when you're worrying about how to arrange an empty shirtsleeve.

I fill out the name cards from the attendance sheet. The attendance sheet lists names and age, income and profession. And in this case, allergies. In one of the last groups we conducted this exact same research, and a man allergic to cherries nearly choked to death when his trachea swelled shut. Doc Peeples had to insert a tube into his neck to allow him to breathe. The man sued The Institute, but to no avail. We are protected from legal action due to our research contract with I Can't Corp, and their law firm "I Can't Believe You're Suing Us."

I write Mary; Robbie; Tina; Shania; Louis; Nikki on the folded pieces of plastic. Two men, three women. In order to establish a rapport with group, I will ask a few questions about them, just to show that they can trust me. I don't care what the answers are. This is ceremony. I have to tell them that I do not represent the company that makes the product I am testing, or the university whose theory I am helping provide research for. I'm completely independent and don't give what is called a "flying fuck" what they think. But this means not being hurt if they hate the product or idea. In this case, they should feel free to hate the pies. But they won't. Peeples' Pies are very good, as pies go. If they crack a joke I can't laugh.

If they say something sad, I can't frown. If they insult me, I can't give a flying fuck. However, if they get crazy or out of hand, I have a paralyzer gun – the FOCUS ON THIS! 2000 – that will render the troublemaker unconscious in two seconds. The paralysis lasts longer, about ten minutes, which is enough time to restrain them until the ambulance arrives to take them away. Also long enough for the Ticketists to stuff tickets in their pockets and in any and all other visible orifices.

I've used the gun only once since coming out of the coma. My doctors say I was a crack shot before. Nice to know.

ENTRY 11

DIGITAL COMMUNICATION DEVICES AND THE INCREASE IN TUMORS OF THE BRAIN, GONADS, AND UTERUS.

Multiple, limited-use digital devices have been the norm the past ten years. Pre-Calamities, the three major manufacturers of Digital Devices sought to create just one device that could meet all needs. They succeeded in creating a three-inch by three-inch all-purpose device that became ubiquitous in the culture. But irrefutable research on over ten thousand cancer patients revealed the cause of tumors of the brain, inner ear, gonads, and uterus in an overwhelming sixty percent of the cases was that single all-purpose device. The CRL, in the interest of public safety, subsidized these manufacturers to find the solution. The manufacturers instead used the subsidies to fund contrary research that indicated that their devices could actually cure several forms of cancer and enhance longevity. When this was discovered by the CRL, they nationalized the industry. A decision was made that instead of having one device to handle all functions, devices would be made uni-functional, so that no one was on one device too long at a time. And then they instituted the maximum length of a single phone call to be no longer than one minute. People now carry a minimum of six devices: one for personal communications; one for emergency communications to police and terrorist reports; a screen device for digital news, and another for non-essential entertainments; a digital reader for words; and a CRL communications device for the latest on the government standards, practices, and for meaningful quotes from leaders that seek to calm the population. You can also purchase medical devices to monitor the body and communicate directly with your local clinic. This business model, though cumbersome, also increased revenue as the CRL discovered that creating more limited-usage Devices delivered an increase in spending on more Devices. That became the plan moving forward: encourage constant consumption of all Devices, which then spun off its own industry of fashions, bags, and boxes that could hold the devices. The CRL then instituted National Device Day, which became a holiday where the CRL initiated a marketing campaign to encourage the populace to purchase the newest Devices, the newest software for the Devices, newest contracts for the Devices, the newest accessories for the Devices, and to use the Devices to communicate with others on their Devices about which Devices they just purchased. The CRL then charged the user seven CRL units per minute. It became the largest revenue creator for the CRL, and enabled them to construct a series of statues to honor the members of the CRL. National Device Day slowly eclipsed Christmas as the largest purchasing holiday. The CRL then contracted the remaining members of the entertainment community to produce a commemorative city-by-city entertainment called "Devices on Ice." In time, Christmas died its own death with the increasingly agnostic population and the newly established obesity guidelines, which sent to rehab anybody in excess of fifteen pounds over the CRL weight limits, which essentially sent the character Santa Claus out to what was referred to as "the pasture," and so Christmas became a holiday without mascot, and therefore, less marketable. National Device Day, on the other hand, has a purple ferret.

The incidence of brain cancers continued to rise, with one in five people, at some time in their lives, developing a tumor. Most of them could be dealt with, as the medical establishment was getting very precise at being able to scoop the affected areas of the brain out with somewhat more optimistic outcomes.

Still, with those incidence numbers, there were a tremendous number of people who were virtually brain dead, or only able to function for the simplest of jobs, which of course the society needs. According to the CRL, this is the price of technology and communications. It should be noted that due to the limited capabilities of each device, the content for each device has also been limited. Films are now no longer than three minutes each – even the mid-century remake of Melville's *Moby Dick*. Articles are no longer than thirty words, books generally run ten pages, and history has been truncated; the Thirty Years' War was shortened to Fifteen. The truncating of language holds true across the globe, except in England, where it is more difficult to express oneself with an economy of words.

—The focus group files into the room. I have placed their name cards where they should sit. I do this every time, and every time they sit where they want and I have to shuffle the name cards to where they are sitting so I can remember their names. Doc Manning finds this repetition most curious and attributes it to the breakdown of rules unless there is a Ticketist nearby.

Everybody stares at my arm. Or lack of. Or at the sleeve that's stuffed in the front of my shirt. "What's wrong with your arm?" asks Robbie, who lists himself as a conceptual artist, which is complete bullshit. Near as I can tell, all art is conceptual, so what does it mean to be a conceptual artist? It's like being a "food chef," or a "word writer."

"They say you focus group people have guns," says Nikki, who lists herself as a sexual therapist, and judging by her physique and the fact she is wearing a tight Peppermint Hippo Lounge T-shirt – which has a fat pink male hippopotamus that spreads across an ample, very strong chest – translates to pole dancer, escort, and sex shrink.

"Can I see it? Guns turn me on." And I believe they do, so I just show her a peek, just the handle of the FOCUS ON THIS 2000, which is in a small drawer underneath the table where I sit.

"That's so cool. Can I touch it?" she asks, and no, she can't.

The others don't like her. She scares them. Her sexuality is right out there, on the surface for all to see. She's comfortable with it, and she knows that the women in the room think that she might even have taken care of their men at one time. They also fear her because she could be a carrier of one of the new incurable sexually transmitted diseases. There has been a whole host of new ones in the past ten years. It's why during the first week of our relationship, Marsha wanted me to wear a condom. Needless to say, pumping my penis and then rolling on the condom cut into the time allotted for the erection. In fact, with the time it took to get the condom on without breaking it (they were also made by the I Can't Corp, this product named "I Won't Believe It's My Baby"), I would be flaccid by the time I was game-ready. And there is nothing that – and this from Marsha – is more of a turn-off to a woman than a limp penis wrapped in loose plastic. Worse, when we succeeded in our race against time, the condom intensified the numbness down there that made sex completely uninteresting. She might as well have been fucking a plastic mold of my penis. So, after a week, we stopped using them, diseases be damned. It was a mutual decision.

Tina – a mani-pedi-acupuncturist with a shivering, big-eyed, small-boned dog nestled in her ample lap – tells Nikki to stop making me nervous, but she is projecting her anxiety onto me. It's how she copes with the fear that sexually transmitted diseases might be airborne.

"I'm not making him nervous. Are you nervous, sugar?" Nikki asks, her thick, shiny, pink lips looking like a talking vagina. "I know you're not nervous. You wouldn't be talking to us if you were. The rest don't know it, but you moderators have to go through an approval process. Psychological tests, right?"

Actually, no. No tests at all. But I can't fall into the trap of agreeing with any of them. It ruins my impartiality.

"We must move on," I tell them.

"She's a sex worker! You got to spray the room after they been in it," says Louis. "They're carriers."

"We're always 'they,' 'them,' to you, huh, fatso?" Nikki shoots back. "Relax, I get tested once a month. I'm clean. And my clientele is not from the hoi polloi. Not from your 'hood, OK?"

Shania, a big-boned, small-eyed African, joins in. "What kind of gun do you have? Do you have a permit? Do you know how to use it? Have you ever used it?" she asks in rapid-fire sequence, not waiting for an answer but instead inundating me with questions I'm never going to answer.

"I need you to put your Devices in here," I tell them as I slide a big straw basket onto the table. They don't want to part with their Devices. They will temporarily, during the first part of the group, be a bit unmoored. But, with their gnat-like attention spans, they will adapt, and then, I will have to remind them to take their Devices back upon leaving the group. Never fails.

Nikki spills her Devices into the basket, then looks at me with what I imagine is her seductive, come hither look, bedroom eyes and recently wetted lips, and says, "I could get used to that. You know, a little nub at the end of your shoulder. I can see the pleasure in that," and she licks her lips again and puts her hand underneath the table between her legs and smiles at me. Nikki's nipples are now very pronounced under her T-shirt, giving the Peppermint Hippo image a bulging left eye and what looks like a hemorrhoid.

Following her lead, the others drop their devices into the basket. Soon, there are over twenty-five of them, stacked on top of each other like a messy pile of black plastic pancakes.

*****

Peeples, in an apron with the words *Peeples' Pies – Pleasure to the Peoples* emblazoned on it, brings two pies into the room: one cherry and one lemon meringue. He tries pie recipes from old dramatic digi's that ran on the television from the last century or so: peach pies from a digi called *Leave it to Beaver*; custard pie from *The Andy Griffith Show*; apple pie from *The Donna Reed Show*; and on and on. He often tells me about his love for these shows, as they present the life uncomplicated. He wonders about their lack of color, and has been researching exactly when color came into the world. But clearly, civilization was broken down into the Age of Black and White and the Age of Color. He told me that when the world changed to color, it got meaner, coarser, and might have had a hand in encouraging some of the less savory behaviors exhibited during The Calamities. He's still researching this.

The cherry and lemon meringue pies were inspired by *My Three Sons*.

These two pies will be the focal point for today's research, before we do anything deeper, like skin graft or stool samples.

I try to attach sensors to the respondents' thumbs and necks, but it's too hard without a functioning second hand, and I look at the mirror and shake my head. I noticed the respondents cringe a bit when I approach them. I assume they don't want to be touched by a one-armed man, like one-armedness is some kind of virus. They kept looking at the end of my shoulder like something might pop out of there and hurt them. Maybe they sense my ability at extremity regeneration. Maybe they're scared of the combination of a new arm suddenly springing from my nub, grabbing one of the pies and hitting them in the face with it. The image in my head makes me smile. I let out a small giggle. This disturbs them even more. Now they think I'm crazy. I'm not. But that would be fucking hilarious.

Manning enters and helps me out. I notice he helps Nikki a little more, as it seems this woman is very aware of how to keep men around her body and she squirms and Ooooos and Awwws when Manning touches her fingers to attach the sensor.

"Did you bake those pies?" she asks him.

"I helped. And do you know what?"

She leans into him, puts her ears close to his mouth as he whispers to her, "We made them from scratch."

"You should taste my pie," she tells him.

"Do you bake, too?" he asks.

"Not that kind of pie. You know, my pie," she coos but Manning isn't getting what she means. She tries some more: My cooch snack, my cherry triangle, my dirty dessert, sugar snatch, and a bunch more inventive names for her vagina. He just smiles. We are wasting time. Move on.

The attached sensors will give us bio-feedback on the physical and emotional reactions as a contrast to the logical ones. Manning and Peeples enter all three into the FOCUS ON HUMANITY data assessor, along with my report, camera images, and sound, and the machine spits out the results, which I never see, but I trust gives them and the companies we do the research for the answers they seek.

"I'm going to show you some digi's," I tell them in my most cool-as-a-cucumber voice. "After it's over, I want you to take a bite out of either the cherry pie or the lemon meringue."

They shuffle in their seats, and I have seen this before: tremendous consternation about being confronted with a decision, a commitment, a choice, no matter how small, how trivial. Since The Calamities, no one wants to take responsibility for anything, lest their decision domino into another riot, protest, crime wave, or just a series of killings or suicides.

"What if I don't like the cherry?" asks Mary, the oldest in the group.

"Then you should eat the lemon meringue," I tell her.

"What if I don't like lemon meringue?" asks Louis, a heavyset man who looks as if there is very little in the way of food he doesn't like.

"Then you should have the cherry," I tell him.

"What if I don't like either the cherry or the lemon meringue?" asks Shania, an even heavier set black version of Louis, who looks like she never met a pie flavor she didn't like.

"Is that true?" I ask her. She fidgets, looks at the two options in front of her, and asks, "Which one is sweeter?'

"That is part of the test," I tell her, once again, in my most modulated voice, even though some dark energy force inside of me wants to fucking strangle these morons and I have never felt that before and can only deduce that this moodiness has to do with the ever-present irritation of my nub.

"You will decide which one is sweeter," I tell them.

"What're you gonna eat?" Robbie the revolutionary asks me, as if what I was going to eat was somehow the right answer to a test that had none.

"I'm not going to eat."

"Is it because of your arm?"

I look at the group, confronted by these two now-threatening desserts, as their eyes dart to my empty sleeve, then to my left healthy arm, then back to the pies, cherry to lemon then back to empty sleeve then to complete arm.

They want to get back on their Devices, but these are the rules: No Devices during the test and that makes them nervous. This is usual. This is why I have to speak in a modulated voice and also carry the paralyzer gun.

"How much can we eat?" asks Nikki, "One bite…" and her eyes go to the nub of my shoulder, "Or the whole thing?" and her eyes to my full arm. And I must say, I like her. She has a certain allure, and she is not afraid to look at my armless shoulder.

"That will depend on your appetite," I tell her. "There is another digi after the one I am going to show you," I say as I scan the room to see their eyes beginning to glaze over from not being able to use any of their Devices for the past twenty or so minutes.

My mind wanders too. All this inane questioning about pies and arms has me thinking of the vague memory images and sounds of two men named Abbott and Lou talking in increasingly frenzied tones about "Who was on first, what is on second and I don't know is on third." It was a chant, I thought, maybe a part of a religious ceremony, and it had such a confusing meaning. I had no idea what they were talking about, though I believe it has something to do with existentialism, as what I know about that philosophy is that the adherents generally confused people in the same way as the Abbott and Lou's "What-Who-I-Don't-Know" philosophy.

Dr. Manning said that before the coma, I was a big fan of ancient television, where people watched endless hours of black and white images on screens larger than that of the Devices. He believes most of the images were ways of capturing the history of the civilization. If that is the case, it is easy to understand why things spiraled downward so fast.

*****

"We ready?" I ask.

"One more thing…?" This comes from the end of the table, from Mary, a woman who looks like she volunteered to absorb all the injustices in the world: dark circles under her eyes, a gray complexion, and a tattered scarf around her head. She has no eyebrows as a result of treatments for radiation exposure. Or she could be a victim of the dreaded outbreak of alopecia ten years ago. I have seen this before. Also, she was part of a test group to try out a whole new slew of anti-cancer drugs, one of which was called Tumerity, which doesn't kill cancerous tumors as much as put them to sleep or slow down their processes. But it also exhausts the patient and the sleepy patients were often said to be, "tumor slow," and the phrase, "She's in tumor hold," became popular.

I know this because the profile cards have to list conditions and drug use, as we need to know everything we can about the respondent's medical past should we want to perform experiments on selected members or offer them certain drugs they might have an adverse reaction to.

"Yes…" and I check her name plate, "…Mary?"

She pulls a card out of her purse and gets the others to hand it down to me.

"In case I die from eating the pies," she says, barely audible, face down to her bony hands folded on the table top, "That's who you should call to get my body."

Now the group is back to being agitated, shuffling in their seats to distance themselves from somebody who could die eating pies, and pissed because the distance puts them closer to Nikki and the threat of a sexual disease. They are between a rock and a hard place, which is a phrase I like very much. Her statement also makes them look at the pies a little cautiously.

Robbie speaks up, big smile on his face and says, "Cut the crap. She's in a tume zone. Show the digi!" I note "tume zone." I have to keep up on the ever-changing vernaculars. I start the digi player and the group focuses on the screen.

The screen fills with a compilation of the worst scenes of human death, disaster and degradation Manning and Peeples could assemble, with some help from the in-house migrant workforce: A woman is engulfed in flames and you can see her face bubble up and melt; a little boy is hit by a truck and practically disintegrates; a group of Islamic terrorists saw the head off a man and place it on his stomach; a fat man disembowels himself; a woman puts a gun in her mouth and blows her brains out; a man slices his penis off and eats it; Chinese children hang from a tree and are hacked to death by two men; a razor blade slices open an eye; a woman has her clitoris removed; a man's head is axed open and children pull out his brains.

There are more scenes of people on fire, being run over by cars, cut in two with buzz saws, smashing on the pavement after suicide jumps, mutilations to every appendage, cannibalism, mouth to mouth vomit exchange, shit eating, shitting into people's mouths, and a man tied by his hands and feet to the bumpers of two cars, the cars taking off in opposite directions, and the man being pulled completely apart as a pack of dogs eat his entrails while he is still alive. It's a fucking parade of the worst of humanity.

Then it ends. I look at the group and wait. Nikki asks if that is all. I say yes.

She eats the cherry pie. Robbie eats the meringue. Mary eats the meringue. Tina, Shania, and Louis all choose cherry. They are very focused on making sure they get a certain amount of pie on their forks, and they think about the flavor, chew slowly, and swallow, then they put their forks down, except for Louis and Shania, who take another piece. Done.

"I need to get on my CommDevice," Nikki says as she starts to punch in some numbers as if I gave her permission, "I have an appointment."

The rest join in, each telling me they have to get on one of the specialized Devices to do specific things.

"Stop. If you don't put those down you won't get paid. The test isn't over. Please." Slowly, they obey. Devices clank back into the basket.

"We gonna get more pie?" Shania asks.

I lift the remote control to the digi player, "I have another digi and after seeing this one, those of you who ate the cherry must eat the meringue and vice versa." I press the start button on the remote.

"Vice versa, what?" asks Tina. "What do you mean vice versa?"

I stop the digi player. "If you ate the meringue, now you must have the cherry," I tell her as I feel a sharp twinge in my shoulder. I wince. Mary asks me what is wrong. I feel nauseous. Nikki asks me if I want some pie.

"No, I'm fine. Can we proceed?"

"I don't like cherry," asserts Robbie, "Never did. Never will."

It is clear their appetites have not been diminished by a digi filled with what Manning and Peeples know to be some of the most brutal human against human scenes ever captured. This is not new. We have seen it before, but month after month, the reactions have become even more calloused and detached, and with the restrictions placed on their Devices, they eat with more determination, as if they are angry at the pie, and eat it so it will cease to exist. They also take bigger bites. They eat to defy the images. Their appetites now have anger to increase them.

Perhaps this will help the food company – and I don't know which one it is – sell more of their product. If they enclose a violent digi with each product that people can watch while eating whatever they are selling, they will buy more. Ingenious.

I turn on the second digi. It is of a single dead white dog, bloated and rigor- mortised, floating down a flooded river.

The disgust on the part of the respondents is palpable.

"How can you show that?" demands Shania as Tina covers the eyes of her bug-eyed little dog. "I'm going to be sick," she says, covering her mouth.

"Please eat the alternate pie," I instruct them.

Nikki and Robbie eat. The rest don't. This is new. It used to be one hundred percent rejection. Now it's two out of the five that find the pie appealing. Even Robbie, who hates cherry pie, or so he says.

"I ought to throttle you," says Louis. "'Cept for the fact that you have a paralyzer gun and one arm."

"It will grow back," I tell him.

They all push away from the table, except Nikki, who tells me she would like to watch that. This was a mistake. This is sharing my personal life with these strangers. I am not supposed to do that. I'm slipping. Not as sharp as I used to be.

"Give me my money," demands Robbie, and I do. Six envelopes, one to each, as they march out of the room. Nikki gives me her card and says, "You and me, we're 'them,' aren't we? Come by some time. I can help you make the transition from who you are to being 'them.'"

"But I won't be 'them' after my arm grows back," I tell her.

"Yes, you will. You'll be a different sort of 'them.' Now, they look at you out of pity and they hate feeling pity. If your arm grows back, and it's not my place to say whether it will or not, they'll look at you out of fear. You're going to be a category of 'them' whether you like it or not."

I look at the card. It's three inches by five. It says: NIKKI SEX: CERTIFIED SEXUAL LITERACY INSTRUCTOR AND CONFIDENCE BUILDER. It has a close-up photo of a disembodied vagina.

"It's mine," she informs me. "And that's close to actual size, so it's tight."

ENTRY 12

LITERATURE FOR DUMMIES AND THE CREATION OF GENDUMMY.

S ometime at the end of the last century, with the advent of complicated and expensive technologies that no one knew how to use, there was a need to explain the technologies to the masses that used them. This is believed to be the event that started the Dummies Literary Movement. At first, the books were written to help people understand computer technology but quickly spread to other seemingly hard-to-master chores: plumbing, electrical work, French, philosophy, politics, public speaking, toilet training, cooking, eating, sex, tooth care, perfume making, floral arranging, piloting aircraft, and the volume that was reported to be the best-selling book of all time: *Ignorance for Dummies*. A whole generation grew up getting the bulk of their information from these books. Marketers called them "GenDummy," and since they were labeled and branded, they got organized. The company grew so profitable it was able to dictate policy to the government and use the influence they accumulated from their bestseller, *Terrorism for Dummies*. The information in this book led to the nuclear attacks on the East Coast, Maryland, and parts of Northern Virginia, including Washington, D.C., which for over two centuries was the focal point of the government of the Empire of the United States, until the corporations decided the government was too expensive, cumbersome to their needs, and unreliable, and did away with it completely.

But the book was blamed for the catastrophes. Over ten million people were wiped off the earth, and many more had their gene codes damaged, which led to an epidemic of freak births and an increase in infant mortality. And so the publisher was outlawed and the inventory burned. Which led to the Dummy Riots by the GenDummies, who were led by the authors – an aging hotel heiress and the multi-racial adopted children of two movie stars – of the follow-up book, *Rioting for Dummies.*

The Dummies were passionate but clumsy in their rebellion. They had explosives and tended to have a lot of accidents with them, twice blowing up their headquarters and killing about a third of the staff. It was clear they hadn't read their own *Bombs for Dummies* books. The Dummies were either rounded up and transformed or they got jobs. The leaders, mostly living off their rapidly depleting trust funds, flatly refused to work. Two thousand sixty-two people died in the riots, and it is official CRL history that the founders were the ones to blame. They were incarcerated in Iceland, under a rock where the Elves lived. As far as the mortality rate of the Dummy Riots, one of the news sites said at the time of the final body count: THAT'S A LOT OF DUMMIES.

—Shoulder on fire! Rip off the fucking shirt! Tear off the fucking bandages! Turn on the fucking water! Splash the fucking nub!

There. Emerging from the fold, a small white bubble. Sliding up and down the tender two freshly healed folds of the skin. Folds like Marsha's vagina, like the picture of Nikki's vagina. White little bubble, out of the shaved vagina on my shoulder. Peppermint bubble gum chewing labia.

Feed the fucker. Cup water in your hands. Shit! One hand. Not a great cup. Fuck. It's growing. Growing things need to get fed. Feed the fucker. Splash it. Cool it off. Make it drink. Drink. Hide. Fuck you.

It doesn't retract. It stops moving. It stops itching. More water. Feed the fucker. Grow motherfucker. Grow now. Give me a new arm. Grow and end the suspense. Show them they're wrong. Show them I'm not crazy. Cooperate. Reveal. Truth. Vindication.

Another bubble slips through a fold! Good, you grow back now! Give me another, here, more water. Good. Three more white bubbles. Pop. Pop. Pop. Lined up in a row. My new knuckles. The beginning of a fist. Beneath that, a whole hand, opposable thumb, what makes us different.

"Let's review, OK, John?"

It's Peeples. In the bathroom. It seems all my meetings will now take place in the bathroom.

My knuckles retract. This is between me and them. Nobody they don't know. Nobody they don't trust. Not that Dr. Peeples can't be trusted, or Manning for that matter. No, these are fine men, but my growth is new, it's young, it should be distrustful. Wary of newcomers, looky-loos, gawkers, tourists. There has been so much destruction. The world is in a boatload of pain.

"Yes, Doc," though the suddenly emerging new hand from my shoulder makes reviewing the groups the furthest thing from my mind.

"Looks like your arm is healing."

"It's growing back, if that's what you mean by healing."

I must continue to think my thoughts. Record all I think and feel. Accurately. In real-time. As it happens. As I feel it. Commit it to memory and compare it to memories past, that's what Manning and Peeples told me to do. My arm is growing back. They want to understand the process. If the arm hides, how will they know? I'm not crazy, I'm sure of that, and I'll stand toe to toe with anyone who says I am.

Then, of course, one of the things I've learned is that crazy people don't think they are crazy. It's the world that's crazy. But that's in reasonable times. Right now, the times are crazy, and so I am not.

I am a focus group moderator, not prone to frenzy. A confident man.

"Let's review. We have to fill out the report for the company we're doing the research for, and we always like how you write them," Peeples says. Of course they do. I am an orderly but imaginative thinker, a brutal editor of my own words, and an accurate yet lively interpreter of the findings. They say I write with swagger. They say I do that because prior to the coma, I was a big fan of gangster digi's. They say I talk like a gangster, write like I talk. They say it's fun to read. Fine. I'm game.

*****

I stand at the entrance of their office. Dr. Manning listens to classical music – Harry Belafonte and Johnny Mathis. Loud. Too loud to enter his office. I stand at the door, my toes atop the saddle of the doorway.

He giggles at a ragged, dog-eared book on his lap: *Jokes for Dummies*.

He has a whole library of the Dummies publications. Maybe one of the largest remaining collections in the world.

Manning smiles ear to ear.

"John, do you know why the chicken crossed the road?"

"No," I tell him, loud enough for him to hear me over the strains of "Chances Are" coming out of the giant speakers on the floor of his office. He plays vinyl disks. They are very pretty. Marsha doesn't have what is called a record player. No one does. Just Manning. He has a lot of old things. Sometimes I think dust is a bit of a life force for him.

He gets up and takes the vinyl disk off the record player and tells me it was for the chicken to get to the other side of the road.

"It's quite a brilliant thought, don't you think?" he asks me.

"It's stupid," I tell him, 'cause it is.

"No, John. It is an unthought-of logical question off a rare observation," Peeples says as he squeezes by me and walks into Manning's sanctuary.

"Chickens rarely cross the road," Peeples says. "The sensation of a different surface on their feet. It gives them instinctive pause. But what the hell. Who knows that? So the human mind reels. It is incapable of the obvious and so it cycles through a series of hypothetical possibilities..." he continues. "To get food, to save its chicks, to exercise, to avoid the axe, to run from the wolf..."

"Or the cat, or the rooster..." adds Manning.

"Or the coyote, right, John?" Peeples says with a big grin on his face and it's not a funny grin, it's a challenging grin, and my mind is back to the attack, back to my finger being sliced from my hand and my arm being torn off my torso, and that memory, fresh with smell and wet and pain, makes me wince. Thanks Doc. How much do I owe you?

"We've calculated over five hundred possible scenarios as legitimate answers to this question," Manning says, and now he sounds like the research master of the human condition that I have grown to love and respect. "But it's one," he adds: "To get to the other side."

"The side we must get to, right, John?" Peeples says.

Manning has the Johnny Mathis vinyl disk in his hands, and turns it over and over and with the dusk light flashing off the disk and the black vinyl going from black to orange and back, it is mesmerizing.

"This was made from oil," he says, as he too is hypnotized by the shape and feel of the disk and the dusk turning the black vinyl to bright orange. "And they don't have much, never did, really, but what they did have they made into a receptacle of music. Fascinating."

"And buttons." Peeples chimes in. "A lot of buttons."

"Why do you say 'they'?" and I can't believe I just blurted that out. You don't question the Docs. It must be the arm, the lack of the arm, my vagina shoulder, my bubble knuckles. I feel a change coming on. I'm changing inside. I'm not just an observer anymore, I want to participate. I want to create a better world for my new arm.

I had heard this in the expert groups, the groups where we questioned the skilled. The enlightened elite, as they were categorized. Doctors of body, mind and physics, grid experts, water experts, shelter builders, legal consultants, inventors. The experts that knew what most everybody else didn't. They too referred to the rest – the great unwashed, the everyman – as "They."

Peeples sits in Manning's beanbag chair, another relic of a past when furniture was not supposed to have shape. "John, we do very important work here." He adjusts to get the right of bulk of beans to support his neck, then pats his hair down over his ears and says, "We seek to understand the previous generations and the generations to come."

I can feel my bubble knuckles moving beneath my shirt.

"My arm is growing back," I say.

"So you have said," says Manning.

"John, why did the chicken cross the road?" Peeples asks.

"To get to the other side," I answer.

"Well, then…there you go." Manning adds.

"Let's talk about your groups," and Peeples brings me right around to what is my job, my insights and questions, my download, my digi-dump.

"The groups still exhibit a callous nature when confronted by death," I tell him. "But they eat the pie, nonetheless. And all existing research should indicate revulsion. Unless the pictures weren't strong enough?"

"They were the most repulsive in existence," Manning says and they were.

"Does anybody think it might have been because this batch of pies might have been extraordinary?" Peeples says.

"Then why didn't they eat them when confronted by the dead animal?" I ask.

"Surely, I jest," Peeples says, very pleased with himself.

Manning informs me it's not about the images; it's about the pie. He tells me we're testing for an additive that can calm the psychotic, the angry, the nervous. An additive that can soothe the masses. To be applied to pie or any one of the other still acceptable comfort foods. A chemical catalyst that can flood the brain with dopamine and slow the reaction to fear and horror in the anterior cingulate cortex. It makes sense. "And so we put a certain amount of this additive into the pie to achieve results."

"But it did not affect the taste. I do love cooking things," Peeples says, "Especially the aroma of the food. The smell of it."

My new knuckles agitate under my shirt. They are either agreeing or disagreeing to the additives, the chicken, the road, the action of crossing it, or to Peeples' Pies. No one knows if The Calamities might return in the event of another asteroid shower. If peoples' brains are flooded with dopamine, their stomachs won't ache, and they won't suffer so much watching their children suffer, and they might not riot. The CRL would pay dearly to maintain peace with pie.

"It has been observed that hungry men can become sated just by having food vibrantly described to them," Manning says, "So we'll flood their brains with dopamine and provide rich descriptions of food to them on the InfoDevices."

I can almost feel that somehow, inside my shirt, in the recesses of my nub, covered in viscera, my new hand was giving the thumbs-up to this caliber of thinking.

ENTRY 13

DOGS AND THEIR CURIOUS REPUTATION AS MAN'S BEST FRIEND.

This phrase, part of the vernacular of the Empire of the United States, was said to have been created approximately fifty years ago in a digi drama – then called television movies – called *The Trial of Old Drum.* It was the story of a dog that was shot by a villain somewhere in the midwestern farm country, where shootings of people and dogs were frequent, especially at high schools and fast food establishments. The prosecutor, one George West, in an attempt to further vilify the man who shot the dog, said, "The one absolutely unselfish friend that a man can have in this selfish world, the one that never deserts him and the one that never proves ungrateful or treacherous, is his dog." Later, that statement was shortened to "Man's Best Friend," though The Institute has no idea why the media would take such license, except that it stuck in people's minds better than West's rather longer statement. The history of the superiority of the dog goes back centuries, to an influential visionary named Buddha – whether this is his first or last name is unknown – where it was written that on the day he died, he summoned all the animals in the country to his side. The Institute has no idea how he did this, as it was surely before communication devices, so we assume he had a lot of helpers, or a special whistle. Only twelve species reached him before his death, among them dogs, and he rewarded all those who reached him with a year named after them. Cats have no such year, as they never showed up for Buddha's death, as an innate lack of obedience is fairly typical of cats, and though The Institute has never researched this, there are stories of cats eating their keepers if the keeper has died and the body goes undiscovered. The timespan for this is usually four days, which is a testament to the loyalty of cats.

Dogs have been used for therapy for certain memory diseases, and seem to offer solace to the terminally ill. For a period in the early part of the 21st century, it was believed they could detect cancers, but it was discovered that this was a rumor started by a certain Purina Dog Chow Company to be able to launch a new line of dog foods that promised to enhance the cancer-detecting abilities of dogs. They named the product line "Down Cancer!" Dogs were also used to help the blind and to help firemen fight fires. With the shortage of dogs as a result of The Calamities, cats were then used to help lead the blind and fight fires. This was less than satisfactory. Due to their instinctive independence, they often tried to escape their leashes and ran their blind masters out into streets or over cliffs, often to tragic results. But The Institute has reason to believe that cats had evolved to a point that this was a bit like hunting for their food, as they knew they could eat their recently departed masters. They also wanted nothing to do with fires, as when the firemen turned the hoses on, they would run away, being terrified of water, never to be found again. It is rumored that most of the cats now live somewhere in Mexico, where they are allowed to sleep all day.

—Home. Lassie's at the door. She sniffs my shoes. I tear open a snack bag of "I Can't Believe This is Dog Food," and dump it into a bowl.

Lassie never rushes to her food. She watches me do this, then goes off and does something else, and somehow, later, the bowl is empty, but I have never seen her eat. Dr. Manning says that's because in Ecuador, the eating of food is a very private matter, especially for circus dogs, who have their bowls stolen by the midget clowns.

She follows me to the bedroom. I sit on the bed. Lassie jumps up onto it and stares at my armless shoulder. "You don't believe me either, do you?" I say, even though I wouldn't be surprised if she did. Nothing she did surprised me. We had been doing some brain cell swap experiments on some respondents, where we would take some cells from the brain stems of male dogs and implant them in a human brain and implant the removed cells from the human and give them to the dog. The purpose was to see if the cell swap helped humans understand dogs better, or dogs understand humans better.

In the case of the humans, their sense of smell increased exponentially. In the case of the male dogs, they just stopped raising their legs to pee.

*****

Lassie examines my nub, sniffing and being thoughtful.

My new knuckles are resting, I'm sure of it. I hear Marsha come home and clank her arrival: bags and belongings and Devices and shoes.

"Look what I did," Marsha says as she enters the bedroom, holding a handful of my shirts above her head, and plops the shirts on the bed. They have all been tailored to have one arm. The right sleeve is altered at the shoulder, sliced at its throat, and heat-fixed closed like the full sleeve never existed.

"My arm is growing back," I tell her.

"Well, until it does, it's better than tying it in a knot."

Lassie licks the folds on the part of the shirt that covers my nub and knuckles. She sniffs and licks, very focused now. She senses something.

"Do you want me to pump?" I ask Marsha in the best seductive voice I can muster. But it's not the moment. I don't really feel it. I don't think she feels it. And I keep thinking of Nikki and her twat card.

"Try on one of the shirts," she tells me and I'm up and my soiled shirt is off and I'm putting one of my Marsha-altered shirts on.

My nub is tight against the altered sleeve of the shirt. No room for my knuckles. They agitate. Lassie comes out from behind a chair, jumps back on the bed, and places her head against my nub like Donna Reed used to place her forehead against her child's to check for fever. I don't know how I just had that memory. It's happening more and more. A flash of an image. Out of time. Out of place. From either the Age of Black and White or the Age of Color. I prefer those from the Age of Black and White. They calm me.

"They're too tight. There's no room for growth," I tell Marsha. She frowns, and asks me how work was.

"I don't understand why I'm doing what I'm doing. I've run the pie test about twenty times since I've come out of the coma. At first it was very interesting, astounding really, as people could still eat even when confronted by human suffering and mutilation. Now..."

"What do you think The Calamities were about?" she asks me. "They made everyone care less about life, as everyone lost a life in their own lives. So perhaps seeing other people suffer reminds them that they must eat to stay alive."

I think about this. On the surface her observation feels profound, real smart, but as a researcher, I am cautious of profundity. But I can't deny, Marsha can be one sharp cookie.

"I just think Dr. Peeples' pies are getting better," I tell her.

Nailed it!!! Objective interpretive analysis that could be construed as irony were it not so accurate.

Marsha leaves the room.

*****

Lassie stares at me. She's absolutely locked in on me.

"Come on, girl, let's go for a walk." I tell her, "Let's go to the dog run, and let you have a day amongst your own kind."

I've never taken Lassie to what they still call the "Dog Park." I never saw the need to go, and Lassie, even though we have driven by it many times, never really expressed any interest, never craned her head out of the car window, tongue wagging and showing that she wanted to be with her kind, frolic in the dirt and mud and shit freely, but that's mostly because I've never even seen her shit. She is very secretive. Manning and Peeples say it's because she is a circus dog.

But the day is sunny, and the reading on the Neutron Meter for atmospheric radiation is at the acceptable level for spending longer than two hours out of doors.

Over the years, with the decline in the dog population due to The Calamities, and the fact that the CRL made it mandatory that all new dogs be spayed at birth, the parks were becoming populated with a veritable menagerie of different types of animals: monkey, ferret, mountain lion, ostrich, rabbit, raccoon, wolf, snake, iguana, skunk, rat, and mole. Most of the animals had to have their containment chips updated before coming, as each would be scanned before entering the park. The containment chips signaled that the animal had been sedated prior to arrival. It was necessary as there were too many times where the mountain lions and the wolves pretty much ate all the other animals except the snakes and the iguanas. It didn't stop the snakes from eating the moles or the ferrets, but it did stop them from biting humans. The monkeys took to climbing the high fences, only to be electrocuted at the top.

So, in order to keep order, every animal was in a stupor. Most of them just drooled and slept in their own shit while their owners would sit outside the fence playing on their Devices. At the end of the hour, hoses would spray the animals and wash the fecal matter down the gutters that framed the park. The whole soup of shit washed down to the ocean, where it created a sludge that deadened the oceans up to ten miles out.

*****

Lassie stuck her head out the car window and stared at the dog park. Today was an unusual one. Somebody decided to bring an elephant. I had heard of this, as a group of animal activists closed the last zoo down and auctioned off the elephants to people with sizable backyards and the money to pay exorbitant water bills. The woman who owned this elephant – and I recognized her from the infoDevice entry that covered her story – became a bit of a sensation when her elephant went on a rampage and plowed through the neighbor's garage and took out half the kitchen. The neighbor sued, but the woman had a lot of money from writing both *Ignorance for Dummies* and *Ventriloquism for Dummies,* and she just exhausted the neighbor with legal fees. The neighbor, defeated and destitute, committed suicide.

The elephant now lives in the deceased neighbor's back yard.

*****

Lassie stares at the activity in the park, then sits down in the back of the car. I want to get her out so she might get exercise chasing monkeys, and frankly, maybe show off some of the skills she learned in the circus, with the elephant there as a trusted partner. That would be rather cool, I think, to see my dog show off a bit.

Today, in addition to the elephant, there are five other dogs, two chimps, an armadillo, and two flamingos. The dogs play with each other in their drugged fashion, the chimps beat the armadillo with a stick and try to pry it open, and the flamingos huddle in terror on spindly, snapable, avian legs.

"C'mon, girl! Let's go have some exercise," I say in my best dog owner voice, waving my arm and running in place to show how much fun it is to be active, as if I needed to tell an animal used to jumping through burning hoops about exercise. She ain't buying it. I don't blame her.

I reach in the back of the car and get my arm around the dog and lift and I can't. I get a better grip and try again and the dog is just too heavy, or the muscles in my left arm have atrophied since the attack. This is not a big dog. She shouldn't weigh any more than fifty pounds max, but shit, she feels like she weighs two hundred.

I start to push Lassie off the seat and onto the floor, but that doesn't work either. She's a cinder block, and I don't have enough strength to move her.

"C'mon, girl, help me out. Let's get out of the car." Mechanically, like someone just going through the motions because they don't want to disappoint, she gets up, jumps down from the car, waddles into the park, right past the chip scanner, which sets off an alarm, and she crunches down on the armadillo's shell. The armadillo owner shrieks, "You killed it!" The chimps jump around Lassie and hit her with sticks, but Lassie growls at them with such ferocity that they run and climb the fence, get shocked and fall to the ground with a thud and now the chimp owners race to the fence and scream at me too.

The screams of the pet owners freak the elephant. The elephant stampedes across the length of the park, builds up a head of steam and crashes through the fence, freeing the frightened flamingos. The dogs run like drunks in every direction, barking in a low pitch and the hoses turn on automatically and wash the electrocuted chimps into the sewage canal. They get swept up in the force of the water and into a chute and are washed down to the ocean.

Lassie leaves the park, gets in the car, and sits. Ezra approaches out of nowhere and starts issuing tickets to everyone, but I get the majority of them.

"You didn't put the dog through the scanner," he tells me as he issues me the first ticket.

"I know, Ezra, she jumped out of the car and charged in."

"Dogs have to be leashed until they are in the park," he says as he issues me the second.

"I didn't get a chance…"

"Killed an armadillo and they are an endangered species," he says as he issues me the third.

"C'mon girl, let's get out of this stupid place," I tell Lassie.

"Denigrating an essential service," Ezra says as he issues me a fourth ticket and marches away to confront the onlookers and owners and issue them their tickets for whatever infraction he conjures up.

ENTRY 14

THE HISTORY OF ALTERNATELY AND NON-ABLED PERSONS IN ENTERTAINMENT AS IT HAS INFLUENCED SOCIETAL PERCEPTIONS.

T he Institute's best research into the area of how those born with deformities –both mental and physical – were treated in society comes mostly from the ancient digi's provided by the digi makers of the past century. In all the digi's, those who were retarded (a term later used only by the retarded, much like the "nigga" word which was licensed in the early part of the century to black citizens only), crippled, mentally ill, without limbs, without fully formed limbs, or with distorted, damaged appendages fell into two categories: villain or victim. They either were evil incarnate, thereby feeding into the already latent fears by others of ever succumbing to such a condition, or they were the hapless recipient of their unfortunate circumstance, thereby eligible for our pity and aid. But it is clear from our interviews and outside research, including some intuitive insights, that neither of these portrayals had anything to do with how these people felt about themselves. It was very hard for them to do wrong, as they couldn't get away with it easily. Being retarded, if they commited a crime, it's not like they could get away fast or lie well (The Institute will use this phrase in its classic definition of meaning "slow," thus less developed than others). They didn't look for sympathy, but they also didn't want doors closed on their wheelchairs or stumps. So the portrayals were mostly created to placate the abled and healthy, and to

warn against the dangers of mating with the deformed, and increasing their numbers, thus putting undue stress on the finances of the state.

—"I'm scared of you, John. I'm scared for you. I'm also scared for us."

Marsha and I sit up in bed. Lassie peers over our sheeted feet. Her head turns left-right-left-right in the direction of whoever is doing the talking.

"What's happening to us? Why do you feel something is happening to us?" I ask her, knowing full well the answer, but using my focus group moderator behavior. It's the arm and the fact it's growing back. But maybe it's also because I sense I'm getting increasingly agitated by little things that never bothered me before. I get these energy surges that turn me anxious, and I'm not quite sure how to handle them.

"John, you walk around the house in a daze, talking to yourself, talking to the dog, rarely talking to me…"

"You don't like what I have to say!"

"Which is what, John? Which is what!?"

I see we are back to where we've been winding up of late. She will not engage me in a discussion of my arm, or its complete regeneration (notice I didn't say merely "regeneration." It's already started that, yessiree! with a fine fistful of waxy white bubbles as proof. So the only thing that's a question in my mind is whether they'll follow through and complete the deal).

*****

Marsha moved in with me about a week after I came out of the coma. We met at a CRL supply store. I was picking up some processed water and artificial bananas and Marsha had her cart loaded up with plant foods, feminine hygiene products, donuts, and some batteries. Our carts got stuck in the narrow aisles, the wire corners of the carts got entangled, and we stood face to face when I smiled at her very sympathetic, honest face. No beauty, but eyes you could trust. At first she was bothered, but then with all the machinations of trying to unhook the carts, it became a two-person operation and we discovered a sort of rhythm and a way to communicate with each other.

"I think if I lift this corner up and you pulled yours away we might free them up," I told her, and she added, "How about if when you lift I first push to the left then pull it away? That might unhook it," and we agreed and that was just what the doctor ordered. Her solutions were logical and well thought out. I liked that a lot.

In time, I discovered that she knew things. I, right after the coma, knew nothing, just the disconnected images of old digi's and language in my damaged memory banks. Untrustworthy information for sure.

She had a grasp on the world. I was floating in its broth. She could take care of me, talk to me, teach me to remember all that I'd forgotten. After we got the carts unhooked, she came back to my apartment and after some light conversation, we went into the bedroom and she groped at my body for a time. I had a tough time responding, as I didn't remember the last time I had sex and had forgotten the dance steps. She asked me if I was gay. I said, "No, this is just awkward. I don't really know what to do."

Somehow, this sent her to what is called "over the moon." I was a neophyte. A greenhorn. Maybe I was a virgin. The idea that she might be my first made her, as she told me, "wet." She put me in her mouth. Nothing. She masturbated for me. Nothing. She manipulated me until I could tell she felt her hand cramp up and her arm go numb. Nothing. All nothing. All for naught. All a stupendous waste of time except as a calorie-burning exercise.

This was the inaugural moment of the discovery of my erectile dysfunction.

Not to let the whole afternoon go to waste, she instructed me on what to do to her. So I licked her. I put my fingers in her. She held my hand and moved it around her clitoris. I got a little improvisational and pinched her nipples, which seemed to punch her ticket. She asked that I insert one of the bananas I bought into her, and I did that too. And then she had an orgasm, and a tear rolled down her cheek and for some primal reason I licked it and it tasted wonderful and at the same time, she liked that I did that.

After the sex, she got up, looked around the apartment and saw my dying, neglected plants and immediately set about to rejuvenate them by feeding them "They Won't Believe It's Not Plant Food."

The plants perked up almost immediately. It was then I realized that Marsha was in essence a caregiver. I needed a caregiver. I need as much care as I could get right now. Everything around me was alien. My neighborhood, the people in it, the way things operated. My Docs helped me get oriented the first week, but she could be my full-time tour guide until parts of my memory flooded back and took their rightful place in the folds of my brain. I could pay her in orgasms and she would reward me further in tears.

And we've been together ever since.

*****

But right now, I terrify her. I threaten the simplicity of her life. I present her with small daily challenges. I know it was hard for her to get used to my flaccidness, but she dealt with it, and we got around it and she has healthy and regular orgasms. I know she lives a woman's disappointment at my inability to ejaculate and impregnate her, but, Jesus H Christ, this lack of a next generation is something everyone is dealing with right now. I know that without me it would be harder on her, and this world is not a safe place for a woman alone. It's rough, chaotic, violent, psychotic, and too, too sad. There are just too many plants dying all over for anyone to tend to.

You are better off being in a miserable relationship than no relationship at all, as at least your misery has focus. At least misery becomes a team sport. You can both work on it. You can take the focus off your own unsolvable pain and blame it on your partner. But right now, I need to put her at ease.

"OK, I'll go see my Docs," I tell her, "I will get a complete evaluation. We'll run a series of tests to see if I am hallucinating. It could be I am having phantom visions of an arm. It is totally possible, as I have read about that in the hospital literature. OK?"

"OK," and it's a little girl's OK, so sweet, and from Marsha, not unsexy.

"Do you want me to pump?" I ask her, responding to the little girl sexiness.

I look over to her. She's asleep, the weight of her worry relieved by the promise of an examination, which reassures her I'm not crazy, because the last thing crazy people want to do is see a doctor who tells them they're crazy.

My nub stirs. My knuckles jostle. Time to visit with my babies.

*****

I turn on the bathroom light. I pull the bandage off my nub and lean into the mirror to get a closer look at the things crawling around my new flesh.

If my eyes were not as good as they are, my little bubble knuckles could be mistaken for maggots, feeding on my damaged, oozing skin.

I rub my eyes. In the mirror, coming out of the folds of skin are four thin, delicate, spindly new fingers. They are wet, just born, boneless it seems. In fact, they look like my flaccid penis.

*****

"Marsha!" I say in a loud whisper as I shake her back and forth in the bed.

She stirs, mumbles, and turns to look at me.

"Marsha, look!" I say as I turn on her bedside light and shove my nub and new fingers into her face. She repels, flops down on her back, rolls over and off the bed.

"What the fuck, John!"

"My arm is growing back! Look, see the little fingers," I tell her as the palm of my left hand becomes a little display shelf for my new fingers, like I just pulled a rabbit out of my hat and am doing the "TaDaaa!"

"Fuck you, you bastard! You're determined to drive me away, aren't you?"

"No...look at my fingers..." But it's pointless. She is more about having been awakened so rudely than the reason for her being awakened. And worse, the reason has disappeared. The finger show isn't there anymore.

"You must have scared them," I tell her, and we lock eyes: hers terrified, mine bewildered and definitely disappointed.

"Get out. Sleep on the couch. I don't want you near me," she says as she throws a pillow at me for emphasis.

*****

Where was it written that in the so-called war of the sexes, when the woman disagrees with the man, it's the man who sleeps on the couch, or packs a lonely bag to go to a friend's apartment or a sleep center. The woman never sleeps on the couch, even when she is wrong, which is more often than they give themselves credit for. And they would never dream of going to a sleep center because they have shared bathrooms and women have been raped, as they are populated by men with a newfound hatred of women, especially those just exodused to the sleep center.

I'm not plotting to end the relationship. I'm not looking to change my life at all. My life is all-new to me, it's unfolding daily, growing, much like my arm. I'm creating a life by speaking my memories to myself and to

Lassie, to make them real, to make them moments, and to commit them to memory, in case I ever go into a coma again. Doc Manning told me all this thinking out loud, conscious remembering, and analyzing of moments was an exercise that would help with hardening memories in my brain and making sense of a world I don't understand anymore. Talking to myself, hard remembering, carves little notches in my brain matter. And a more complicated looking brain is a smarter brain. Makes sense to me. And it's Doc's damned orders.

Plus, when your talk to yourself, you're giving speeches, sometimes to imagined audiences. And you can see them in your mind listening to your every word, sometimes even applauding you. It's healthy. It's good to be king in your own head.

I prepare the couch. I turn on the EntertainDevice and flip through the sites looking for something that will put me to sleep and calm my little babies growing out of my wound.

I'm blasted by a title: THE FUGITIVE. The Announcer introduces the story: *"Falsely convicted of the murder of his wife. Reprieved by fate when a train wreck freed him enroute to the death house. Freed him to hide in lonely desperation. Freed him to search for the One-Armed Man he saw leave the scene."*

I watch as scenes of a gray-haired man – a Dr. Richard Kimble – stares at the body of his dead wife. There is commotion, tension. He didn't do it, it's obvious. He's a doctor after all. Then, in his car's headlamps, a scruffy looking man with one arm: The One-Armed Man! He's not just unshaven, he has a heavy brow. He's almost a Neanderthal. And the One-Armed Man runs away, guilty, HE DID IT! The One-Armed Man is a criminal! All One-Armed Men are criminal! All One-Armed Men cannot be trusted! All One-Armed Men don't shave! All One-Armed Men hate women!

My heart sinks. I'm a One-Armed Man. I'm a criminal. This is why Marsha is scared. She is living with a criminal. I'm sure this is popular fare, and that over 65% of the adult population has seen the story of Richard Kimble. So now, when Marsha sees me, her mind flashes to the One-Armed Man, eyes in headlights, frozen for one second, then running away, blood under the fingernails of the hand on his only other arm. She's afraid I will murder her. That's it. This is going to be hard.

I look at Lassie. She is eating one of Marsha's prized plants, the Tracepta, an exotic meat-eating plant invented to process bacteria for pharmaceutical lab work. This depresses me some more. This is a very expensive plant. A rarity. I let this happen. But of course, I am a criminal. And now my dog has murdered her plant.

I pour myself a glass of wine and shake salt from the saltshaker into the glass. I change the channels, looking for something that will take my mind away from The Horror of the One-Armed Man.

And then: Three men in an old airplane cockpit, from the Age of Black and White, just like the One-Armed Man story. One of the men has no hands. Maybe this was an era where they were trying to make as many stories as they could about men without limbs.

I wonder whether it was a cost issue: that digi's about men with fewer limbs cost less, as if the actors charged by the limb. There were a lot of shenanigans with labor unions back then, so maybe this was a negotiating ploy.

The uniforms on the three men give them away as soldiers. Somewhere in a memory, I sense it takes place in what was a World War, which is what they called the wars in the 20th century that everyone wanted to participate in, and because it's a plane of some size and technology, it must be the number two war, the really shitty one.

The youngest has no hands. Instead, his arms end in hooks, shiny metallic hooks. He lights an ancient cigarette with practiced dexterity. The other two men look on with much the same expressions Marsha has when it comes to my new arm. The armless man notices their discomfort, and says: "I can dial a phone. I can drive a car, I can even put nickels in the juke box," and though I don't know what that is, I assume it is a pretty nifty trick and judging by the sound of the name of the box, I assume it is a box that offers some level of juke. Then he stops and gets sad: "I'm all right, but…" then one of the older men, maybe they are his bosses, asks, "But what, Sailor?" And this confuses me, as they are not on a boat but in a plane, and so I think it might be a flying boat, which is new to me. And the Sailor holds up his shiny hooks and says: "Well, see, I got a girl."

The two older men look at each other and they seem to be in pain. The Sailor continues: "Wilma's only a kid, she's never seen anything like these hooks." And that reminds me of Marsha. She has never seen anything like my new fingers, but she's hardly a kid. I wonder how old Wilma is, and whether Sailors were allowed to have sex with children as compensation for serving in the conflict. I start to stir the salt in the glass with the finger of my left hand, but think again, peel off my bandage and hold the glass up to my nub. My new index finger, the intelligent one, slides out of the fold and stirs the salt for me. Employment. Good boy.

Now the Sailor with the metal hooks is on the sidewalk, in front of a house. He looks scared. The two older men watch from a taxicab. A woman runs out of the house. She is very pretty, very fresh, wearing a lovely dress that seems to be made of summer breezes. She has a big smile on her face, and I conclude this must be the Wilma the Sailor spoke of, the "only a kid" person. She is hardly a kid, with breasts and a full mouth and not an ounce of baby fat.

She runs to him, then stops and her expression changes. She sees his hooks. The Sailor drops his bags. Wilma approaches him slowly, like he might have a disease, but it's the sight of the hooks that slows her. And they do look like a lethal early technology, some sort of torture device. He could possibly decapitate her with one swipe of his hook. He might snip a finger off, rip open a nostril, or cause great sexual torture. So she must be careful, but this is her man, and now he is home and she must trust that he won't do anything crazy. And from my memory, I do know that a lot of these men were considered heroes. They had given up their lives in the defense of whatever the government at the time deemed necessary to defend or destroy. In some cases, as this one, they gave up their hands.

She hugs him, but somehow that does not make him happy, and he just stands there and he can't hug her back. He doesn't think she will accept him, and her hug feels perfunctory. But she is hugging him, so she is accepting him. It's him! He's the jerk.

"Hug her back, asshole," I whisper loudly at the screen.

But he doesn't accept himself. He feels like I did when I left the hospital and all the athletes, with their torn tongues and broken limbs, stared at my nub.

But then you can see Wilma's face, and you can see she is scared, in unknown territory, over her head, and I wonder if she is thinking, "What else is missing?"

My new index finger gathers up the tear that is tickling the side of my face and takes it back into its nub home as one of the older men in the taxi car says as they drive away: "Gotta hand it to the Navy. They sure trained that kid to use his hooks." And then the other older man says: "They couldn't train him to put his arms around his girl, or stroke her hair."

I'm feeling so sad.

A title comes on the screen: *The Best Years of Our Lives.* I have no idea why they would name it that. These don't seem to be good years at all, not to mention best.

*****

Marsha is screaming at me now.

I take time to listen and make sure I'm not dreaming she is screaming, and after what seems like a full minute, I'm seeing Lassie with the green mash of the Tracepta leaves around its mouth. This is a very rare plant.

Marsha is screaming at me now.

ENTRY 15

DUMPLINGS AS A REPRESENTATIVE FOOD MODEL FOR PERFECT PORTABLE NUTRITION.

The Institute – with its interest in global nutrition – tracks the international popularity of the dumpling food product to the later part of the 20th century, then finds it disappearing as a food product during the height of The Calamities (though at this writing, we are not concluding that The Calamities are over) due to the emergence of the I Can't Corp. The Corp sought to remove all other food choices from the market and thus ensure a monopoly for their own products. It was harder to do in some Asian countries as dumplings are more culturally ingrained and I Can't Corp's militias found it harder to police Asia. The English and Irish gave up dumpling eating, but this might have to do with the quality of dumplings in those countries, and the fact that the I Can't Corp made food stuffs completely to their liking, as they had a long history of enjoying bland foods. But it was in the middle part of the 21st century that there was resurgence in dumpling consumption. Though the I Can't Corp's militias tried to confiscate shipments of dumplings, they were soon being made clandestinely in people's homes. There were arrests and trials and many home dumpling makers went to jail.

The Institute believes passion for dumplings has to do with the backlash against ubiquity and a lack of choice in food categories. After a period, simply put, people want different, even it different looks the same, as is the case with dumplings. Though the I Can't Corp could imitate many food substances to a near identical facsimile, they were terrible at dumplings, and to this day, The Institute cannot figure out why, except that many workers might have also harbored a love of independently made dumplings and sabotaged the formula. The CRL, sensing a potential revolt in support of the nascent dumpling movement, now called the Dumplinks! (with exclamation mark), overruled the I Can't Corp embargo and allowed limited shipments of dumplings from China and Thailand. These are priced way above I Can't Corp products, and so are only available to the more moneyed in society. The Institute finds the dumpling phenomenon has many common sense attributes: they are usually made with real meats and vegetables, and are uniquely portable. As such, they are both healthier and a better survival food, as they can be carried in the pocket or palm of hand and stay relatively fresh over time. The most popular stuffings are pork, shrimp, and vegetables (mostly soy), which are still readily available in those parts of the planet less affected by climate change or that have created alternate forms of growing vegetables and cloning meats. The Jewish community, sensing a market opportunity, also entered into the newly unregulated dumpling business with a larger, denser dumpling, made entirely of dough, without stuffing or nutrition. The CRL ruled those could only be used for self-defense.

—I struggle up, look at Lassie, who sits surrounded by the chewed-up leaves of the plant. I gather up the remaining petals, which undulate in my left hand. My babies react, they seem to spread out in the skin fold, like they are stretching, but they are reaching, I know it. They are reaching for the Tracepta leaves. They want the leaves. They want to be fed. They want to learn. They want to experience the world.

Marsha watches the whole thing with her arms crossed and her foot tapping. She is royally pissed. She is one of the few registered caretakers of the Tracepta as she had proven herself enormously skilled in plant technology on the infoDevice survey: "So You Think You Can Plant!" In fact, she won first prize.

"We'll get another one," I say, as I turn away from Marsha and lift a leaf to my right shoulder and slide it under the bandage. I don't need to alarm Marsha any more than she already is. I figure if she won't accept the fact that my arm is growing back, she'll never accept that it wants to be fed the leaves of her favorite plant.

The fingers grab the leaf. At least that's what it feels like they are doing, pulling it to them, squeezing it, then, just as fast, they stop. I feel the bandage. My babies are gone, slid back into the slit. My shoulder throbs, but a good throb. They must be chewing the leaves in there. Nourishment. Growth. Spring!

She is screaming at me now. Her mouth opens and closes and the veins in her neck bulge. My body is overcome by a tingly warmth and my mind sees blackened oceans and slick, oil-rich pastures, a lavender sky with three blue moons. It is a vision alien to me but not unknown. It calms me, yet also fills me with the desire to travel.

I am lightheaded. Maybe the plant is poisonous. Maybe that's what Marsha is yapping at me about. But I can't hear her. Maybe its poison has made me deaf. Now I'm a one-armed man and I'm turning deaf. I can only sign with one hand, destined to be only half understood. I'm fucked.

*****

Dr. Peeples and Manning. Hovering over me. Why?

Lights behind them. In silhouette. I need to ask them where I am.

"Where am I?"

"In The Institute, John," one of them says and I don't know which one as they are just two flat-black identically coiffed shapes against the harsh hospital light, if that is indeed what it is and I am not dead and that light is not the heavens opening up to accept me into The Pearly Gates Lounge, which I don't believe happens but you can't deny a ton of people have written that it's true and seemingly, millions of people want invisible friends, so…you have to think about it a bit, it's the only mature thing to do. I might be dead. I could be dead. We'll see. Here we go.

"Am I dead?"

"You had an event," one of them says. The fact that I might have hosted an event seems relatively benign, not the thing that causes one to wind up like I am now, unless the event turned ugly, which has been known to happen in these brutish times.

"You fainted!" and it's Marsha's voice cutting right through the bullshit of my daze. She sits off to the side, craning her neck to see what they are doing, which seems to be a lot of pressing down on parts of my body and tapping me with what is either a digital tuning fork or a neon green lightning bolt.

I look to my nub. It's still a nub. If I was dead, I believe my ghost would have both arms intact. I am not dead. This is good. The beginning of a good day. Top of the morning to my one-armed ass. I am not dead.

"Suddenly your Doctors appeared and I hadn't even gotten around to calling an ambulance, so I consider that an extra layer of weirdness," Marsha says. "But, I guess you have better insurance than I have!"

I do. Much better. I have The Institute.

*****

"Why aren't you taking blood, urine, samples, taking digi-images of his insides?" and it's Marsha again, my little Florence Henderson (a talented, singing Civil War battlefield nurse I remember from a digi about this especially nasty time in human history).

"We don't know why he feels this way," and as my eyes adjust to the light, I can make out that it's Doc Peeples talking. "It might just be disorientation."

"And we don't do those things much anymore, Miss…" and that's Doc Manning 'cause he can't remember Marsha's name.

"Marsha," I tell Doc Manning, and I wish he would remember.

"What kind of doctors are you?" she blurts out.

"Marsha, they're my doctors!" I snap, as only a man who is not dead can.

Doc Peeples takes the bandage off my nub and pries around the wound with his fingers and I never noticed this before but they are long and thin and look like grownup versions of my own babies.

That makes me smile.

Doc Peeples always stood with his hands in his lab coat, like all the reassuring doctors in the Age of Black and White – the same ones that carried the deathly black bags into the homes of the infirm – so this was really the first time I have ever seen his fingers. They are lovely.

"He thinks his arm is growing back," and then Marsha can't help but add, "How crazy is that? Give him something!" Yes. A pill. An "I Won't Believe I'm Crazy" pill.

Doc Manning sits down next to her, takes her hand, and applies a coat of paternal calm. "There is no magic pill I can give him to convince him his arm is not growing back, or one that will convince you it is," he says and he almost had her nodding until he got to the second part of the sentence.

"I don't need a pill to tell me the whole thing is crazy!" she says, and she's tearing up a bit, just at the corners of her eyes, not enough for me to stick my tongue in there.

Doc Peeples rises from his little nub exploratory and tells me I'm healing nicely, then slides his fingers back into his lab pockets and I smile, knowing my growing babies are progressing nicely.

"Did you see the fingers? They're in there," I say as I pry the centerfold of my wound apart with my fingers and display my shoulder orifice to both Manning and Peeples.

"Fucking Jesus!" and that's ol' Marsha again.

Peeples shakes his head. "No, John, I see nothing," he says as he tapes a fresh bandage over it as if he is pulling the curtain on a stage show.

"There! Nothing!" Marsha says. "Finally, a decent doctor thing to say!"

"They never come out when you're upset!" I remind her, as it is true that so far, I have never seen my little babies and Marsha in the same room together.

"Fine. I'll wait in the car with the armadillo-eating dog," she says as she marches out and slams the door behind her.

"She creates a great deal of stress to you, doesn't she, John?" Doc Manning asks in his calm paternal tenor.

"And she offers me a great deal of comfort. She's a good person. We have a calm life. And she accepts that I can't get an erection without the machine," I tell them. I don't like that Manning doubts my partner. I'm feeling a little insulted, Doc or not. "I can't find a single instance on the InfoDevice of a human arm being able to grow back," I tell him.

"The information on the Devices has been scrubbed so as to not alarm the populace of any normal abnormalities," Doc Peeples adds, "Or histories that might cause unrest. The CRL's mandate, given to them by the United Corporate and Governmental Governance Board, Inc., is to keep the population relatively calm until we can dig out of the mess caused by The Calamities."

"What is real is that you believe it is. That is what we know," adds Manning. "Your struggle is in convincing those around you. You risk shattering their entire belief system if indeed it is growing back. That is the greatest dilemma you face. That is the resistance of the species."

"Remember the chicken, John," Peeples says, "You must get to the other side." He goes to a medicine cabinet and pulls out a vial filled with fairly large pills. He hands them to me.

"Take one of these a day, John. Fortify yourself."

"What are they?" I ask as I hold one in the palm of my left hand.

"Supplements. Balancing ingredients. Good stuff. Too many questions, too little time. You must trust us, John."

"We are your doctors," they say in unison, and it is almost musical.

"Oh, I do. I would never not trust you," I say and I hop off the table and remove the wires from my penis and testicles.

*****

"Dumplings!" I say as I climb in the car and I can almost taste their chewy little goodness. I have a huge desire for dumplings. Veritable veggies or vat processed pork, my appetite is on fire. If the price isn't too high, I'll order, "I Can't Believe It's Not Tofu!" as a side.

Marsha drives. We don't say a word. Lassie sits on the back seat like one of the lion sculptures I saw in a digi-album of a library in New York that was one of the Useless Things That Got Destroyed in the first nuclear war.

Marsha signals and is about to merge onto the Suri Cruise Cruiseway. I hate these roads. They're dangerous, with no enforceable speed limit and every car built to go a different speed. Plus, it's the most used route by the many terrorist factions. People don't dare stop on them for either a flat tire or an accident for fear of drive-by thievery, road ragists, or Ticketists issuing triple-penalty tickets.

"Don't take the Cruiseway," I say as she approaches the PayBooth and comes to a crawl as the scanner scans the license plate. "You know I don't like the Cruiseway! It's too competitive. Take the side streets, please, Marsha, take the side streets."

"It's faster. You want dumplings," she says and she is all business right now, dictator of her world, ignorer of mine.

My nub throbs. The stress of the ride seems to be affecting the wound. Lassie merely watches out the window at the cars speeding by. The Excess doesn't go fast and we are outperformed by the cars of the poor; the Hondelet Rancids, Mercedes Thrusts, and the Chrybitchi Scar. A Rancid in front of us veers out of its lane and bangs up against a Scar, then careens back into the lane then over to the next and wings the Thrust.

It's bumper cars now, as this affects the flow of traffic, which has no rhyme or reason, and other cars screech to avoid hitting cars that have slowed or sped up to avoid the altercation. A TeslaTaTa 2000 smashes into a BMVW 21 series and then three cars spin out of control and dump into the barbed wire ditch on the side of the Payway and are immediately set upon by a gang of Stemmers, who strip the tires off the cars and take the drivers' wallets and all their Devices.

One of the drivers is obviously a criminal of sorts and he fires his pistol at one of the Stemmers, who then fire back and kill the driver, and I note that this is new as Stemmers only ever really fire at advertising.

I can see the wrecked and robbed drivers in the sideview mirror shaking their fists at both each other and the Stemmers as the Stemmers drive away in their tiny Nissiat Minutias – looking very much like pictures I have seen of clowns in the circus – and then I see them immediately set upon by three Ticketists as their Ticket-Taker 1000s spew out what is surely thousands of CRL units, practically covering the Stemmers in paper.

One of the drivers attacks a Ticketist and he is set upon by the other Ticketists as they keeping printing tickets and soon he is covered in reams of tickets representing many more thousands of units and he becomes so upset, he just cries and he's given yet another ticket for that.

"Get off here!" I tell her because I hate the Cruiseway and my nub aches worse than I have ever felt before. I believe it senses danger, and being mere babies, my fingers don't want to get damaged in my womb of a shoulder.

"It's faster, you want dumplings. The best dumplings are three exits away." "Now! I'm begging you, Marsha. Get off at the next exit!"

She glances at me, and I must look like I am in some kind of pain, because she pulls off the Cruiseway, hits a side street in the flatlands, makes a couple of what could be construed as hairpin turns in the slowest car in the remaining world and slams to a stop in front of a building. I look up and smile.

Dumpling World.

*****

Water. I wash down the cookie-sized pill my Docs gave me. The nub is quiet. Off the Cruiseway. Away from the stress. About to eat. Drinking water. Have to pee.

Marsha marks her territory in a booth. I go to the bathroom to piss out my mist. The water went right through me, and yet, at the urinal, it still comes out as mist. I don't ejaculate like most men, or pee like them either. The only liquids I seem to share with my brothers are blood and tears, and even then my blood is dark and oily and my tears devoid of salt. Peeples has reassured me that my bodily functions will return to normalcy in about a year. I guess I can look forward to sprinkling the toilet and leaving wet spots on my pants like other men. I guess it's a mark of virility. I like the mist.

And now, as I spray my gentle mist into the toilet, it seems I have awakened my babies. I pull the gauze bandages away, and Holy Shit! Now, alongside the four fingers, is what looks like a thumb. Glory! I touch them all, lift them gently up and let them curl down again. They are now getting a tinge of fleshy pink at the tips, my fleshy pink babies. I pour some water in the palm of my left hand and feed them a bit of moisture. They dip their tips into the puddle in my palm, then slide back into the slit.

Go to sleep my babies.

*****

I return to the booth. Marsha already has several small plates of dumplings on the table. A woman and her young daughter sit in the booth opposite, and the young girl, no more than eight, stares at me, then at my nub. I smile at her.

"Don't stare, Misery," the mother admonishes. Parents of the past ten years had taken to tragic names for their children, lest they get too optimistic about the future. The most popular were: Misery, Burden, Woe, Ache, and Ruin, with no delineation between boys' and girls' names as in the past.

"But Joyce," Misery says, "He has no arm…"

"Shhh!" Joyce scolds her, and Misery goes back to her dumplings and her can of "I Can't Believe It's Not Cola!"

The waiter brings two large green drinks to our table.

"Margaritas?" he says. He places them in front of us, and Marsha picks hers up and raises it in toast.

"I can't not be there for you, with all that you've helped me with in the past and all. It would be cold to just up and leave you."

"I can't quit you," I tell her. It's a phrase that suddenly swam up to the top of my damaged memory. "I can't quit you." Sounds good.

We toast.

"What have I done that you even talk about leaving me?" I ask her.

"You must try to get it in your head that your arm is not going to grow back, John. It's a fantasy, that's all it is. I don't want to think that I will be burdened with a crazy man for the rest of my life."

"My lack of a right arm disgusts you, doesn't it?"

"It's hard to look at, yes. It makes me sad."

"So if I were to get really sick, you would leave me?" I ask, as I can't fathom that. "You would quit me?"

"No, not if you got radiation cancer, or leukemia…"

"Lupus? Melanoma? Alzheimer's?" I ask, poking around to see which sicknesses would push her over.

"They can cure Alzheimer's now, you know that. And everyone has melanoma. It's natural."

"So it's the diseases of the mind that bother you?"

"I'm not strong enough for that," she says as she sips at the edge of her drink, the salt on the rim leaving the glass and sticking to her upper lip. I watch the salt melt into that part of her lip, crystal by crystal. This is as good as pornography to me. If I was not afflicted by the unnatural need to mechanically create my own erection, I would have one now.

But I must return to her attentions…

"They always suspect the one-armed man. Because he has one arm. He is the real fugitive," I say as the images of Kimble and the one-armed man in his headlights run in my head.

I look at my drink, bright green, slushy and, like Marsha's, also heavily salted on the rim with large, rock salt granules. The Council of Culinary Practices deemed salt to be toxic but mostly it was because the I Can't Corp had come up with a substitute and didn't want any competition. So, salt like this is hard to find in the stores and even rarer in restaurants. That's one of the things I liked about Dumpling World. They didn't play by the rules, even though they'd get ticketed about three times a week.

I lick the salt from the rim, take a sip of the drink, then go back to the rim again. The salt is delicious, better than the drink. I run my tongue around the entire rim, taking off all the salt. My mind is lost in salt pornography.

"We'll get you a prosthetic arm, John. They made incredible advances in those before the disasters."

"But then I'd have three arms and would be in a worse situation than I'm in." I yell to the waiter across the room. He rushes over and asks if I'm all right, all the while diverting his eyes from my nub.

"More salt, please," I ask, handing the drink back to him.

"Do you want another drink?" he asks, "I have to charge for this one and you didn't finish it."

"No, just more salt on the rim, OK? Same drink."

"Sir, we dunk the rim in salt before we pour the drink, so we have to throw this one away."

"John, drink this one and we'll get another."

"I want to drink it with the salt," I tell her and I'm getting agitated. My nub is beginning to itch again.

"Just get him a small dish of salt," she says as she pretty much solves the dilemma in one all-purpose solution. But the waiter looks around as if we asked him to mount and penetrate Lassie in the backseat of the Excess.

"I can't bring salt to the table..." and as he says this, I swing my nub out to face him, and wiggle the shirt end around to shake him up a bit and let him know that I am a desperate man.

"Pleeease!" I beg, the nub wiggling the cut end of my shirt. His eyes are full pupil against white and he runs off and it looks like this form of pathetic begging has worked. I now have a new use for my nub: puppet shows.

"Maybe not having an arm can be useful," I say to Marsha and she looks at me with a Final Days expression, which comes to her easily, as every day for the past twenty years has been touted as Final.

"Can you watch my daughter? I have to go to the ladies room," Joyce the Mom asks Marsha, and I can tell she is avoiding looking at me.

Marsha says, "Of course," as the waiter brings a small dish of salt and a new drink with the rim drenched in it and I immediately lick the rim and make my nub roll against the cloth of my shirt like a puppy having his tummy scratched, which of course sends the waiter scurrying off again and I can't help but wonder after all the crap of the past years, why my little puppet nub would freak this guy out, unless he has been living in a cocoon.

I finish that salt and apply more from the dish to the glass, lick that, then just dip my finger into the dish and eat it directly. My body is warm, the nub quieted, but I can feel my new little hand pulsing. It feels good, it pulses softly, almost like it's massaging the wound around it.

Marsha tears up and runs to the bathroom. What the fuck did I do know? I look at my reflection in the chrome of the napkin dispenser. I'm covered in salt. Misery – the little girl – looks at me, and I spoon some salt into my mouth and smile at her.

"What happened to your arm?" she asks.

"Coyotes bit it off."

"Coyotes ate my cat," she says and you can tell she loved her cat. "I don't like coyotes. Does it hurt?"

I like speaking like this. Little simple sentences, each with its own unique thought, especially to a person who's purely curious and not repulsed by the subject of my arm or lack thereof. She might really like a puppet show right now.

*****

I like children, from the ones I've met. We really only have two age groups in society anymore. Either very young or old. The middle ages are pretty thin, with The Calamities claiming most of them in the riots and wars.

"It itches sometimes," I tell her, "and sometimes it hurts a lot. My doctors gave me some pills, so I'm hoping that helps. I just have to stay calm, and I like salt."

"I had a cut once, and it itched like crazy. My mother was afraid it was getting infected so I had some shots, and I got sick from them and had to go into the medical warehouse for a whole year."

"Would you like to see it?" I ask her.

"Really?" and how I wish more people were like this little girl. What happens to them that they suddenly reach an age where all they want to do is destroy stuff? I push my shirt off my shoulder and pull the bandage down. Misery sits down across from me and I point my nub in her direction. Her eyes go wide as a pie.

"Can I touch it?" she asks and of course I say yes. She reaches her little finger across the table and I am warm inside, teaching this little girl and she not afraid or disgusted and I wish she were older and was my girlfriend. In my head, an image of a large man with a flat head speaks to a girl by a lake. In my head, a flower is exchanged.

And she touches me, and I feel the little finger on the wound, then I feel my babies stir and it feels like they are joyous. I look to the nub, the slit, and see my four little babies slide out of the slit and curl themselves around the little girl's finger.

"Don't be afraid. They are my new fingers," I tell her and she isn't afraid.

"They're like babies," she says as she lifts her finger up a bit to see if my fingers will hang on to her tiny finger and they do.

"I had a baby brother last year, and he would hold onto my finger too. He died in an explosion at the daycare," she says as she relives the memories of her baby brother in the fingers growing out of my shoulder.

"No one believes me when I tell them my arm is growing back," I say, and now I'm moving my shoulder around and her little finger and my little babies are doing a little dance together.

"Plants grow back," she says, "if you water them."

"So you don't think it's strange?"

"You're not strange, so what you think isn't strange. And it looks like they are growing back to me. Where is the thumb?"

"Deep inside. It's really new, maybe not as ready to come out."

"C'mon out, thumb thumb thumby. C'mon, and play with me like the rest of your hand," she says in a sing-song and sure enough, I feel the thumb stir and it slides out of the slit and takes its place next to the other four babies. Misery meets it with her thumb and she starts to play a little game with it.

"I'm going to thumb wrestle it," she says as she gently hops her thumb to both sides of mine.

"Be careful, it's brand new. No roughhousing," I tell her, but I didn't have to. Misery will cause me no pain. She is as gentle as they come and sure enough, both her thumb and mine are now dancing alongside each other and Misery giggles. Then I giggle with her. I have never been happier than I am right now. Not in my short memory.

This is glorious. This is as right as right can be.

"Misery!" Joyce shrieks as she bounds down the length of the restaurant toward her delightful little daughter. Misery startles and recoils from the playground of my wound. Marsha follows on Joyce's heels, and she looks as pissed as Joyce is horrified.

"His arm is growing back, Joyce!" Misery tells her and at that, Joyce grabs Misery by the arm and yanks her out of the booth.

"Don't hurt her," I say, "we were just playing."

"He has little fingers growing out of his arm, Mommy," and she says "Mommy" now because I bet she is negotiating against a punishment. In a society where all the children call the adults by their first names, suddenly calling them Mommy or Daddy or Mister or Missus was an adroit play for forgiveness or for toys.

"The world's not safe for children with people like you wandering about," Mommy Joyce tells me as she pulls little Misery out of the restaurant.

"Jesus, John. You are so totally out of your head."

I am covered in salt. My drink glass is empty and Marsha asks me if I have a drinking problem, "because if that's what this is, I can handle that," she says, "Together, we can be strong. And you and I are all we have in the world, and frankly, John, I'm scared every day. I've lost my parents. A lot of my friends too. Either they got killed, died, or turned into survivalist assholes in the mountains."

I look at her and now she's as vulnerable as I have ever seen her. I smile at Marsha. And with wet eyes on the verge of letting loose a backwash of delicious salty tears, she smiles at me, and touches my left arm.

It's time to go home, and I've only had one dumpling.

ENTRY 16

THE MEANING OF DREAMS AS IT RELATES TO MEANINGLESSNESS.

The Institute embarked on a study to examine the current dogma on the meaning of dreams and nightmares. It had been accepted that dream imagery during sleep had deep metaphorical meaning to the dreamer. The Institute did over twenty studies on dream imagery as professed by their chosen respondents. The Institute studied the four most common scenarios of dreams: Chase Dreams ("Help, I'm being chased!"), Flying Dreams ("Look at me, I'm flying!"), Naked Dreams ("Oh no! I'm naked!"), and Teeth Dreams ("Horrors, my teeth are falling out!"). There were countless other "types" of dreams, but The Institute did not believe those had much value. In studying the meaning of the dreams, The Institute needed to know whether the person having the dream was going through anything in real life that the dream would represent. So, in the current psychological literature of the latter part of the twentieth century, the "Chase Dream" scenario came to represent avoidance or fear from an unknown attacker about an unknown issue or threat. However the literature of the time also suggests it represents ambition if the dreamer is the chaser. In our studies, those having Chase Dreams were found to be neither under threat or particularly ambitious. The "Flying Dream" scenario has been identified as representing the dreamer being in control, especially if they control their flight. Except when they don't or fly too high, and become afraid in the dream. Difficulty achieving flight was described as being indicative of difficulties in controlling one's own circumstances. The Institute finds that these myriad numbers of interpretations to the Flying Dream scenarios indicate that none of the studies has a clue as to what Flying Dreams mean, and so The Institute dismisses them as merely man's innate desire to fly without an airplane or any mechanical device. In the vernacular of the culture: "Big fucking deal." Likewise, the Naked and Teeth dreams have been analyzed as being metaphorical of certain insecurities or even, especially with the Teeth scenario, the advent of menopause in women. But since menopause was essentially abolished in the early 2020s, and this dream was still being reported with some regularity, The Institute disregards this interpretation as that of a male-dominated psychiatric community. The Naked scenario we can only assume causes consternation because during the time of Naked Dream research in early 21st century, the population had grown either obese or anorexic due to the stress of The Calamities and generally poor nutrition. In some old digi's of the music of certain eras, there was a phenomenon of the California Dream or of California Dreaming. The Institute concludes this is another meaningless scenario having to do mostly with weather. In summary, The Institute concluded that dreams, in the vernacular of the culture, "Don't mean shit."

—Marsha straddles me. She rocks back and forth, rubbing her pubic bone against me, tightening her vaginal muscles, cupping my testicles, pinching her nipples, sucking her fingers, biting her lip, sticking her finger in her ass, pinching my nipples, dragging her nails across my scalp, sticking her finger in my mouth, her usual ritual repertoire of orgasm-inducing actions that keep me busy withstanding the pain of her pinching my nipples and scratching my scalp. But she doesn't look at me. She insisted I wear a T-shirt to bed, so as not to see my naked nub. It all feels a little desperate to me. Like she is fucking me to accept me. We didn't speak in the car back from the dumpling restaurant, but as soon as we got home, she turned all hellcat. It was fun, but now, it's at an intensity I haven't seen before.

She is wet, very wet inside, and as usual, I do find some comfort in the wetness. I await the orgasm, await the salty tears that hopefully will drip from her eyes into my mouth.

"Are you all right?" I ask.

"Yes, just shut up, shut up..."

OK, but I feel like I could replace myself with a stranger and she wouldn't know it. I now have no personhood even though this entire experience is all about my manhood.

My right shoulder feels like it's being tickled from the inside. I can't scratch it; I don't want to break the rhythm of Marsha's humping. I try to bite it to stop it from itching. I strain to bring my shoulder to my mouth and bite it like a cat bites its fleas.

And now, one of my baby fingers is in my mouth. The index finger, the bravest of all the fingers, the one expected to do most of the heavy lifting and the one with the intelligence to know where to point, has slid itself into my mouth, like I have seen babies do when they put their hands in their mother's mouths.

It slides over my teeth and plays with my tongue, then my thumb joins it and the two of them pinch my tongue and motherfucker that hurts.

I scream.

Marsha stops grinding on me, slows her breath and looks at me with a smile I have never seen her have before.

"Did you come?" she asks, and I realize she thinks my scream was about an orgasm. Sorry dear.

"I bit my tongue," I tell her, and am not sure it was very convincing.

"You didn't come?"

"My fingers came out of my shoulder and pinched my tongue," I tell her and hope hope hope that she doesn't have the reaction I'm afraid she'll have, and she slaps me across the face establishing a world record for dashed hopes.

She gets off of me, crying, not from orgasm, but sad tears, scared tears, and I try to lick them but she pushes me away, throws a pillow at me, and I know, like a bad dog, I have been banished to the living room couch once again.

"You're trying to drive me crazy, aren't you? To get me out of your life," she says, and I guess this one is going to have to go in her column.

"No, Marsha, I'm not. I wouldn't do that. I don't know anything about myself except for the time we have been together. That is the sum total of my memory of me, minus the imagery and language that floats around in my head and I have no idea why." I have nothing to be sorry for. My arm is growing back, whether she wants to believe it or not, accept it or not. Shit, she should be throwing me a baby shower for the arrival of my new arm.

"Goodnight John," she says and I have nowhere to go. Worse, I'm feeling things I have never felt before. I don't know what it is to be angry, but maybe this is it. I don't know what it is to be sad, but maybe this is it.

I was a happy man. I woke up every morning. I went to a job that treats me well and have been told I'm good at, by bosses who tend to my every need. Though I can't seem to master the easy erection, I have my machine and that keeps my girlfriend in weekly orgasms, which is not a bad life, on the whole, compared to others less fortunate.

Onto the couch.

*****

Two men dancing. They are very good.

They wear black jackets with stiff white shirts. The jackets are short in front and long in back. Their shoes are very shiny. On both sides of their neck, two black triangles meet in a knot. This looks familiar. I have a memory of this. It's just one more of the floating memories that knocks on the front door of my brain once in a while and asks for a seat on the couch.

The dancing men hold walking sticks, but not to walk. To help them dance. And they dance. Together, each with the same movements. And there is music.

They sing. I don't know what it is. I'm trying, but it's not clear to me. But it makes them happy and so it must be good. The suddenly Marsha spins, runs, leaps, and lands on the spot the two men have just vacated with their dancing, which is comprised of kicking their legs out thus moving them forward and occasionally spinning around on the pointed toes of their shiny shoes.

What the hell is Marsha doing in this digi? Did she have a career on the stage, in front of the camera? Is she hiding a whole other life from me?

And they all sing, both in unison and solo, and now I can make out the words as I strain to listen:

"*Watch your hell crush, crush, Uh oh,*
This means no fear, cavalier,
Renegade, steer clear!
A tournament, a tournament, a tournament of lies,
Offer me solutions, offer me alternatives,
And I decline.

> *It's the end of the world as we know eight,*
> *It's the end of the world as we know eight,*
> *It's the end of the world as we know it and I feline."*

I know this song. I have heard it before. But I can't for the life of me figure out why the lyrics are about knowing the number "eight," or why they "feline" which means cat and I don't understand this, but it's a dream, so maybe it's not supposed to make perfect sense.

I'll stay here a little longer. It's pretty funny. It relaxes me. And they dance well, so that's nice to see.

Marsha tries to sing along. She can't. They either drown her out or she can't keep up with the lyrics. I must help.

"The other night I dreamt of knives, continental drift divide..." I shout to her, but that just befuddles her more and I have no idea what it means or why I know these nonsensical lyrics.

I have to make sense of this. The dancers don't have noses. Why not? Where are their fucking noses and who thought THAT was a good idea? Marsha has a nose, so what are they trying to say? This might be the reason this genre died out sometime in the latter part of the Age of Black and White.

One of them kicks an approach towards me, big leg in front of the other, shiny shoes flashing. Truly fun to watch. He is a very talented person. He has no nose.

He is the Dancing Man Without a Nose. He smiles wonderfully. Without the nose, the mouth is more pronounced. All eyes on the teeth. He spins, plants a foot and says to me, "You have been chosen. You will forever change the future." And of course he can't be saying this to me, it's all the digi, to the wider audience, not me, but he really looks like he is looking at me.

"That's right, John. That's why you're here," and shit that's Marsha and she is calling me by name and I'm wondering if this is one of the more interactive digi's where they can scan your name and make it audible in the dialog, but Marsha stopped that service because it was too expensive and the charge of seeing that little boy in *Shane* yelling out to the cowboy to come back but instead of "Shane" it's your name actually ruins the effect to some extent. So, that's not it.

"Who are you?" I ask him, and I am struggling to get past his teeth to get to his eyes, but without the nose I seem to slip straight up to his forehead. I settle on talking to the place his nose should be, and of course, I can't help but wonder at the same time why the fuck I am talking to the screen.

"How do you breathe?" I ask and he waves his hand in front of me as if my words were mist and he wanted to clear the air between us.

"I am your best friend," he tells me and then he tells me how proud he is that I was chosen. He tells me of a wonderful place where there is peace and quiet, and where everyone lives in homes that look like salt water taffy.

He tells me this place has more oil than they need and less salt than they'd like, and that is why I am here. His teeth are truly inspiring.

"Did you make the homes out of salt and waste it and that is why you have no more salt?" I ask. Marsha has now positioned herself behind the man and is tap dancing side to side, smiling and making goofy gestures stage right and left. He laughs and his laugh echoes and he says, "No silly. You are so silly. So silly silly silly." And I tell him to stop it and my voice echoes and then he leans in close to me, like he is going to kiss me and I look into his eyes and his pupils look like black water circling a drain.

"You will protect us from what might cause us harm," he says and then takes out what looks like a gun, sticks the end of the barrel into my arm, and squeezes the handle. There is a sound of a pillow hitting a wall, then he pushes against my shoulder and I fall back and I keep falling and I scream and he says…

"John."

I choke to breathe. I grip the arms of the chair.

It's Marsha. She is back to wearing normal clothes. No longer dancing. I look at the screen. It's black. There is no man without a nose in front of me. Good.

"You were having a pretty violent dream. You were yelling it's the end of the world. And something about noses."

"Yes, I guess. I thought it was a digi. I thought you were in a digi."

Marsha smiles at me, and kisses me, which right now is nice, especially as she has a nose.

"Dreams always mean something. You have to figure out what you are going through and how the dream might offer an answer. Can you tell me more about it?" she asks. I search the now nonlinear collection of images.

"There were dancing men. They sang about the end of the world and the number eight. You were dancing too, and singing, and they didn't have any noses. And they told me I was chosen to do something important," and the more I think about the dream the further it sails down the tunnel of my memory, which is pretty damned dark and quick to send memories packing.

Marsha sits on the ottoman in front of the chair and says, "Yes, of course, the men are your doctors, the dancing represents their bedside manner, the number eight is a mythological number representing doubt, and the noses represent the thing you are missing: your arm. The important thing you're going to do is accept the loss of your arm and show everyone how a man and woman can overcome all sorts of adversity. You will give hope to many," and shit! that sure was simple.

*****

"I made these last night," and she holds up four shirts.

She spreads them out on the bed. Each shirt has the right arm heat-fused at varying lengths, from about one inch away from the nub to one a full foot, nicely done, real natural, like they were made that way to begin with.

"Don't ask me why, but if this helps you, then..." and she drifts off, letting her handiwork speak for her devotion to me.

She is my Wilma, hugging her man but unsure, going along with it, trying to accept my rapidly changing condition, which is far less odious than the sailor's hooks. But Wilma shouldn't have worried so much, as eventually his hands would have grown back, and I think I fell sleep before that happened in the movie, and maybe that was the meaning of the title – *The Best Years of Our Lives* – as it was probably about his hands growing back, and yessiree, they would have been great years. I hope it doesn't take years for my arm to grow back like it did for that sailor.

"Thank you," I say as kiss her on the cheek, take one of the shirts, and then take off my nightshirt, and Marsha turns away in nub avoidance.

*****

I think I'll wear the first shirt in the series, with about an inch of room. This makes sense. A start.

I take one of the pills Peeples gave me. It's hard to get down, like swallowing my fist. I carefully wash the nub, cleaning it with soap and applying one of Marsha's many moisturizers.

I probe the slit of the nub with my finger, deep into the slit, and I feel around, looking to make contact with my babies, to wake them – Hello my babies! – to alert them to get back to the business of growing. I can feel the wet soft flesh of the inner workings of my healing and the complicated fleshy nest of my new fingers.

They are deep in there, hibernating. I sense they are late risers.

I towel off, and put on the shirt.

It's tight to the nub. Too tight! Proof it has grown.

I have again been vindicated.

This is very exciting, and I yell out to Marsha, "The first shirt is too tight! That means my arm is starting to grow!" and she yells back, "That's nice, John."

Lassie watches me, so I show her too.

"You see, it's too tight. A couple of days ago, it would've fit just right." The dog snaps its head in the direction of the front door, and I hear Marsha greeting Ezra. Lassie leaves to greet him. She likes Ezra more than I do, and right now, I'm not liking him at all.

I grab the second shirt, with a skooch more room in the nub. I slide it on and roll my shoulders to test the fit. Expectations are high. There. It works. I am freshly and crisply dressed. The second shirt with a full three inches of room at the nub does the trick. I look like not having an arm is a natural thing, and that if I have a shirt made just for me, there must be a whole bunch of stuff made for one-armed people. Makes me feel almost normal.

*****

Ezra stands next to Marsha in the kitchen watching her make his sandwiches. There are several tubs of "I Can't, Won't, Shouldn't Believe" products on the counter: ham, chicken, cheese, and a new line of game meats they just came out with comprised of a mixture of deer, lion, and wildebeest, or so they say. They call it, "I Can't Believe I'm Not Hunting," and like their other products, it's become a big hit.

"John, well, look at you with the new shirt," he says as he peels off a ticket as it's his way of saying hello. I take it, crumple it up, and throw it in the garbage can, and as soon as I do that, he issues me another for throwing that one away.

"They mount up, John," Marsha says as she layers factory-made game meat one slice atop the other.

"I'm sorry," I tell him. It was rash of me to challenge the status quo. I have overstepped my boundaries and the only thing we have that keeps the precarious order is the boundaries given us by the CRL. Perhaps I am having a reaction, both to my changing body and the pills needed to bolster my system. Or perhaps I have become more confident as I see that I will soon be able to show the world I am right by flipping them the bird with my new fingers.

"I'm on prescription medication, Ezra," I confess, "I hope you can excuse my little…" and he finishes my sentence with the word, "snit."

"Yes," I tell him, "Snit is a good word for what I did," and yes it is, even though I have never heard that word before, it sounds like what I did. I snitted. Ezra punches out a ticket for my being in one.

"The scene at the dog park was interesting, don't you think, John?" he asks me. "Certainly a lot of commotion. A fair amount of destruction too."

"You didn't issue me a ticket," as it comes to me he didn't and that surely was a big-ticket issuing moment.

"I felt bad for you. You were merely a bystander. I should have issued Lassie the ticket. But, frankly, I thought the whole thing funny. And truth be told, I hate the people that go to that park," he says as he issues me a ticket for not issuing me a ticket.

"Here," and Marsha hands him his bag of sandwiches. He takes it, shakes the bag and says, "Exactly ten. Good," and heads to the front door.

"How are you feeling, John?" he asks, one hand on the door knob, which tells me he doesn't want a long answer.

"Confused. But I'm getting over it."

"Just keep remembering what you see, what you feel."

He sounds like my doctors now. I tell him my arm is growing back, not in a snitting way, but just to see what he would say and if he was going to issue me a ticket. He doesn't.

"Well, then you are either a man with no arm, or a man whose arm is growing back," he says as he opens the door and leaves.

And they must teach doctors to speak in riddles too.

ENTRY 17

THERE IS SOMETHING WRONG
WITH SUBJECT JOHN.

T he Institute has begun to worry a bit about Subject John, as he has begun to exhibit a more questioning nature. We accept some variance in our subjects as to their cynicism, as we suspect they will adopt some of the behaviors of those around them in the attempt to fit in, but John has been getting positively ornery. We understand he must be going through some degree of disorientation as to the issues involving his arm, or lack thereof, but The Institute is willing to allow this to play out. We had hoped to learn more about behavior from his sexual dysfunction, but apparently his mate had none once a mechanical solution could be provided. What is of concern to us, in watching him in the men's room scratching his wound, and in sensing his more combative nature, is whether the pain and rejection will cause him to do something violent. If we continue to suspect a downward spiral, we will have to abort the study.

—"I don't remember ever having a dream," I tell my Docs in their office. I tell them about the dancing men with no noses, and the one who sounded a lot like Manning, and about the adventure he told me I was about to go on and I asked them what it meant. Then the gun to my arm, the sound of the shot and the feeling of falling.

Their mutual side-glances to each other while I told them my dream didn't escape me, like they were worried about what I had told them.

103

"All right, cut the mutual side-glances like I'm a nut job or something," I tell them. "Is there something wrong?"

"It could be the first time you remembered a dream. It's common that people don't remember their dreams," Manning says as he flips through an ancient book filled with pictures of Palm Springs houses before the calamity. He shows me one of the houses; it's glass from ground to sky, topped only by a heavy sloping roof. It looks like a bird. "What does this mean to you, John?" he asks.

"It means that people in the desert shouldn't build glass houses," I tell him and it's true, it's so hot out there. "Costs a fortune to keep cool. They must've been rich."

"Indeed, the owner was a man who seemed to give hope to people, as that was his last name," Manning informs me. "I'm sure he was well compensated."

"In fact, John, you never remembered dreams before the coma, so this could be a good sign. A jogging of the part of the brain that causes memory," Peeples tells me as Manning keeps flipping the pages of this huge book.

"What does it mean? The man with no nose?" I ask.

"It means nothing. Dreams mean nothing. It's a dishonest to say they do. You have this dream again, and I bet he'll have a nose," Manning says as he shows both Peeples and myself a picture from the book of a luxuriant stretch of perfect green grass that surround little pads of even more perfect grass.

"And what does this tell you?" Manning asks.

I look at the pastoral scene. I recognize it a bit. I sense a memory pushing through the folds of my brain. I see men with short-sleeve shirts and hats of all sorts. I see some of them wear sleeveless sweater vests over their short-sleeve shirts, as if their arms are prone to warming but their bodies are constantly cold. And they swing metal sticks and swear at little balls. When they put the ball into a little hole on one of the carpeted surfaces, they are happier. Then they drink.

"It's golf," and that name just spits out of my brain and right out of my mouth. "The CRL outlawed it years ago, or they outlawed the areas they built to play the game, when the water dried in the deserts. And they outlawed it to punish the rich for hoarding their money during the early Calamities."

"They are greedy and frivolous against their reality," Peeples comments, and his use of the word "they" startles me.

104

"But the point is that you have had a bit of a breakthrough in memory retrieval," Manning adds as he shuts the big book down and slides it into the shelf with the other big books.

"Why did you say 'they'?" I ask; "Why are they 'They' and not 'Us'?"

"Are *you* them?" Manning asks, "Would *you* go to the desert and build homes made of glass and divert precious resources for the sake of a game only very few could afford to play, and that fewer actually enjoyed when they did? Would *you* do that?"

"No," and it's true, I wouldn't do that and can't understand how stupid you'd have to be to build glass houses in the desert and water the sand until it grew grass and then walk all over that grass swearing about how much you hate the game you invented that requires the grass to begin with.

"Sometimes, right now, I feel like a 'they,'" I tell them.

"The arm?" Manning observed.

"Yes."

"You know how they treat those with less, or who are different," Peeples adds. "We see it every day. I see it when I give a patient a diagnosis and they're afraid to share it with their loved ones. I see it with my patients who have lost all their hair from the radiation. I see it with the mother who just gave birth to Siamese quadruplets, attached at the sides of their bodies, sharing four legs and two arms, but with four heads across, and worse, not even looking alike."

And my mind races to picture this: the poor mother burdened with walking her quadripeded and different-headed conception inside the mall, like she had a small crowd with her; or trying to arrange a game of musical chairs with other children at their birthday party, but due to their condition, having to use a bench. Indeed there is ample reason for everyone to feel like a "them" or a "they" amongst their own species. It's one of the great curiosities that Manning and Peeples seek to discover the answer for, in order to solve this in some way, either through education or pharmaceuticals.

"One of four things will happen to you, John," Manning says, "Your arm will grow back and you will be back in the swim. Your arm will grow back and they will still not accept it as they don't believe arms can grow back. Your arm won't grow back and they will think you are crazy. Your arm won't grow back and they will regard you as a "they," as you are a man without an arm. Your arm…"

"Five," Peeples adds as Manning goes past his allotted assessment of possibilities of my arm/armless life, then adds his own, "Your arm won't grow back and you won't care and they won't consider you a 'they,' just a lesser 'us.'"

"That's a long shot," Manning chimes in, "In the meantime, remember the chicken…"

"The road," says Peeples.

"The crossing," says Manning.

"The Other Side," adds Peeples, "Now, we have a group to prepare for. Review the project at your desk. We're on in an hour."

*****

In the men's room.

I pee my yellow mist into the urinal. This urinal device is not meant for those who evacuate their bladders in a fine yellow mist. The urinal makes me a "They/Them." That's rich, isn't it? I get to be insulted by the urinal because of how I pee.

I stand in front of the mirror, thinking about the man with no nose, the chicken, the road, and my nub.

I pull the shirt off my nub, peel the gauze bandage off to free my babies and rub my hand over the fresh skin, coaxing my babies to come out and play.

"C'mon, we're alone. C'mon out…" I coo to them, encourage them, like the late-night motivational speakers Marsha watches that pace the stage, back and forth, with the "You are blessed, you are capable, worth it, deserve it, have it, do it, it's not so bad, death is vital, life is temporary, give to the cause" sort of nonsense that the CRL encourages to reduce the suicide rate and they take a 75% tax on all donations to boot.

A rumbling. Slowly, my babies pour forth from their slit, index finger first, then the middle, then the fourth finger and the pinky. The thumb is last, but LOOK! Now a palm! A whole new palm! My new palm! A fleshy little pillow, devoid of folds or lines, like the single cheek of an albino baby's butt.

"Let me see you!" I practically scream out, "Come out, all of you!"

Now, I have a hand! My new hand. I touch it with my older, established hand. I want my left hand, the veteran, to teach my rookie right hand how to *be* a hand. How to do hand-like things. I touch the new palm. It's still moist. I don't sense a strong bone behind it yet, and even my fingers are more rubbery than the fingers on my left hand. There is no infrastructure yet. I can imagine it all taking shape in the ballroom of cells and cartilage and tendon and calcium, each spinning around the other, dancing together to the sounds of the blood band, changing partners, taking shape, a party in the making. My little debutante party.

I lace my old fingers with my new fingers, being careful not to damage them. They feel like holding some long, thin dumplings, or tube pasta that Marsha boils from time to time. I concentrate. Move. My veteran hand unlaces its fingers from my new hand, and pulls away, hand stretched out, fingers wide. My new hand mirrors the act, slowly, almost like it has to observe, absorb, and then do. But they do, and now they need encouragement. My veteran hand gives them the thumbs up. My new hand returns the gesture. My veteran index finger and my rookie one engage in a bit of swordplay, then my new middle finger rises up and "flips me the bird," and though I have no idea why it's called that, it means to go fuck yourself. My new hand has a sense of humor.

There is no reason to put the bandage back on. They need air. They are not part of a wound anymore. They need to breathe. They are alive. They are me. I put my shirt back on. I stuff some towels in my pocket. Today, they will be free.

*****

In my cubicle.

There is a folder on my desk, but it's empty. I don't know what this session will be about, the questions or exercises I need to put the respondents through, or their profiles, which is very important as I need to know what their station in life is in order to properly assess their cultural and economic bias.

Nothing. I got zip to work with here.

I see the card from Nikki Sex, the therapist/dancer/escort woman whose vagina is in full laminated color on her card.

I remember the reaction the others had to her. I remember that no matter how smart she was or how prominent her nipples were, she was very much considered a "they" by the others in the group. Different and separate from them. Lesser, and she knew it. And she dealt with it. She was proud of it. She seemed to wear her "They" as a shield. It made her seem oddly superior to them. I liked that. I wonder, as a therapist of sorts, and an outsider, if she could tell me how to deal with how I feel, like the outsider, the "they," the one who is different.

I wonder if she can make me stronger. I wonder whether a sex therapist would be repulsed by my nub, as Marsha is. I wonder if my babies will show their tips to her. I wonder if I should call her.

"What is that, John?"

It's Manning, hovering over me, looking at Nikki's flesh pink card.

"It's a vagina, Doc," I tell him as I hand him the card, "Just a lonely little vagina. One of our respondents. She gave it to me after the group she was in."

He turns it around a couple of times, upside down and sideways, looking for an angle where the disembodied pudenda would make sense to him, as I really don't think he has seen too many of them, at least not in this form. Yes, in many of the tests we have done, the female subjects have been naked, but Manning is usually behind the mirror or at a distance, and these tests were mostly gynecological or esthetic in nature, not sexual, as Nikki's card seems to be. Also there wasn't any type printed over the live vagina to obscure it. Nikki's vagina is surrounded with her contact information, thus perhaps disguising it for him. I also think a detached vagina, with no owner to give it context, is perhaps a bit abstract to him, as it would be to most people, I think.

"Yes, I remember her now. She wanted me to try her pie."

"Yes, but you know she meant her vagina?" I enlighten him. He looks at me as if I just spoke to him in some alien tongue. I do believe he has no idea what I am talking about. I do believe he needs to read more recent texts.

"Where are my documents for today's group," I ask him as I take the card back. He puts his hand on my left shoulder, and tells me that today's group will be a bit different, and I will be both moderator and participant.

Fuck that. I don't want to be part of them. They are them to me.

"That's impossible. I won't be neutral," I tell him.

"Nothing's impossible, John," he says as he saunters down the long cubicle-lined corridor, "After all, your arm is growing back, yes?"

"Then you agree with me! It is growing back," I shout after him.

"Get to the other side, John. Remember the chicken," and he's gone.

ENTRY 18

THE INSTITUTE ENAGES SUBJECT IN THE ALIENATION TEST.

One of the tests we conduct to analyze the level of acceptance or rejection of the population to one another is called the WORKSHOP 6. The Institute had hoped to name it something more memorable, but the consultant brought in to create the naming conventions for The Institute was killed in a rock slide during the last earthquake. So we called it Workshop 6, and the "6" just denotes that when we came up with the name, it was close to 6 pm. But, it's a test we've used several times in the past and find quite effective. It seeks to place those most damaged and deformed individuals in the same room, along with two people not damaged, to see the sorts of alienation that occur. We put two undamaged in the group as with two, they feel more free to act on the fears and hatreds of being in the room with the damaged. We will use Subject John in this test as one of the damaged to see if the group reacts to his specific damage and shuns or accepts him. It is a risk, but one worth taking at this time to sort out how to get to the core of John's new more aggressive attitudes. Plus, with Workshop 6, all these freaks in one room is truly a memorable sight.

—The respondents file into the room. Since I had no information as to their names, sex or occupations, I was unable to prepare the seating. But in they file, each making a run for the cookies and water against the wall.

Shit. Workshop 6. I hate Workshop 6.

I tense. My breath is short. I'm feeling tension. I got a room full of "Thems."

There's a guy whose skin is spotted pure white and cocoa brown. He's neither African nor Caucasian, black nor white. I look to see if he is splattered with paint. Nope. It's skin. It's not a burn. It's ugly.

There's a woman whose head looks like it was split down the middle and it healed all a-kilter, with the right side higher than the left. Her left eye is off on the side of her head, and her hair is in patches, though she tries in vain to use the longest of her hair to obscure her hideousness. That's a birth deal. That's some rotten DNA. She reminds me of pictures of rather odd paintings by a man named Picasso, the subject's features painted without regard to anatomy. I asked Marsha if people once looked like that. She rolled her eyes. She was wrong. They do.

There's a man, or a boy, I can't tell, in a wheelchair. He's just chest and head, no arms or legs. A human pillow. He wheels himself around using a hose attached to his chair. As he blows into the hose, the wheelchair activates and he tilts his head left or right to make a turn. He has maneuvered over to the plate of cookies and is masterful at using his forehead to tip the plate and slide a cookie off, after which he lashes it with his tongue, which is unusually long, almost six inches by my estimate and about one inch wide. He has completely mastered his infirmity. He's going to be interesting to talk to, even though I have no discussion guide. I'm swimming in the deep end of the freak pool.

There's a man with a hand that resembles a lobster claw; a bald woman without a chin who looks like she is being treated for one of the tumors; and Siamese twins, sharing one torso, two heads atop one set of shoulders with three legs to keep it all up, a pile of human on a tripod. They all attack the snack table like a swarm of locusts.

Then another respondent enters: a white man, about forty. His skin is chalk white, his hair is thin and looks like it's given up the desire to be hair. He wears a black suit and shiny black shoes. His shirt is chalk white and he blends in with this to be a seamless white expanse of shirt, collar, neck, and face. He walks with his hands clasped in front of him, shoulders hunched over, like he is terribly embarrassed by something, and wants to slink in unnoticed. He pours himself a cup of water and sits next to the Siamese twins, who eat their cookies in synchronized movements. The girl on left bites then the girl on right follows, each with the same size bite. Their movements resemble pistons, up and down, timed and accurate.

They chew with their mouths open, at the same time, and look like fish sucking for air. It takes them no time to finish the cookies, then sip from their cups, wipe each other's mouths, primp their hair and arrange the middle third leg to hang over the far right one.

Then there are two last respondents – a man and a woman. They're different from the rest. There is absolutely nothing unusual about them at all. They pause at the door, scan the room, and look at the card in their hand with the room number on it, then at the door to match the number on the card. They do that twice, then look at each other, though they should be strangers. They are more like each other than anyone in the room, as no one in the room is like each other at all. Except me, of course. I'm more like the couple, as is the Chalk White Man. He is like the couple. I wave them in. They see my nub and pause.

"Please come in," I tell them as they still look like they got off a train at the wrong stop in an alien galaxy. "There are cookies and water on the table there. Serve yourself and take a seat and we'll get acquainted with each other."

"Chocolate chip!" the Twins say at the same time, and that unsettles the couple even more. The Twins meet eyes with the normal-looking man in the black suit, but he looks away. Human contact seems to unsettle him, especially when it's two humans on three legs sharing one torso.

The couple slinks over to the snack table. The man picks up a cookie, but it's clear, in scanning the room filled with the human oddities, that he's lost his appetite. As has the woman, who pours a cup of water, and drinks it while staring into the cup, looking like there is something unidentifiable at the bottom of the cup.

The man's eyes run the length of the table, past the Spotted Man, the Picasso Head, the Human Pillow, the Tumor Sufferer, the Lobster Hand, and all the way down to me. His eyes settle on my nub, and he puts the cookie down.

The couple take their seats, close to each other and some distance from the others. The Siamese twins smile in unison at them and say at the same time, in the same high-pitched and nasally accented voice, "De quai ka quai!"

The man asks, "What?"

The Twins say it again, "De quai ka quai!"

The man asks "What?" again.

"De quai ka quai!" and this time the woman asks, "What are you saying to us?"

And the Twins laugh in unison. Big joke, it seems. "De quai ka quai! It means nothing. But people think it means something because of the sound and syllables. We have a lot of fun teasing people with this. We're from Montreal."

"Please don't speak to me again," the man says.

By this time, the others had settled into their Devices, talking, reading, watching, writing, ordering, doodling, gaming, listening to music, and watching the digi's. But mostly they were hiding from each other, except for the Twins, who had no Devices and just sat there, smiling and staring at the group and at me. Apparently, in Montreal, smiling and staring is what people mostly do.

I haven't a clue what to do. I don't have a list of questions, no format, I don't even know these people's names, jobs, salaries, hobbies, nothing. Manning and Peeples have set me adrift in a room of strangers, and in this case, one of the oddest collection of strangers I have encountered post coma. I have no map and so I sit and say the only thing that was never part of the script and questionnaire:

"Hello."

What I get back is a series of disinterested muffled greetings, except from the normal two people, who seem to be too horrified by being surrounded by this group of damaged and disabled.

The Siamese twins say, "Bonjour!" bright and perky, and look to the room to see if the rest will mimic their politeness. They don't.

Manning and Peeples enter the room. They don't acknowledge my forlorn look caused by the guilt I have in not being prepared. I expect to be scolded and I hate that feeling and I wonder why I would feel that now as I have never had feelings of inadequacy before, and this from a man with erectile dysfunction and no arm. Why do I feel so out of my skin, so off-kilter? My nub tingles, and I think this is bullshit. They didn't prepare me. That's their job. That's the routine. Fuck the forlorn look. I muster a bit of macho.

"Would you all put your Devices down and turn them off, please?" Peeples says.

I'll just explain the command… "Yes, the Devices tend to disturb the focus of the interaction and…" Manning cuts me off.

"Quite all right, John. We'll take it from here."

Peeples gathers up the Devices and puts them on a separate table in the corner, stacked on end like slices of "I Can't Believe It's Not Bread."

Manning hands out sheets of paper and pencils. This is a first. Usually I write on a DigiPadDevice. It enables me to check response boxes, type responses, and doodle my impressions of the respondents in the margins. Manning pays close attention to my doodles, as he says they are the emotional impression I'm having of the respondents during the sessions.

The respondents look at the paper and pencil like they are moon rocks. The Twins bite the one pencil in two and share the two halves.

Pencils are rare these days. They haven't been used in years, as there has been a moratorium on using trees to make them, and of course, no one really writes anymore.

The questions are essentially multiple-choice, color in the boxes, or check them off. I thought it was going to be more related to the physical infirmities of the respondents and the oddness of the atmosphere of the room, but it's actually these:

- What is your favorite fruit?
- What is your favorite vegetable?
- Do you like night better than day?
- Hot drinks more than cold drinks?
- Cats over dogs?
- Coffee or tea?
- Fast or slow music?

and the last question:

- What's the one thing you would change about yourself?

That's an essay.

"Please fill out the questionnaire. Don't share with your neighbor. Be truthful and honest. Think about what you are going to say. You have thirty seconds. You can begin now," Peeples says with clear staccato authority and steps back to the wall with Manning, as they both lean against the wall with their hands behind their backs and the backs of their heads tap-tapping the wall, which sends little waves through their shiny, silky perfect hair.

No one's going to be able to fill out the essay box. Most people have forgotten how to write. The rest can't do it in defined spaces.

Then I notice the Siamese twins seem to be writing long form, which is a tribute to the Montreal school system. I get busy with my questionnaire, hating that I have to do this at all, wondering what the game is here.

Normal Couple are getting antsy. They look up from the paper furtively, as if they didn't want to get caught staring at the others, but I can tell the paper means nothing to them. Might as well be in another language. I wonder if they can read at all, but they're dressed well and seem reasonably intelligent and these concepts are pretty basic: a test on simple everyday likes and dislikes.

I write that I would have liked to have normal erections and be able to project semen across a normal-sized room at will, like I've seen in many of Marsha's sex digi's. I write that it would be interesting to have the pleasure sensation that many men try to describe during the ejaculative process. If I could do that I might, being a rational man, be able to add some clarity to the descriptive oeuvre. But I add also that it's not so interesting that I'd want to change anything about my life to have that. It might be nice for a couple of days, but the thought of having the ability to project semen across the room at will makes me nervous.

"Pencils down," Manning says and I think he enjoyed that. He heard that in one of the old films from the Age of Black and White. "Instructional propaganda" he called them. He has a whole library of these. They were mostly warnings about unknown things. There was the one about the disease young people got if they went into a bedroom together, though it's never quite clear what exactly they did, but there was a tremendous amount of guilt. Then of course if you didn't get a horrible blistering disease, you got pregnant, which was actually portrayed as being worse than death.

I'm assuming that they had sex in the bedroom, but that was never portrayed, so it's a little assumptive on my part. Whatever it was, they will never do it again. These were made to save parents the arduous chore of raising their children. At least that's Manning's interpretation.

The ones he thought very funny were the "Duck and Cover" films that advocated getting on the floor and covering your head to survive a nuclear attack. He got a real charge out of those. Peeples thought it so curious that he ran some experiments with children and had them in the duck and cover position in one of the clean rooms and saturated them with gamma rays. Three days later their hair fell out and about six months later they died. The Institute compensated the families, and Duck and Cover was proven to be a scientific fraud. Peeples submitted a report to the CRL and they thanked him in a form letter and reimbursed The Institute for the settlement monies, but Peeples returned the cash and got ticketed for refusing CRL subsidies.

But somewhere in that library, somebody said "Pencils down," and it stuck.

Manning puts his hand on The Spotted Man's shoulder and asks him what is the one thing he would change about himself, and he – black skin spotted with white spots or white skin spotted with black spots – tells him he wishes he knew how to cook better. And as soon as he says that, the Normal Man gasps and the Normal Woman keeps her eyes on her test paper. Lobster Hand raises it and says he likes cats better than dogs, his music slow, and coffee over tea. On the last question, as he holds the test paper in what must have been fingers before they fused together and thumb before it swelled up to the size of an eggplant, he says he wished he had studied harder in school and pursued his talents in swimming. He says that now, with his lobster hand, it's hard to perform his job well, which is bagging groceries.

One by one, the respondents spout out their favorite things and then what they would change about themselves. Tumor Woman doesn't wish she was healthy, she wishes she didn't have children who will be sad when she dies, and the Siamese twins don't wish they were separate, they wish they liked the same things. Nikita, the one on the left, loves vegetables, dogs, day, tea, hot drinks, and fast music while Narita, the other one, likes fruits, cats, night, coffee, cold drinks, and slow music, and it's constantly a source of strife.

Worse, Narita is a lesbian while Nikita is a heterosexual. This makes dating and their social lives difficult. Except, Nikita says, for her dates, as the men always want to watch Narita and her date have sex, but somehow, Narita's dates don't like men watching them. Lesbians can be difficult.

Then comes Chalk Man. He talks but no one can hear him. Manning asks him to speak up.

"I don't like the sound of my own voice," he says almost inaudibly. "Does anybody else here not like the way they sound?" he asks the room. It goes silent as the respondents think about it. And truth be told, it would seem to be a living hell to not like the way you sound to yourself. Like hating what you see in the mirror. Not just because you feel crappy about yourself for some reason, but actually hating what you see in the mirror. Not psychologically, but physically.

"Every time I speak, I want to shut up," Chalk Man says, fidgeting with his hands below the table. "Right now, I speak, but the sound of my own voice hurts my ears. If it was another person, I would move away, leave the room. But I can't leave the room. I can't leave me behind. So I don't talk. Or I whisper to reduce the impact of my own voice on my insides. That's enough. I can't stand to hear anymore."

"We like our voices," say the Twins. Tumor Woman says she likes her voice better on the days it's not weak from the chemo and laser radiation treatments on her tumors. And it goes on down the line, with everyone sort of agreeing that their voices are just swell to them. Their voices are no better than Chalk Man's. But this is the road he has decided to travel, poor bastard.

"Of course, because it's not supposed to happen!" says Chalk Man. "You're supposed to like the sound of your own voice. You can hate a recording of your voice but you can't hate it in your own head." And he pretty much exhausts himself on that. He leans back on his chair, like he just got a lot off his shoulders. And he smiles a bit, like he actually did. But maybe he's smiling because the vibrations of his own voice have subsided.

Manning looks at me. It's my turn.

"Coffee. Dogs, but dogs more like my dog than dogs in general, and there aren't many like my dog. He's a circus dog. Music I just don't care much for at all. I like vegetables, especially in dumplings, and if I could change one thing it would be my erectile dysfunction…" Nailed it. Concise. Clear. I'm a pro at this.

"That's fucking enough!" It's Normal Man. He flings his test across the table, then Normal Woman joins him. "I agree, this is some kind of bullshit, some kind of set-up on everybody here against us," she says.

She has a brittle voice that drifts from whining to accusation to indignant, and her eyes are mean. His too. They might be made for each other.

"What do you mean," Manning says as he looks to his attendance sheet to get Normal Man's name, which he says is "Steven?"

"You're kidding," Steven says. "Look at you," and he looks at Lobster Boy. "You have a disease of the arm, a skin disease, and there is no cure for it, and it gets worse I hear. I hear it takes over all your limbs. And you wouldn't change that. That's not the thing you would change. And you," and he looks at Spotted Marvin. "You have to whiten your skin. Or you have to darken it. But you have to one or the other. And all you want to do is learn how to cook?"

Then he turns to me and glares.

"And you fucking don't even address that you're missing an arm! You just want a hard-on? Are you fucking kidding me?"

"My arm will grow back," I tell him calmly as he is quite agitated and my calm voice has worked in the past to disarm the disgruntled.

"That's it!" says Normal Woman as she gets up and marches out of the room. "I'm nobody's fool and I'm not going to be a guinea pig!"

"You're all a bunch of freaks!" Steven says, "All the freaks of the world in one fucking room. It's the freaks that make the world a bad place. We have to see you, we have to feel sorry for you, we have to be nicer to you, help you, forgive you, the CRL treats you special, gives you bigger chances, makes stairs normal people can't climb, builds apartments with sinks so low you feel like a freak. All just to make you feel equal to us and us to feel less! To make normal the new freak!"

That's true. Instead of trying to fix the infirm, the crippled, the less than abled, the CRL focused on reducing the able-ness of the abled. So stairs were built that were unusually steep, and then laws put in place that forbid the normals from using the ramps. But it kind of worked. You can't help those who have less to work with without taking away the abilities of those who are better equipped.

"Can't do anything about my spots, asshole! I can do something about eating better. And you telling me if you were hungry and I made you a gourmet meal, you wouldn't eat it?" asks Marvin.

"You're all freaks!" Steven shouts.

"I just wished I was smarter. Then people don't care so much what I look like," says Lobster Boy. "I can't do anything about the one day my whole body will look like this. So I might as well be smart, so I know better how to handle it, or have more things to think about all day long. Plus, women still like really smart men, no matter how ugly they are. And they like lobster. So..."

"We are sisters," the Siamese chime in, "why would we be apart? Nobody cared in Montreal."

"What the hell is this a test of, anyway?" asks Steven. "To see how I would react in a room full of freaks? Why? Is the CRL thinking of forcing them to live in my apartment building? Is that it? Forced integration with the fucking freaks!"

"My arm will grow back," I add to the chorus.

"That's fucked up," says the Human Pillow.

The rest of the respondents look at me like I'm the freakiest one in the room, insensitive to the plights of everyone here, and a liar to boot. They've accepted their ordeals, their Siameseness, their swollen appendages, bodies without extremities, with tumors and spotted skin, split skulls, and strange-to-them sounding voices. I have not accepted my one-armedness, and in fact have been communing with the soon-to-emerge, reborn second arm and I tell them that, "I can talk to my new fingers," which doesn't go over so well either, judging by the furrowed brows on Picasso Head. It makes her head look even more abstract.

"Why do you say that?" asks Manning, finally speaking up to break the hubbub that has taken over the room. Picasso Head tilts her head to the side and now, with her red stringy hair and olive skin, resembles an autumnal landscape Torso Man wiggles his body in his wheelchair and blows into the hose. The chair activates and rolls over to me, and Torso Man just sits there and stares at the nub.

"I want to watch," he says as he tips his body forward in the chair with the force of his large head.

"Jesus!" blurts out Steven.

Fuck normal Steven. Fuck him and his fucking normalness and his lack of faith in me and his absence of curiosity and his fucking fear of all that is different.

I don't have to be moderate now, as I am not the moderator. Now I can get pissed and I do. "Fuck you!" I tell him and that freezes him a bit. And it sounded strange in this room, where I ply my trade, try to be moderate, calm, attentive and non-judgmental, even though, in the past five months since coming out of my coma, I have heard opinions that make me wish I was still in one.

But I am being judged. Time to push back.

"John…" Manning says to calm me, but it's too late, and I pull the shirt off the nub and the bandage off the wound.

"Look! Keep your eyes on the nub! See the folds!" I command them like a magician about to reveal his greatest illusion.

"What is this, the fucking circus?" says Steven.

They all lean in over the table to get a good look at the nub, and I talk to it, trying to coax my babies out.

"Come on, come out, show them how you grow in me," I say seductively to my nub. I smile at the group, especially the Siamese twins, as they seem to delight in watching me speak to my nub and wait expectantly for it to explode in fingers just like flowers bloomed in the predictable springs of long ago.

"Great. I suppose if an arm comes out, it means there are just three more weeks of winter," says Steven and I have no idea what that means, but I am desperate to shut him up and to embarrass him to the group, to make him the damaged one, the disabled one, the inferior human.

Manning watches intensely as I pet my nub and push my finger into the slit to see if my babies are napping within reach.

"Do you see anything?" asks Chalk Man.

"No," answers Torso Man.

"Give it a moment," I tell them, "They're in there. Freshly grown. I have even begun teaching them some of what they need to know as fingers and thumb..."

I hum a little tune to my nub, something to entice just one finger to snake out of the slit like a boa comes out of the basket when the snake charmer plays his flute in a part of the world where that still goes on.

But nothing. Nothing happens, and the respondents start to leave, one by one, by wheelchair, by walker, and they take their tumors and spots and hated voices with them. And the Siamese twins smile and approach me, and one of them actually touches my nub and they both smile and tell me that if it does ever appear, they would like to see it, and that Manning has their contact info.

"We are going back to what's left of Montreal," they tell me, as most of Canada was nuked by the Empire of the United States after the Ottawan terrorist attacks. In fact, Montreal is about the only place in Canada that is still livable, much to the chagrin of the remaining and quarantined Torontonians.

The room is empty. I sit at the head of the table and observe the mess left by the group. It's all crumbs and crumpled paper plates and balled-up napkins. I noticed many of the respondents had trouble eating and swallowing the cookies, as certain levels of their infirmity demanded forms of drug and chemotherapy and thus they in all likelihood had trouble with their saliva levels. The pencils are broken or dull and the test papers are either scattered on the table or are on the floor, left there in a fit of pique by many of the respondents to both the test in general and my statement about my arm in specific.

I have never felt so lonely. I feel as though I will be in the "They, Them" club for the rest of my life.

No one can see my babies except me. No one, except for the little girl, will accept what I feel about the coming of my new arm. And as Manning said once, the opinions of children don't matter anymore, as they will all be dead or insane in a matter of ten to twenty years, depending on how badly their bodies were affected by the radiation, mercury, hormones, and minerals in the air, water and food supply, and the daily loss of hope and constant diet of fear.

I am back to the sensation I felt when Marsha was wheeling me out of the hospital, except now all the world is that corridor and the inhabitants are even more damaged than those football players. I am a man without an arm who has no evidence whatsoever that it's growing back. I have checked the digi-info and there is nothing, *nothing* that says that an arm can't grow back. In fact, back sometime in the early part of the century, and before the Great Calamities and Acts of Enormous Stupidity, they were actually working on some regenerative theories but apparently they failed? Nothing in the digi's says this and they are all I have to go on. Dr. Peeples, being about the body, makes no commitment and that's only because everything he does and says is measured. If he said it would and in my case it didn't, than he would feel terrible.

I am angry. This group has made me angry. I didn't need this today.

ENTRY 19

SUBJECT JOHN QUESTIONS HIS DOCTORS AND SO QUESTIONS HIS EXISTENCE.

At this point, research organizations of note will regroup when a set of assumptions have been altered by circumstances beyond their control and will alter the desired results of the research. The stakeholders of the studies need to be notified of a change in direction or a result that might not be congruent with the desired results of the stakeholders. The Institute is now progressively more worried about Subject J and his changing demeanor. He has begun to question his doctors, and so questions his connection to reality. We will access his progress and report in further entries.

—"How the fuck do you think I feel?" I ask Manning after he asks me, "How do you feel?" Really? I just spent an hour on the receiving end of hatred by people who will never grow their limbs back. I'm ahead here.

"You've become a 'they,'" Manning says, shaking his head at the pages of a very large book. The title of the book is worn away but that book sure as shit's got Manning's attention.

"I just don't understand this form of communication," he says as he hoists the big book in front of him as if he is about to give a lesson.

"One part has a drawing of a man," he says, "with a turban, lying next to a woman on a bed of nails, and the woman is asking, 'How come we never sleep at my place?'" Manning looks up from his presentation and I can tell there is something we both don't get. And I now feel very much like a "them." The panel next to it is a drawing of a very muscular man and woman flexing their muscles like peacocks flex their tails. They are naked except for a leaf covering their privates. The caption says, "Adam and Eve in the Garden of Fitness." Below that is another black and white drawing – they are all black and white, by the way – of a man talking to a woman at a bar saying, "I may not be Mr. Right, but I know Mr. Right, and maybe if you sleep with me it will make him jealous."

Manning shakes his head.

So do I. I don't fucking get it. But I don't get much these days.

"These feel separate, random," he says. "There is no cohesive thought. And yet, they must be important. Look at the size of the book," and he holds the book up with both hands to make his point. It's huge. The Biggest Book I've ever seen.

"It's called the New Yorker Cartoons." Manning says. "They must have been decipherable only by people that lived in New York." Manning gets up and pulls back the folding doors of his closet and reveals a whole shelf full of these huge, oversized, hard-covered books.

"They call them coffee table books. They were part of a low-slung table created specifically for only one kind of drink: Coffee."

That makes sense. The book is thick. You can put things on it. Coffee especially. But there isn't much coffee drinking anymore, so nobody ever reads these books. This much I know.

*****

Peeples probes my nub with a pen. I chime in, "I have a table Marsha refers to as the coffee table. We don't drink coffee, but we have a table named after the drink."

"One wonders the level of importance the drink achieved for the culture to begin naming furniture after it," Manning says, closing the door to his closet and imprisoning a veritable Columbia of coffee table books.

"I can find less and less information about anything, every day. I have tried all the Devices, all the screens, and it seems that the information is just disappearing. On so many things. Like it's being wiped out. Or it doesn't make any sense whatsoever."

"A lick of sense," Peeples says. "It's a very good phrase. A lick of sense. A short, wet, lick of sense. It's over as soon as it starts, dries fast, and you forget it ever happened or why. Then you have to lick it again, and the process starts anew, and no one is satisfied and nothing moves forward, which in and of itself doesn't make a lick of sense." I look at Peeples and from my expression I think I have made it clear that I don't think what he just said made a lick of sense.

Now Manning has the podium: "There is evidence we have gathered and collated this past year that the population is getting stupider and stupider. No, that is judgmental. Their brain's ability to absorb and synthesize information is shrinking. For millions of years, their brains were always expanding, becoming more capable, pushing them past the ape, the elephant and the octopus."

"Am I part of this..." and now I'm fishing for what I'm going to say next... "Great Stupidity." There. I said it.

Peeples finishes his examination. He puts his skin swabs, his light-up pens, and his pasty hands in his pocket.

That's bad. That's a sign of deep thought, bad diagnosis, and a pocket full of crap. "You have impending issues," he tells me. "There is evidence your arm might be growing back. So, you should understand it's possible. There is evidence it might not happen, so you should keep it a secret."

"Really? A secret? So when my arm does grow back, and Marsha says, "Holy shit, your arm grew back!" I should say, "Shhhh! It's a secret."

These are my fucking Docs. Come on!

Manning steps up: "They tried to regenerate limbs, long ago."

I can't dislike Manning. I like Peeples' Pies, but I'm neither here nor there about him. Peeples is my body person. But, Manning did all the heavy lifting post coma. He introduced me to Marsha.

"So why should I keep my arm a secret from her?"

"It was a failure, like so many things they tried," Manning says and he is in a bit of a zone. "Windmills for energy, tapping into the sun, ending cancer, cloning failures. A history of drastic failures. Any one of them might have altered..." Manning stops. Peeples takes his hands out of his pocket and then puts them back in.

"They altered the genetic makeup of certain animals so they would be bigger, with more meat, then gave that up to grow meat in protein greenhouses, but that meat, though chemically identical, had no texture." Manning is shaking his head again. "It happened once before. During the Rise of Inc. The takeover of the governments by the multi-nationals. And from what we can detect, they had the public bamboozled into thinking it was the government that was taking over the corporations. But it was the other way around the whole time. Much was erased. But the people rose up, mostly out of not being employed. En masse. And then the wars began. Almost like a diversion…" Manning ponders this, chin in his hand, "No, just like a diversion," he concludes, then plunks down in this chair, clearly exhausted. "It's no wonder we're getting the results we're getting."

"It's the 'them' thing again," I say, "You're saying 'them' again. Everyone else is 'them.'"

Peeples is over by his table, putting the nub-moistened swab under a magnifier. "John, we're researchers. Everyone is 'them' to us. 'They' are all test cases, things to learn from. We don't look at the world as if we are actually in it, but more alongside it, taking its pulse, watching them bicycle down the street. We don't even tell them when we see a pothole. We can't. We must let them fall into it. Then we must gauge their injury and conviction towards getting back up on the bike again."

"We don't help the chicken cross the road, John. We seek to understand why," Manning says in a tired voice, eyes closed, hand on forehead. "And you know this, as a moderator. It's imperative you keep a safe emotional distance from them also. To you, they are also 'them.'"

"Then why did you put me in the same pond as them? I could no longer be objective. I was part of the test. I don't want to be part of the research!"

I feel so separate from the goings-on of my world. I woke up and in short time I had a new girlfriend. That was comforting. But I don't feel love. I feel fortunate, as Marsha is tolerant of my limp maleness. I know, today, we just try to survive as well as we can.

"In this case, John, you were part of the research. A very important part," Peeples says. "And your swab test has come out inconclusive."

"So I'm insane, is that it?"

"No," says Peeples as he pushes back from the lab table, "I'm just not a good enough doctor to know what to look for."

I don't know how to react to that. For the past six months these two were my only contacts to a world lost deep inside my memory. My doctors had a greater sense of the past, of the history, my history, my health and well-being, both mental and physical, and now one of them is saying he is a charlatan?

"Only kidding," he says, which elicits a giggle from Manning.

"I can't go on like this," I tell them both as I get up. "I can't be a 'them.' I already take too much heat for not being able to have an erection. I want my arm to grow back. Now! I want to prove them wrong, celebrate the win, and go on with my life."

Manning looks at me with tired, dry eyes. "You honestly think you'll be able to do that when your arm grows back?"

"Are you taking the pills we gave you?" Peeples asks.

"Yes, every day."

"Cross the road, John," Manning says and then nods off into a deep nap.

"Double the dosage, John. Two tablets a day, and make sure that you have the opportunity to salt your food," Peeples says as he leaves Manning's office and heads down the hallway, whistling what my memory recalls is the theme song from some ancient digi involving a man named Andy Griffith, which was something that was made during the Age of Black and White, and remains a favorite of both Manning and Peeples.

I don't know why. There is a lot of whistling.

ENTRY 20

SUBJECT SEEKS ADVICE ON HIS FEELINGS OF ALIENATION FROM AN OUTSIDE EXPERT, FURTHER CHALLENGING OUR EXPERTISE, with ADDENDUM ON NATIONAL LEADERS DAY.

S ubject John has harbored thoughts of seeking advice from outside The Institute, and we are concerned that bad or less than factual advice will skew his experiences, or have him react in ways that are hard to predict or make predictions on. However, we must be careful that if seeking advice is a natural progression of the human experience, then we should not intrude on this. But we don't know. The Institute has seen the aspects of frenzied behavior based on faulty information, and many of the occurrences during the man-made Calamities were due to proselytizing by evangelicals, fundamentalists, and terrorist factions. Both individuals and large groups acted in ways contrary to self or societal preservation. We shall have to access this as it unfolds.

ADDENDUM: JULY 25 is National Leaders Day. This event exists so that the population of the former Empire takes a moment to remember every single person in the history of the Empire that led people through some event or invented something to advance civilization and the human condition. The CRL sanctioned a list of twenty leaders, mostly titans from the corporations that had much to do with the economic growth of the country during the second half of the 20th and first ten years of the 21st centuries. Most of these leaders' contributions were eventually *discredited, however, but there was very little memory of more politically historical figures – generals, adventurers, religious leaders, etc. – by the population, as the worship of the corporation grew beyond that of governments and religions. The most notorious of these titans had their records expunged or rewritten by the CRL, or twisted into lessons of accomplishment and great human endeavor. For example, many of the instances of overt greed exhibited by many financiers were translated into human spirit and the satiation of desire, and that seemed to impress the public, and without the facts, they could know no better.*

The list also had a lighter side, with an entertainer named Michael Jackson, his chimp – who they say was clairvoyant, a sports man named Peter Rose, and a very black man named Al Jolson, whose hobby it was to sing about how much he loved his mother, which the CRL found to be a vital message with the ongoing disintegration of the family due to The Calamities and the Crashes.

School children have to study one week for this day, and every year, they have to learn a new fact about the approved Leaders, facts the CRL adds to at their leisure. The histories have become incredibly expansive and a bit mythological, with Jackson and Jolson responsible for both electricity and refrigeration, respectively. More importantly, the creation of a new holiday was good for business, as each historical personality got his own action figure, with changes from year to year to combat obsolescence. This year, the Michael Jackson chimp was programmed to defecate chocolate candies into a diaper that doubled as a serving dish. It promises to be very popular.

—Parking garage. Car door closed. Window down. I reach into my jacket pocket and pull out Nikki's little vagina card.

My babies stir. I pull my shirt off my shoulder and three little porcelain fingers curl around the lip of my bandage, peek out at me as if to say hello.

They stretch for Nikki's card. They're curious about anything that is in my veteran hand, like the younger child wants everything the older sibling has. I give it to them. They turn the card over, index to middle, middle to fourth finger, and then back again. Like a magician, they turn the little shiny laminated vagina over and over amongst them, like they are sharing her, passing her around, like three boys playing with one girl who got too drunk at a party to care that there are now fingers all over her vagina.

I'm going to visit Nikki. She's a "them" and I need to know what that feels like from a person who seems to be a straight shooter and suffers daily for doing nothing more than being a sex worker/stripper/surrogate/psychiatrist. In talking to her in the group, I sensed acceptance of and interest in my condition. Which is more than I'm getting from both my girlfriend and my Docs.

My new hand emerges from the slit. It reaches for the steering wheel.

"You want to drive?" I ask it. It strains toward the wheel. I lean forward, nub toward wheel, and the hand takes it. It doesn't so much grip the wheel as just lay itself on top of it. It looks comforted by the wheel. This is good. It has memory. It has purpose. It likes to drive. When it comes out completely, I'll let it do most of the driving for me. I will drive with my new hand on the wheel. I will probably get ticketed for driving with one hand on the wheel, but that's the price of giving a new limb a sense of identity, so Ezra, bring it on.

I'm going to visit Nikki. I must spend non-moderator time with one of "them," especially *this* "them" so I know how she is handling her "them-ism." The address on the card is an abandoned strip mall. There's a family in the alley between two of the buildings. They're eating a dog that's rotating over a fire that's contained in an old coffee can. Slow going I'd say. But it is a small dog. Without the skin or tail, not sure what kind.

A Ticketist gets off his scooter and issues them a ticket. How he expects them to pay, I have no idea. But he has to meet his quota, and it's up to the Department of Tickets and Warnings to pursue this. Right after he finishes printing out the ticket they offer him part of the dog's right leg. He takes it and gives them another ticket for offering food not approved by the Department of Culinary Conformity. And as he takes off, dog leg in his mouth, he is immediately stopped by another Ticketist, who gives him a ticket for eating while on his scooter. They often give each other tickets. The CRL considers it a process that keeps them honest, and shows the general population that no one is above the law. Except for the CRL. And, I believe, my Docs.

I knock on a door, the one the card tells me is hers. The doorbell hangs from some wires attached to the doorbell hole and not only looks like it doesn't work, but that it could be dangerous, and the last thing I need is to suffer electric shock and paralyze my good arm. That would be funny if it happened to someone else, but I want no part of that. I knock twice again. I hear a muffled "Just a minute."

I stand at the railing and scan the city from my perch. The family of dog eaters has left their camp, leaving dog bones and a smoking fire and assorted plastic and cardboard containers. The street is empty today.

It's July 25, which is National Leaders Day, so for most, it's a holiday, and if people don't have to work, they'd rather be safe at home, or they hide in the few approved malls where they can buy Leaders Day crap.

The door opens. A woman. Robe and slippers. Her head is covered in a plastic shower cap. She looks to be in her late, very unhealthy sixties. She has a cigarette in her mouth that burns at the tip, and she sucks on it then blows out smoke. It's both strange and amusing, as I haven't seen these things recently, but know them from the digi's, as a man named Bogart used them a lot. He was a hard man, as I remember. Weary. Spoke oddly. She's hard too. And weary. Speaks normal. Maybe they are related, if not by blood then in spirit.

I hold the card up to see if she recognizes it.

"What happened to your arm?" she asks and now she blows the smoke in my face. It's a curious scent. I wonder if it smells like the inside of a lung.

"You can't have one," she says as maybe I was gazing at her cigarette too intently. "They're too hard to come by. I have to grow half my own tobacco because I can't always count on the smugglers," and she snatches the card out of my hand and moves it back and forth in front of her eyes so as to find a focus in her failing eyesight, which could very well be caused by the cigarettes she so loves.

"You want my daughter," she coughs, "But I don't know if I should let you in. What's wrong with you, walking around like that, making all the rest of us feel sorry for you or guilty that most of us have two arms?"

"It will grow back. Soon. I wanted to talk to Nikki," and as soon as I say that I know I've made a mistake, as this is the statement that gets me in trouble just about all the time. "I don't mean to make anybody feel anything. I just wanted to talk to Nikki."

"Lots of men, some women, want to talk to her. But you gotta pay for that. You know how much she spent on these cards. This is high gloss stock. Makes her pussy look almost real. So you gotta pay."

She lets out another cloud of smoke from her mouth. It creates a barrier to entry. I take out some CRL units and hand them to her.

The gatekeeper lets me in.

The apartment is even more dog-eared than the mall it sits in, but tidy in terms that their belongings all sit in little piles, in the corners, under tables, and stacked up on the walls like boulders. There is an organization to the junk. The piles are made up of either tightly folded clothes or tightly tied plastic bags. Without doubt, most of it useless. But there is honor to the junk in the neatness. These are people who can't let go of the past.

It's essentially one big room, with a large antique beanbag chair, and a huge dining room table covered with what looks like bonsai gardens in separate ceramic planters. There is a door off the room. I assume it's a bedroom, or an office.

"Did you make an appointment? I don't remember hearing you call. Did you book on a Device? I don't remember that either. You a Ticketist? Better not be. I'm done with those assholes. They got us for almost a thousand last year and that's with Nikki paying some of it in trade. Cocksuckers!" and she doesn't stop and I don't bother answering any of her questions. I'm in moderator mode, just listening.

"I'm not a prostitute, Mom," and it's Nikki, standing next to the bathroom door in a sheer robe with nothing on underneath. Her breasts are enormous. They have the same shape as the breasts of the women in some of the porn digi's Marsha showed me in hopes of inspiring me to a less mechanical way of achieving an erection.

She has a big blond hairdo. I don't remember her having blond hair. But women change hair color a lot, I am told. And styles.

Mother of Nikki pours herself a large glass of "I Refuse to Accept It's Not Vodka," and sucks more from the cigarette, and when she does, it seems she shrinks a little, like the tube is sucking the life right out of her.

"You want me?" she asks. "I'm old but still pretty tight."

"Mom!" Nikki barks.

"I wanted to speak to Nikki."

She laughs, then barks back, "Nikki, we gotta talker!" in a voice that's been chiseled by her sixty-plus years inhaling smoke and imitation vodka. The whole apartment smells like smoke, and the paint on the walls seems to have been affected by it. My thoughts paint a picture of her graying insides. Not pretty.

"I'm just going to slip into something more comfortable," Nikki says as she goes into the bedroom and I can't imagine what could be more comfortable than wearing a sheer robe over your naked body except to be floating in a tub of saline solution. "And leave him alone, Ma. He's way out of your league."

"He's got one arm," Mother of Nikki shouts out, "And says it's going to grow back. Yeah, that's out of my league all right, 'cause it's fucking insane,

OK?" She wanders over to the kitchen sink and spits. Then lights another cigarette and pours herself another glass of imitation CRL-sanctioned vodka.

"Want one?" she asks. I don't. I don't drink much. It doesn't agree with me. Marsha had a bottle of the "I Refuse" vodka in the house once. We drank it together. It tastes like a wet dog smells, frankly. I don't know what real vodka tastes like, but why it was desirable to have something that promises to taste like it I just don't know. Marsha says it tastes nothing like vodka, which she tasted as a child, but it's the only approved hard alcoholic beverage we have. And people need to drink these days, and the I Can't Corp never mastered wine, apparently.

Marsha got very relaxed the night she drank it and we had sex, but she didn't sweat or cry and just went right to sleep in a very drugged way, snoring and drooling. I never felt anything from it, but Manning and Peeples discourage it. They say it affects the organs and weakens the tendons, so your organs, after a while, become unattached to your insides. That's not a very scientific explanation, but I understood as much as I wanted to. In fact, there are people who have died of "I Refuse to Accept It's Not Vodka" who just about spilled out of their skin into a puddle on the floor.

*****

I wander over to the table filled with bonsai plants.

There's an artificial grow light above them and a watering tube that attaches to a small water container on the floor. The tube drips hummingbird amounts of water into the large shallow planters. It looks very scientific. This is more than a hobby.

Under the bonsai trees, there are small human figurines no bigger than one inch tall. Each bonsai garden holds a different set of human figurines. They're arranged in some kind of scene. One has a whole pile of figurines at the base of the tree with blood all over them, and five soldiers have their guns pointed at the pile as if they just shot the people. Another plant has a scene with two men raping a woman, while a third has a man and a woman, with child, running away from figurines of men chasing them with a pack of sharp-toothed dogs.

There's a bonsai tree with a branch holding a figurine that dangles by the neck from a rope; male figurines tearing apart a female figurine by the arms and legs; a bonsai city-scape on fire, figurines running from it with arms and legs on fire.

"Don't you even think of touching them," Mother of Nikki says. "Been making them since the beginning of the first decade. Used to be nice scenes, funny scenes, sexy stuff too." She walks over and fixes one of the figurines I thought was dead but had just fallen. "They helped me through many of The Calamities, or at least my share of them. I could make the horrible stuff I saw small. I could play God," she says and exhales a cloud of smoke over the bonsai collection, giving the scenes of rape, murder, mutilation, panic, executions, and suicides the added atmosphere of fog. Nicely done. Makes her smoking make sense.

"I don't write. This is my journal," she says. Her memories immortalized in tiny pieces of plastic. I wonder if she was a participant in any of them.

Nikki comes out of the bedroom wearing the same sheer robe, but now, a pair of furry boots that reach to her knees.

"I wasn't expecting anybody, especially not you. I didn't really think you were into this sort of thing." I don't really know what sort of thing I was supposed to be into, so I flashed her card.

"You kept it," she says, "Did you play with yourself?"

I look at Mother of Nikki. I'm uncomfortable talking to the almost-naked-except-for-the-boots-daughter about masturbating to her calling card. Mother of Nikki is gluing more figurines together when she looks at me, at my nub, and snips the arm off of one of them with a pair of tweezers. Another memory immortalized, this one about me. Glad I could contribute. Hope she puts me alone under one of the trees. Maybe with a small dog to keep me company.

"I don't want to have sex with you," I tell Nikki.

"I'm not a hooker. That's what those fools in the group thought. But I'm not what they think I am," and she points to the far wall of the apartment with three diplomas on it: The Montessori School of Sexual Functioning, The University of Eros, and one from Yale.

"I'm a PhD. Sexual surrogacy with a master's in plastic surgery for secondary sex characteristics. For a while, I did a lot of trannies. I was good. You could never tell. It was all about fold construction."

She sits on a chair and lights up a vapor pipe to smoke what looks like some medication, judging from the little prescription bottles scattered on the table.

"I liked to use extended ear lobes, the kind you get when you get older. We ran a marketing campaign to convince the aged that extended ear lobes was a sure cause of heart disease, so they would donate them. Then we attached them to the newly constructed vaginal openings of our patients. They made for pretty good foreskins too. The lobes had just the right amount of wrinkles to make it believable," she says as she opens her legs and presents her vagina to me. "I had it done to myself."

"I have noticed a lot of old people without ear lobes," I say, though frankly, I haven't seen many old people since coming out of the coma. They are mostly sequestered to the areas outside the metro zone, for their own safety, and because the CRL doesn't want any carcasses lying on the street, feeding the coyotes and homeless families.

"Let me see it," she says.

Since she has allowed me to view her vagina, I'm guessing she wants to go organ for organ. I un-Velcro my pants, reach in, and pull out my penis. Out of the corner of my eye, I see Mother of Nikki snip the penis off the figurine she just snipped the arm off of while she gazes at my flaccid cock.

"No," she says, "the nub. It's what you think makes you a 'them.' Me, I'm a 'them' because they think I have sex with them for money. But that's not why I should be a 'them.' I should be a 'them' 'cause I'm not even a woman, and they don't know it. If they did, if just one of them did, they'd report me. Or kill me."

Oh. And now I feel a little foolish, limp dick hanging out of my pants in front of mother and daughter. So much for assuming things in today's world.

"Do you have water? I need to take a pill," I tell her and pull the pills my Docs prescribed from my top pocket.

Nikki pours a glass of water from the tap, but it's cloudy and yellowed. She dumps it down the drain and tries it again.

"They're not filtering here this month. Guess I have to buy. Dammit, that's gonna cost!" she says and she's upset.

"I can pay you. I will pay you well," I tell her. "I want to talk about what you feel. As a 'them.'"

"Always the researcher, aren't you?"

"There's a lot I need to know. Not for The Institute. It's personal."

She pours a glass of I Can't Corp vodka, hands it to me, then takes a swig from the bottle. I swallow two of the pills, and wash them down with the swill. It should be called "I Can't Believe I Drank This Shit!"

"Come on, let's go to the bedroom. I want to get comfortable," she says and leads me to the back bedroom where she can get more comfortable than she already is.

*****

Nikki takes an army of pillows that cover her bed and arranges them into a cocoon-like arrangement. Then she lies on them and open her legs.

"Can you tell it's phony?" she asks.

I can't. It looks real. It looks like the image on the card, just slightly larger but not as colorful or shiny. My nub starts to itch. I think it's the pills. It always itches after I take the pills. That's because it's healing. When it stops healing, it won't itch anymore and I will have my arm back.

"Show me," she asks as she plays with herself, but this doesn't seem to affect her like it does Marsha. When Marsha plays with herself, she moans and makes other little animal noises. Nikki's expression is that of deep in thought, like a philosopher touching his chin to achieve ideation.

I pull the bandages off my nub.

"Come closer," she says. I do. I stand right next to her, lean in over her, nub to her face. She licks it.

"It itches," I tell her. She rubs it with her right hand, her left occupied with stroking her vagina. She sticks a finger into the fold of my nub.

"Be careful," I tell her, "It's sensitive."

"I'm a doctor," she says, and indeed her touch is soft and knowing. "This is it, isn't it? This is why they all look at you funny. You're supposed to get a replacement arm. It's the law. The CRL can't have people wandering around with reminders of The Calamities. The CRL wants no visible memory of them. Do you know that over thirty percent of the population in the Southern Section are without either an appendage or an organ? Just prosthetics, made by them. They look kinda real, but they work like shit. CRL always cuts corners. Once there was a shortage so bad for arms, they sold legs to those that needed arms. That was freaky. Made everyone look like orangutans."

"Does it disgust you, like it does my girlfriend?"

"Like I said, I'm a doctor. And I have seen everything. Now why don't you take your pants off and let's get you hard. That's an appendage I know all about, having had one myself back in the day."

"I can't do that."

134

"Of course you can. It's what I know how to do," she says and she uses both hands to fumble with my Velcro opening. She reaches into my pants and pulls out my penis and she puts it in her mouth. I don't stop her because it's her house and she is a doctor and a certified sex professional. I'm thinking, as she takes me in her mouth, that maybe I will find something out. Something I can take back to Marsha. I will tell Marsha that we don't need the pump anymore, that she just has to get some diplomas in sex therapy or go to Yale.

I watch her do it. She looks up at me as she does. And it's making me sad. I feel nothing. I feel worse than nothing. I feel both numb and repelled. The whole concept of a person devouring a part of me reminds me of the coyotes. I am wondering why I should trust this stranger to take a part of me into her mouth, where her teeth live, and where she could easily make me penis-less with a simple swing of mood. Then I would be a man without an arm or a penis. And in the case of the penis, I have no confidence that it would ever grow back. My arm has been useful to me for as long as I can remember. My penis was never a "star" part of my body.

My nub burns now.

"Come on, what's the matter," she asks, as my penis has turned to the texture of the limpest of pasta, the kind Marsha makes too much, the kind that makes me like dumplings best of all the prepared foods.

I'm thinking about the last time I saw Marsha and what time is it now. I'm thinking this has been a very long day indeed, maybe one of the longest since coming out of the coma. I must go home. I must have dinner with her. I hope it's not pasta.

"That's good, thank you," I tell Nikki.

"Is it good? Is it really, really good?" and she keeps on inhaling my penis and then, "Am I the best you ever had?"

I want her to stop but I'm afraid of stopping this therapy ahead of its time, as maybe any time now she will cure my problem. Perhaps this line of questioning has something to do with the process. I better play along.

"Yes, it's really, really good and you are the best I have ever had," I tell her as I think language might be part of the therapy but I still feel nothing. Maybe there are more questions to come. Marsha never asks questions. She usually just tells me things; I'm so wet; I'm so horny; You're so hard; I like you inside me; I'm going to cum. All expository statements. The questions might be the way to go. I hope they get more challenging.

My babies pour out of the nub. They flex themselves with what looks like new knuckles. I can tell they are knuckles because my babies bend like the fingers on my good hand in almost perfect ninety-degree angles.

They stretch themselves to Nikki, and reach for the top of her head as she bobs her head back and forth on my penis.

I follow their command and lean to where they want to go and they grab a handful of Nikki's hair, and it comes right off her head. Nikki stops, pulls away, touches her bald head, and screams.

My babies retract back into the nub, bringing the hair with them. The wig sticks to the end of my shoulder. I look at myself in the mirror and it looks like my nub has exploded in hair.

"You bastard!" She gets up, pulls on her robe, and takes a gun out from underneath a pillow.

"Get the fuck out! You're a freak! An asshole. You're less than one of 'them.' You're a monster. Give me back my hair!"

"My new hand did it. They pulled your hair off. Look!" and I pull the wig off my shoulder and show her my new completely operational and fairly strong fingers. She points the gun at me. She looks angry. She looks crazy. She is not impressed with my new fingers. Her wig is more important. This sucks. Here I am with my fingers running around stealing wigs and all she's concerned about is how she looks.

"You're a fucking freak! Get out!"

"I meant nothing. Look at them. Look at my fingers! Like I was said! My arm. It's growing back. They were reaching for you. They grabbed your hair. I'm sorry. Bad fingers! Bad!" and I can see myself in the reflection of her dresser mirror. There is nothing. Just the folds of the nub. Fingers gone. Into hiding. Done with their deed. Playing a game with me. Making my life difficult. Shit! But, if I were new fingers, I'd hide from her too.

She fires the gun – BANG – in the air – BANG – at the ceiling – BANG BANG – a chunk of ceiling smashes on the floor. I run out of the bedroom. Mother of Nikki swings a bottle at me. She misses. It hits the wall and smashes, spraying both me and her with the liquid and the glass from the bottle. She goes at my exposed penis with a pair of bonsai pruning shears, snipping at it. I stuff my cock back in my pants, grab the door knob, and run down the staircase and to my car. Door not opening. Scared. Clumsy. Door opens. Car! Let's go. On road…

I'm an asshole. The doctor from Yale said so.

ENTRY 21

THE INSTITUTE'S CONCERN ABOUT SUBJECT JOHN INCREASES.

The Institute is concerned about the project as it relates to Subject John. The implants have yielded rich, immediately recordable data of his observations. However, since the unplanned incident with the coyotes, and the loss of an appendage, The Institute is noticing continued questioning of processes by the Subject. It seems he is beginning to doubt his Doctors, which is contrary to programming and general nature. Subject John's motivation to seek the opinion of one of his focus group respondents is out of character, and certainly contrary to the effective execution of his job. He put himself at great risk. Now The Institute understands that Subject John might have been coerced by the representation of the respondent's vagina on the business card, but as it seems from his thought-voicings, the vagina and subsequent oral memories resulted in a shooting. A threat to his life also threatens the project. We are assessing the situation.

—Home.

Lassie greets me at the door. I think she might have even opened it.

The apartment reeks of bland. It's not a decipherable smell. It goes neither sweet nor sour. But it greets you with an olfactory wall of dullness.

"We're having guests," Marsha yells out from the kitchen, "Why are you late? Why didn't you call?"

I walk into the kitchen. Marsha is toiling over the stove, a big steaming pot in front of her. She lifts a spoon out the pot. The spoon carries her spaghetti. Her dreaded pasta. The source of all the bland right now. My mind flashes back to my limp, white penis in Nikki's mouth. My penis; the pasta in her mouth.

Marsha takes a single strand of the stuff and flings it to the ceiling. It drops to the floor without completing the mission.

"I went to see a sex worker."

That just came out of me and I didn't intend it to. I have enormous guilt at how the incident with Nikki turned out. I should have suspected a potentially hazardous situation. I am intuitive, as evidenced with my insights as regards my arm, but I should have sniffed this out. Framed and mounted diplomas are very potent documents that can thwart intuition.

Marsha looks at me as if I just said something in some bizarre ancient language that hurts her ears. Her eyes well up just like before her orgasm. I wait for a tear, as that would be nice. To lick a tear before dinner, like a cocktail, an aperitif. Salt would help give her pasta some flavor.

She turns back to her steaming pot of stringy mush, and calmly stirs it.

"Why?" she asks. I notice that she is not upset. There is really nothing to be upset about. I'm a researcher, and this was research. I didn't go there seeking sex. I might have discovered something interesting for Manning and Peeples, some new piece of knowledge they could add to their vast data bank of human insights. Something they might have adapted and sold to the CRL to help in law creation and enforcement, or even something they might have sold to the "I Can't Believe" people, as they are doing research all the time on taste, nutrition, and what new real-food doppelganger they might want to invent next.

Yes, the part where Nikki took my penis in her mouth might have been outside the normal research parameters, but I can justify that by saying it was part of my personal discovery, and as a sex worker, she has the required skills to cure me of my dysfunction. She is a certified professional, and part of the sex worker movement was to help those whose libidos went haywire when the CRL began putting both anti-aging and hormonal products in the food chain.

"She was a respondent. I did not seek her out," I tell Marsha, and she continues to make the pasta into more of a mush, just stirring and stirring. Now she stops, turns off the stove, and pours some "I Can't Believe It's Not Tomato Sauce" into another pan. "I needed to know how an outsider feels in this society."

"Did you have sex with her?" she asks.

"She gave me a blow job," and upon saying that, I could just have easily said no, but somehow I am hard-wired to tell the truth. I don't attach any significance to the act with Nikki. Pure therapy. I could have said, "We played chess." And I should have.

Marsha yanks the pot off the stove and the spaghetti dumps on the floor. We both jump out of the way as the water and white pasta worms create a steaming lake in the middle of the kitchen floor. Then Marsha charges, and hits me in a windmill-like fashion.

I have one arm to defend myself. I block as many punches as I can.

"I did not go there for sex. I went to ask questions."

"Was one of them, 'Will you give me a blow job?'" and she's screaming and crying now, at the same time. Her face is wet from tears. I feel badly, as I imagine this is something she just doesn't understand. There is much about me she doesn't understand, and there is much I don't understand about the world.

No matter, as right now, with all her tears, I want to lick her face.

I am strong enough with my one arm to pin her against the refrigerator. She kicks and lands a knee between my legs. I have seen that done in many of the digi shows. A man gets kicked between the legs, and it cripples him. There must be a very specific place to kick, because all Marsha hit were my testicles and I don't feel much except the force of the kick. I lick her face.

She squirms away from me, yelling, "You pig. You fucking pig." And she cries more, and I lick more tears. They taste different than the orgasm tears. They are less sweet. These taste much like metal smells. Now my nostrils are filled with pasta and metal. It's a mix where neither scent complements the other.

"I didn't mean to hurt you. I didn't enjoy it at all," I tell her. This doesn't seem to help at all, and frankly, I am out of explanations that might calm her.

"She is a 'Them!'" I tell her, "I'm a 'Them' and a 'They' and it seems, a freak! That's what I went to find out about! How it feels. How am I supposed to feel," and it's either fatigue or this statement but she slows down.

"We had a good thing here. I was safe with you, and you with me," she says, all punched out. Not much damage done to me. My good arm is really good.

"I have one arm, Marsha. And since I left the hospital, everyone is different to me. You, people in the street, the Ticketists, Manning and

Peeples, the focus group respondents. I could feel it when you wheeled me out of the hospital. The stares. From people in worse condition than me. Feeling sorry for me when it was I who should've been feeling sorry for them. I have become a 'They.' I have joined the lowly ranks of 'Them.' And I don't know why. My arm will grow back, so why do you all treat me like I'm crazy when I say that?"

"John, I had one of the pills your quack doctors gave you analyzed. They're salt tablets. They're giving you nothing. And do you know why?"

I didn't. Why would I take salt tablets to heal, or cure, or change me? What did the tablets have to do with my arm growing back? I know I like salt, no, love salt, but this hardly seems like the type of prescription that will be effective in the regeneration of my arm.

"Because, John, you're crazy. They gave you salt! Nothing but salt pills. Not even salt-based tranquilizers they give to those suffering from nervous breakdowns, schizophrenia, depressions, mental conditions. Just fucking salt. A placebo. They thought maybe they could calm you if you thought you were taking something that was going to help you."

"They've never said anything about any mental instability!" I shout at her.

I have never shouted before, not in anger, maybe to make myself heard from a distance, but not uncontrollably. This is the first time I can ever remember shouting. The vibration in my skull caused by my volume gives me a pain in my head.

"They don't tell crazy people they're crazy!" she shouts back at me. We seem to be speaking at mutually unnecessarily high volumes. Lassie sits at the entrance to the kitchen taking it all in, head turning back and forth in the direction of the loudest. Her ears pop up and down and flap a bit, and I think it's due to the volume.

I lick more salt off Marsha's face. And I don't even remember deciding that was going to be the next thing I would do. I'm worried. Maybe I am crazy.

She slaps me. Didn't see that coming. So fast. Whack. Sting. OK! I don't think it's out of anger, like we see in the digi-shows. It's a slap to wake me up, to make me come to, to get me out of my trance, which I'm not in, by the way.

"I saw fingers, and a thumb. And they work. They bend. With knuckles. Which means cartilage. They can point, and hold the steering wheel and I can share a sandwich with them. They come out when I'm alone. I can feel them moving, growing inside of me. They even pulled the wig off the sex worker when she was sucking on my penis. I think she has cancer. She might have also been a man once."

This flood of information seems to weigh Marsha down. And hearing me say it, I can see how it was a barrage of just too many unacceptable new things at once. Again, telling her we played chess would've been wiser. The weight of these revelations presses her shoulders down and she sinks into a chair at the kitchen table. Her head needs to be held up by her hands, and her slippered feet sit in a puddle of hot water and spaghetti.

If she had any tears left, she would shed them. Her eyes are red and sunken into her orbital sockets. Her face is pale, her hair tired, dull and stringy. Pasta-like.

It seems I have drained the life from her. Which is what the crazy do to the sane, I suppose. Suddenly, her head snaps up, her eyes are more alert.

"We're having guests!" she says, "So get ready. Put a fresh bandage on it. It's leaking. We'll talk about your little escapade with the hooker..."

"She's not a hooker. She went to Yale!"

"Fuck you, Yale!" she barks as she gets on hands and knees and scoops the spaghetti off the floor and back into the pot. "Go see your horse!"

I have no idea why she would say that. I have no horse. No one has a horse. No one has had a horse for years. We believe they may be used by I Can't Corp to make their meat dishes, but that would be saying that I Can't Corp actually uses meat in their doppelganger meat dishes, and that's giving them a lot of credit.

"Go see my horse? What are you talking about? I don't have a horse," I tell her and I wish she would stop obsessively scrubbing the floor and look up at me.

"Your Yale horse! You bastard!"

Now I have a horse from Yale and I am wondering if perhaps all this with my arm, my erectile dysfunction, and just life in general is taking a toll on her. We've seen it before, little nervous breakdowns, little personal emotional challenges, all leading to a colossal meltdown. This must be what it looks like.

"Stop talking gibberish! I don't have a horse, much less one that went to Yale!" I yell at her, trying to break her obsession with her believing I have a secret life as a jockey or a polo player. I don't.

"Horse!!!!" She yells right back at me, "W-H-O-R-E-S! Horse!"

Oh for fuck's sake, I'm thinking.

"Oh for fuck's sake!" I'm saying. "There was no intention there. Nothing done with the idea of cheating on you. That was research gone bad, that's all. Now..." and I'm looking at the pot with the spaghetti flopped into it, "Are we having that for dinner?"

I just cleaned the floor last weekend with one of the harsher cleaning agents Marsha keeps buying even though I tell her the fumes are dangerous and are really meant for more industrial type cleaning jobs. The cleaning fluid I used on the floor had a mixture of bleach, chlorine, and some acids. And now, the vapor residue of that is on the pasta and it's going back into the bowl, and Marsha will boil the water again, and the pasta will turn to even worse mush, or it might even just evaporate and turn to gases. And I fear the house will explode.

"I'll make something else," I tell her.

"Like what, John. You can't cook."

Right now, I would really like to tell her she can't either, but why ruin what has turned out to be a perfectly delightful evening, where my girlfriend knows I was given a blow job by a sex worker, thinks I'm crazy, and my doctors have been giving me useless salt pills, and I am about to eat toxic spaghetti. This calls for wine.

"I'll go get some Chinese food," I tell her and don't even wait for a response. I grab my keys and now, I'm back in the Foyota Excess, ready to chug into town in my horribly flawed vehicle to pick up food for some people I don't know nor care about at a shitty Chinese take-out place that probably cleans their floor with chemicals ten times more toxic than ours.

ENTRY 22

THE LACK OF SECURITY IN THE FLATLANDS AND THE INSTITUTE'S INCREASING CONCERN OVER SUBJECT'S MENTAL COMPETENCE.

D ue to cuts in CRL budgets, security in the flatlands was in effect for eight hours a day – all daylight hours – which were actually the hours that needed security the least. During the nighttime hours, neighborhoods set up their own security forces. The CRL-approved security alarm company – SAFE&SOUND – employed its own armies of security, with weapons. The need for security in the inner cities was so high that the standards for qualifying became lax, and pretty soon, these forces were essentially arming the criminals. When the CRL forces went on duty, there was usually a period of shooting and arrests during the first morning hours, but over time, night security knew well enough to get off the streets or risk challenging the better trained and equipped CRL forces, in addition to being issued tickets by the Ticketists.

The group that did the most damage to the system of vetting applicants for SAFE&SOUND was the pedophiles. For some reason, they had higher IQs, were more tech savvy due to their underground activity, and knew how to peel into the data base and the CRL's profile lists and revise them or make them completely disappear. In time, they were able to start a cottage business helping others erase or alter criminal profiles or create distinguished ones from scratch.

This group came under investigation when they changed the profile of a serial killer and created a fictional one of him as the inventor of a very popular line of flavored mayonnaises. He ran for a local political position based on his fictional expertise with mayonnaise until the real company stepped up and refuted the claim. The media sided with the candidate – they would always back the individual over the group – and attacked the real company for taking credit for many of the flavors. It really didn't matter what evidence they had – being a four-hundred-year-old mayonnaise company – the fabricated candidate had so much charisma that he got elected, and was able to start up his own condiment company from the left-over campaign funds. It all came crashing down when he raped and murdered his head of flavor research, his personal secretary, and his former campaign manager, all in a single night in a hotel room in the best part of the city of Cleveland.

The authorities discovered him kneeling before the bodies, entrails in hand, dipping them in jalapeno-flavored mayonnaise and fennel -flavored relish. The headline in one New York tabloid was *Condiment King Comes A-Cropper,* while another was: *You Want Fries With That?*

When the authorities investigated his identity they managed to track the re-coded files back to an address of convicted pedophiles in San Diego. They were arrested, made a deal with the authorities if they confessed willingly to the whole scheme, and shared all they knew technologically.

Years later, the identity re-coding concept was perfected by a vitamin and household cleaning products multi-level marketing conglomerate called Herbavore that needed cheap security for themselves and their wealthy distributors. To get approval to arm them from the CRL, they altered the bios of some of the most violent members of society. It became another income stream so they stayed with it, clearing countless felons and worse and making them security men and offering their services to apartment buildings, stores, businesses, and gated communities.

They were able to hire out their security forces to their competition under a separate company name, and there was a series of mysterious murders of CEOs and COOs at those companies. Most of them went bankrupt, guaranteeing Herbavore a monopoly.

They found a convenient side business in security alarms and were able to create their own demand by first having the security men (and women) rob the properties, then installing the alarm, then creating an atmosphere of fear to keep the monthly payments high. The CRL knew about this, but, as was noted earlier, they only work six days a year, and the sixth is a half-day, and the revenues cast off by the company more than compensated the budgetary needs of the CRL.

Nights in the flats are violent. Shootings, beatings, car jackings, car murders, and general vandalism perpetuate. The Institute wished Subject John would not venture into this area, for fear of attack and altering the research yet again. But it cannot impede the Subject's curiosity and other human needs.

—I hate it here at night, but I'm hungry and I don't want tainted pasta. I see a Chinese-Somalian restaurant on the corner. There's a parking space right in front of the place and an armed guard at the entrance. I will have to pay him about one hundred coin units to not damage my car while I wait for my food, and the meal itself will cost about four hundred units, so all told, tonight's take-out dinner will cost me two weeks' wages. God, how I wish Marsha could cook.

I get out of my car. I'm surrounded by Stemmers.

Six of them. They come up to my waist. One of them pokes my armless side with the barrel of his rifle.

"Where is your arm?"

"I lost it to coyotes."

"You lie!" says the littlest one with the half-smoked tobacco roll dangling from his chapped and beat-up lips. I think he is the Stem Leader. The rest of his tribe chimes in with the Stemmer's taunt; "Liar, Liar! Pants on fire!"

Stemmers never believe adults. They were taught never to trust grownups or people who were taller than them, and since they are mostly ten- and twelve-year-olds, that means just about everybody.

"Look!" and I pull my shirt off my shoulder and let the nub speak for itself.

They all take a step back, their wizened child faces lighting up in both delight and fear.

I look to the nub and it does nothing, no life, but somehow the intricacies of the scars, the folds of fresh new skin, seem to fascinate them.

The Stem Leader slaps one of his baby soldiers as he doesn't like the sudden shift in attention from him to my nub.

145

"He's a liar!" says the Stem Leader, and he tries to light my pants on fire with his tobacco roll. When that doesn't work, he takes out a small blow torch and tries it again. They like to illustrate their metaphors. It gives them more meaning, I suppose. It's just hard lighting pants on fire.

"He's a corporatist!" he shouts.

The Stemmers surround me, and emit a peculiar sort of half-scared, half-angry energy. They jostle each other, their knuckles white from holding their guns and baseball bats too tightly. I look at the guard at the door of the restaurant. I would like some help. I think that if he got involved, with his fire power and his fierce Chinese-Somali features, they would back off. The Stemmers were not big on killing people. They like to set your pants on fire. They like to destroy property, as their official T-shirts say: *We like when it goes BOOM!*

But the Chinese-Somali restaurant guard turns away. He's not interested in getting into a tangle with the Stemmers. Though they kill infrequently, if they are unsuccessful in lighting your pants, they bite like hell.

"I want to order some food," I tell the Stem Leader, wave a couple of coin units in the air, which he promptly snatches out of my hand, which are then promptly snatched back from him...

By my babies.

My newly hatched fingers sway back and forth as if they are conducting a sonata. They turn the coins over in their fingers, over and over, back and forth. I take them back with my veteran hand and drop them into my shirt pocket.

My babies are chalk white and long, perfectly tapered, longer than the fingers on my veteran hand. More evolved, both daintier and somehow wiser, like there was nothing they couldn't do, but there was much that would be beneath them.

These fingers were meant for lifting spoons and touching silk and fur. They were meant to pour the champagne. The veteran hand was meant to pop the cork.

The Stemmers surround my nub, and the fingers hypnotize them. Their little heads and eyes follow the gentle wheat-like sway of them, then the rhythmic opening and closing from open palm to fist then back again.

My babies goad me to stand under the street light so they might have more of a stage to impress the little monsters.

There is an arm inside of me, trying to emerge, to push out of my nub, and the force of this, the sensation of this, takes me in the direction it wants.

I'm helpless but to flow with the tug. When my babies wave right, my body tilts right. If they wave down, I feel an extra force pressing down at my knees.

I position the nub under the small puddle of the street light. My babies bathe in the glow. They are beautiful, emerging from the single source of my nub like Tubastrea, and they move with the night air as if influenced by the motion of the sea.

They pull me toward the Stem Leader. He is frozen in his spot with his now unlit tobacco tube dangling from his lower lip, stuck there with dried drool. First, my babies caress his baby face. He coos, as if he suddenly discovered his first ten years of childhood. My babies caress him like the mother he never had.

It strikes me that my babies were equally willing to show themselves to the little girl in the dumpling diner. What is it about children that they trust over adults?

"Do you see them?" I ask the Stem Leader, as I want to make sure it's not me who is hallucinating this encounter, that it's real and that it's not me who is crazy, but just the rest of the world that acts that way.

He doesn't answer. The other Stemmers surround him, make a line behind him, waiting their turn to be caressed, each one straining over the head of the Stemmer in front of him.

Then the smartest baby, the index finger, points to a little spot on the Stem Leader's chest. The Stem Leader looks down to see what it points at, and the index finger flies up and tweaks him in the nose. A short flick, right under the tip of his little pug nose.

His head goes back in reaction to the soft assault, then, fast and swift, the fingers form a fist and bop him on the top of the head.

As his head goes down from the harder assault, my new fist uppercuts him under the chin and his head flies back.

Then, as his head returns from the uppercut, my tapered index and middle finger fork out and poke him in the eyes.

He falls back on his little toddler revolutionary ass, shocked and blinded. The others move away, giggling at the predicament of their Leader.

I cannot help but feel that my babies have learned that series of hand moves from my own foggy memory bank. The memory is from the Age of Black and White, "The Kinder Age," as Dr. Peeples calls it. My memory is a faded digi of three men, with vastly different haircuts, slapping and poking and hitting each other with their hands, fists, frying pans, and large, flat, freshly caught fish. My memory says they are called Stooges. My hands are now my Stooges.

How utterly delightful! My babies have gone slapstick.

*****

"Kill him!" the Stem Leader shouts.

They point their guns at me, and from the looks in their eyes, I'm not sure that they've ever fired them or that they're even loaded. I do feel a sense of impending doom, though. But I also feel calm. I don't care really. They can riddle me full of bullets, tear me asunder, turn my flesh to butter. If my arm is growing back, then the rest of me will too. I will sprout up again. I am invincible.

I should just kick them away. Let them bite pieces off me. I'll show them the meat and skin replacing itself in front of their eyes. I look at their eyes again. Their guns at the ready to blast me. And now I see resolve in their eyes. They see a threat. Shit. I suck in a whole lot of air, and hold it.

Then, they fall. A blur of a two-by-four piece of wood, out of nowhere, strikes them down. Their guns land on the street, one of them goes off, and the bullet hits my front window and smashes it. So much for the unloaded guns theory.

The Stem Leader raises his pistol and at the moment he fires, the wood smacks his arm upward, sending the bullet into the night sky.

I fall against my car, try to climb back inside, but my one-handedness slows my escape to the false, windowless sanctuary of the Excess.

"Run away," I hear from a huge booming voice.

It's deep, basso, and it comes from up above.

It must be God, wielding a two-by-four, come to rescue me from the slapstick of my babies and the temper tantrum of the Stemmers.

I look to the direction of the voice and see a man who must be eight feet tall. He has a thick forehead that lords over his eyes, and hands the size of ancient coffee table books. He keeps swinging the two-by-four at the Stemmers, scattering their guns. His size and voice scatters their bravery and they run out of the glow of the street light, into the night, as if in fast motion like the films of the police from a place called Keystone during the Age of Black and White.

*****

"Every day I grow," the Giant tells me.

"I have no arm. But it is growing back," I tell him. "Did you see the fingers?"

"I see only Stemmers. I hate them. They bite me."

He yells at the security guard, "Do you see them attack my friend? You do not help? He comes to buy food. That is good for business. He offers to pay for your help. That is good for you."

I hear "friend." And that's nice. I don't have friends. I have doctors and a girlfriend, and those relationships are tenuous at best.

The Chinese-Somalian guard shrugs his shoulders and looks the other way. I can tell he is scared of the giant. The giant has a big voice.

"My name is Alex," he tells me. "Alex Stone."

Somewhere in my head, I know this name.

"Two weeks ago, I was seven foot five inches tall. Month before that, seven foot one. First month after operation, six foot two, no more," Alex tells me as we wait at the restaurant counter for my order of canjeero, wrapped pork and vegetable dumplings, side of cornmeal, mushrooms, sambusa, and sausage made from everything. He has ordered also, but twice as much, as he says he eats almost all the time now, and this is his seventh meal of the day, and there will be one more before sleep.

"And sometimes, it's not tall I get, but feet get bigger, then hands, then I get tall. I go some weeks with huge feet and hands, they look like they don't belong to me."

"Why did they operate on you?" I ask. Makes sense, as his growth could be purely glandular, or a medical fuckup. There are a lot of those.

"They say to remove my spleen, for blood disease. I don't remember much before that. It was five or six months ago, I don't remember."

I tell him I too was in the hospital five months ago. I tell him about the coma, and how I don't remember much before it either. I tell him about my penis, its dysfunction, and how my arm was torn out by the coyotes. He takes it all in stride, especially the part about the arm growing back. Either that or the heaviness of his upper brow makes him look like he's falling asleep, which gives me the impression that nothing really impresses him. I wonder if unusually large people can be impressed. There is almost nothing physical in the world they don't have some sort of mastery over. I should ask the Docs to do a project on that: *Abnormally Large People and Their Impressions about A Normal Sized World*. Or maybe catchier: *Big People. Small World.* Yes, that's it. The Docs like catchy.

"My doctors tell me my memory is gone because of blood disease. I look up for disease that destroys memory, I don't find. They tell me it's new. I believe them. They are my doctors, what to do?"

"I feel the same way about my doctors," I tell him. I'm starting to feel less trusting of them. I ask them questions and the answers are always so vague. "But you know the InfoDevices can't be trusted. They've wiped out entire decades of information," I say to reassure him that doctors can be as misinformed as the rest of us.

"At first, the people make fun of me for way I talk," he says, gesturing with his hands and making a little wind storm. "I don't know what they talk about. Is how I talk. You have accent, not me. Why they make fun?"

I have no issue with the way he talks. I've heard worse. I heard people so traumatized by The Calamities they would start each sentence at the end and speak it backwards. Or one guy who just dropped all the consonants. Of course, the devices themselves were wreaking havoc on language. The shorter your words, the faster you could communicate, so that last sentence might sound like *Shrt ur wds, fst u com*. But I can tell this hurts him, so I let him know he is not alone in the "being ridiculed' department.

"At first, when I couldn't get an erection, I thought my girlfriend would no longer be interested. But it was when my arm started growing back that she started treating me like a freak."

"I get erections too much. I get erections that are sometimes sixteen inches long, my penis grows so big. Women want the penis, but they don't want me. I don't care, the fucking I don't feel anyway."

"Me too, I don't feel so much with sex. But Marsha likes it. And I do like lying down. Lying down is one of my favorite things to do," I say and that's true. I believe I'm happiest when I am lying down staring at the ceiling, looking at the tiny little world up there. I can see into cracks, see microscopic bugs cross the ceiling, whole colonies of new mold.

He shakes his head.

"I cannot lie down anywhere. No bed big enough. I sleep on floor. Now my back hurts. What is happening to me? My doctors tell me to think hard, very hard, about what I live through. They say for my memory."

"My doctors said the same thing. I read that it does help with recreating memories and that the committing of memories to your brain can jog other memories. Though that hasn't happened yet."

"They tell me to talk to myself when no one is around. I look like crazy person coming down street, with big hands and feet, talking to myself. People cross the road to get to other side. Like the chicken," he says, once again, shaking his head in what is a profound sadness, and I can't help but feel we are kindred spirits, Alex the Giant and I. We both have no emotional memories of our pasts. We can remember facts and some of the past, which helps us understand why things are the way they are now. We both don't feel like everyone else does about sex, and physically, we are changing. His struggles are greater, as he is growing more and all I'm doing is growing back. Where it stops for him is anybody's guess. I know my arm will return to match my other arm, or will be slightly improved.

"Do you feel like a 'them'?" I ask.

"I don't feel like 'them.' I am different from them. I grow every day. I had job at Big and Tall Man shop, but then I grow too big, and I am taller than all my customers, so I make them feel small. I go from M to L to XL to XXXL to Four XL Special. I get fired. I had job at car washing place. I could wax car roofs no problem. Two at a time. I get fired because I can't vacuum inside, cars so small. Nobody want to hire eight-foot man with way of talking not like them."

I sense he's exhausted. All that constant growing, stretching of bones, expansion of skin. I have a feeling, based on my carefully honed observational skills, that he has grown an inch talking to me now.

Our food comes in grease-stained bags. Alex holds out his hand, and his bag, easily the size of a large grocery bag filled to the top, fits nicely in the palm of his hand. This confirms my feeling about his recent growth.

The counter lady, a nasty looking Chinese-Somalian – this is not a good mix of genes – scowls at him.

"You pay now, then leave. You scare customers away."

"Hey, he's a paying customer. You shouldn't talk to a good, peaceful paying customer like that!" I say as I mount my defense of my new friend.

"You go too. You one-armed freak. You scare customers away!"

I pick up a salt shaker and throw it at her. She ducks and the shaker hits a wall. The salt explodes onto the floor. I can smell it. The beautiful smell of salt.

I drop to my knees and lick the salt off the floor. It's delicious.

"You freak! Get outta here!" she yells as she hits me with a long metal ladle. The guard outside points his rifle at me. Alex Stone steps in front of me and glares at the guard. The guard shoots.

It's all slow motion. I can see the bullet emerge from the barrel, spinning, then it divides into six pieces, then those six pieces divide into twenty. The metal shards scatter all over Alex's torso, but now, with his size, and what I feel must be enormously thick skin, they stick to him like pushpins.

Alex's fist rises to the ceiling and comes down with a thud on top of the guard's head. The guard goes down like a sack of potatoes. Alex picks me up and we run out of the restaurant.

"I'm shot up!" he says, and indeed, there are trickles of blood, thick winey blood, on his too-small shirt and pants. "Take me to doctors!"

I help him into the Excess. It's not easy, but with the windshield out, he puts his feet through it and rests his legs on the front of the car.

I get in, start the car up, and we race like speedy slugs down Sunset Boulevard, nearly hitting even slower-moving criminal pedestrians as we go.

They're the Completely Forgotten. They wander the neighborhoods every night looking for a place to sleep. Infirm, with lousy equipment to help them walk – like a four-wheeled walker down to its last wheel.

Many are completely crazy, with no idea they are crossing the street. They have a tendency to pause mid-crosswalk to make great speeches and gesture to great imaginary things as if they had a crowd in front of them and they were the inspirational leaders of a small country. I like watching them.

According to the InfoDevices, they were once called homeless people. Good authority – doctors and Devices – decided to give them a name aimed at making the populace understand nothing good was ever going to happen to them. They decided to give them the name of the solution they applied to the problem: Completely Forgotten, in the hopes that you would stop pestering the CRL for a solution.

*****

It's a series of "Turn here, go here, turn now" on the way to where his doctors practice. Then, a short, sudden, booming basso: "Stop now! Is here!"

It's the Institute. FOCUS ON HUMANITY. My place of work.

Alex struggles out of the car, leaving an oily blood schmear on my seats and dashboard. "Leave me!" he barks, and the volume shakes the windows.

"I work here," I tell him. "My doctors work here also."

"They will take care of me. They take care of everything," and he bounds off to the building, hands swaying back and forth to balance his big looping strides.

"Are their names Manning and Peeples?" I shout out. But he's gone, into the parking garage.

*****

I don't know what to think. He has the same doctors as I do. I have never seen him at The Institute during the day, never seen him at work.

152

I know he doesn't work there or at least I think he doesn't but now what do I really know?

Why wouldn't we have brought somebody like him in to test? He has a fascinating condition; it would have been interesting to test him against a control and gauged the levels of acceptance or rejection of his condition against several demo and psychographic types in a control.

What is it about him that makes me feel different? Something organic, something primal. I feel love for him. But I'm not a homosexual. But could I be? Are the changes in my biology, the stress to my system, making other changes in me? Psychological changes? Sexual changes? Philosophical ones?

He saved my life. He saved the life of my babies. I should feel something for him. And I can't say it's sexual. Though I can't say what that would feel like. What happens when you're sexually attracted? Do you achieve a certain state of arousal in just thinking about the person? I don't know. Since the coma, this is something that was wiped out, if it was there at all.

I will ask them tomorrow. Now I can only hope he can get the help he needs.

I hear paper rattling. It's the bag of food. My babies are reaching for it, touching the bag where it's been folded closed, trying to get inside of it.

All they get is greasy from the food that has seeped through the paper.

ENTRY 23

THE INSTITUTE ASSESSES RISK
OF SUBJECT'S ENCOUNTER.

This last entry by Subject John is of concern to The Institute, as no contact was to be initiated with other participants during the process of the test. We needed each participant to move independently of the other, so there would be no sharing of experiences, which could influence or taint the interpretations of those experiences. Also, the power of two or more respondents together, the extremes of their conditions, their natures, and required behaviors, might affect the reactions of the populace to the test subjects. If two or more people are experiencing the same behaviors and dilemmas, the outsiders tend to isolate those behaviors. They don't identify as easily with those behaviors. Or they think it is part of a greater movement and adopt those behaviors as a way of joining the greater. In truth, The Institute has no idea how to handle this situation, and most of our positing is highly theoretical and perhaps of no real value to the reader. We apologize. We will have to monitor this situation.

—I park on the street. It's a nice open space right in front of the building. Rare, and it should not go ignored. Plus, I want the Excess to air out. It smells like greasy Chinese-Somalian food and oily giant blood.

I see people in the windows of my apartment. I see the silhouette of Marsha with her friends. They are laughing, drinking, moving from kitchen window to living room window. I'll have to be introduced to them. This is no night for strangers. I wish I called the shots here. One day, when my arm grows back completely, I will. But it's no use alienating the very person who is going to have to eventually accept my regeneration.

Marsha held off on introducing me to her friends for fear we weren't going to be together. Fair enough. It took a bit to get her used to my flaccid penis, and the fact that I would not be giving her any babies. Even if I could, who would bring a baby into this world? It's not fit for adults. So maybe Marsha has given up on babies and has come to terms with the fact that for the rest of her life her womb will be an echo chamber, and that's why tonight, I get to meet her inner circle.

I asked Manning and Peeples if they knew of any friends I might have had, anyone who might have visited me during my long coma, but they drew a blank. Nothing. No one. In reacquainting myself with my apartment and my belongings, I found no contact numbers or voice records. I seemed to have always been a loner.

And now here come Marsha's friends. She wants to make community. That's good. There is so little of that left.

But after the day and night I have had, this couldn't be further from what I want to do. I'd like to lie down and stare at the ceiling and let my mind see inside the cracks up there, create my little worlds, stare at the plaster pattern on the ceiling until it comes to life and swirls around like an ocean. Sometimes a small spider might scamper across, or maybe I will watch one build a web. I can see it ejaculating its proteinaceous silk from its spinneret glands, crossing it over and over and making a honeycomb. On rare occasion, some other poor creature will get ensnared in the fresh sticky web and the host will spin more silk around it, taking it hostage before paralyzing it with its poison. Then I watch the spider eat its prey, turning it in its tentacles and chomping away on it. I can see it all in fine, fine detail, as it devours first the stomach, then the head. I have very good eyes.

I will tell Marsha I will pump for her all night long if she just sends them away. I will tell her I have come to the conclusion my arm isn't growing back if she will just let me lie down in my bed and stare at the ceiling. No I won't. Who the fuck am I kidding?

*****

"Honey, I'm home" is really what I tell Marsha.

I like that expression. It's calming, as if nothing in the world is wrong and the spouse will be incredibly contented that her husband was finally home, though where he was all day was anyone's guess. It seems that many of the family entertainments from the Age of Black and White dealt mostly with the children and wives of the family. The man was absent most of the time, until he popped in and said, "Honey, I'm home," and that was the code for dinner. These dinners were the opportunity to talk about the day, to wrestle with adolescent issues of sex, homework, greed, or religion. It's a good idea, these dinners. But they're a relic. Most apartments can't handle a table large enough to put families around. And it would seem that in serving all the "I Can't" products, you might as well ladle up some "I Can't Believe This Passes for Conversation."

"Honey, I'm home" is familiar. I believe there was one show that said it a lot. It was something about woman and her strong-jawed husband, who was a doctor, and it would seem that they were about as happy as a family could be. Now I am having more thoughts. More connections. About Alex Stone. The giant, his name and how it sounds familiar. Alex Stone. Dr. Alex Stone. That's why the giant's name is so familiar. Dr. Alex Stone was the husband's name in the "Honey, I'm home" show. And the wife and mother was named Donna Reed. My memory is coming back. Foolish little triggers. The giant was named after Alex Stone. And you know, come to think of it, even with his heavy forehead and huge hands and feet, with his teeth the size of a baby elephant's toe nails, he looked a little like Alex Stone. I'm invigorated by being able to take a memory and make a connection to the present. This holds promise. Maybe the secret to creating emotional memories lies in my ability to connect the dots between past and present, like the Stooges incident with the Stemmers. The actions of my babies were influenced, it seems, by those three men, though I have no idea why those men hit each other so much. I do remember finding them somewhat humorous and thus I was overcome by a slightly pleasant sensation when my fingers did the same to the Stem Leader.

I'm progressing.

My brain's in overdrive. The memory of the images and characters from the Age of Black and White is now spinning into the Age of Color and the gods that were portrayed. The three Stooges are now replaced in the gallery of memory by Men who flew in bright red capes, Men who had grown large and green and temperamental, Men who dressed like bats, Men who acted like my beloved spiders, Men transformed by chemicals, insect bites, or their miserable childhoods, Men with hammers and lethal shields. They were rebellious, and often became threats to their creators. But they served the greater good.

The memories are sketchy, but I am making sense of them. These are the gods the public wanted to believe in before The Calamities. Things had gotten so bad that traditional religions no longer offered solace. They were corrupt, morally bankrupt, so we created more gods, better than the ones they already had. New and improved gods.

They too were made in the image of man, as gods must be, each with a specific strength and a specific flaw. They fought greed, avarice, aggression, and power, and the people cheered them, but were afraid of them at the same time.

My mind's on fire. These gods were glorious, exhilarating. The documentaries made about them were rich with adventure and music and thrills and loss and victory and there were many.

If these Men existed, and were capable of superhuman feats, why is it so hard for Marsha to believe my arm is growing back? She might not remember them. She might have been too small. The records might have been expunged. The CRL might not have wanted their influence, and the false hopes they inspired, to survive. Then the CRL would be the new god, omnipotent, the final word, the only deity worthy of worship. Maybe I am one of them. Maybe I am a god. I offer hope to all those limbless people out there. Maybe I was crossed with the species of lizard capable of growing new limbs.

It's an opinion.

*****

Back in the moment. Marsha's friends.

Two women and a man, sitting in the living room. They look at me like an octopus just walked in the door, albeit one with one less tentacle.

Lassie's at my feet, sniffing and accessing, gathering information, man's best friend gathering his master's experiences from the viscera of the day. Marsha's face turns from happy to horror at the sight of me.

A blond female friend is the first one who says anything. "Wow, he's got one arm. Good for you girl!" she says, smiling her approval at Marsha.

"What happened to you?" Marsha hammers, "Where have you been? You look like hell. Go clean up. Is that the dinner?"

I can see myself in the hallway mirror, with the greasy bag of Chinese-Somali mashup, and a shirt that's splattered in little flecklets of blood. I can accept these questions and observations, as I look exceptionally disheveled right now. Ornery even.

And why wouldn't I? I have been insulted at work by those in worse physical shape than I, given a penile sucking by a hairless prostitute from Yale, berated by my girlfriend for innocently and ignorantly entering into that meaningless momentary relationship, and assaulted by the devil's children. I have had my car window smashed by same, was insulted by a shop owner and shot at by her Chinese-Somalian security guard. And bled on by a giant, who winds up having the same doctors as I, and an affliction that gives me pause about their expertise and the technology they profess to master.

And to top it all off, for the most part, the hand that is pushing out from the end of my shoulder, the one that doesn't exist, the one that can't grow back, the thing that marks me in the minds of those I care about as being mentally unhinged, is the very thing responsible for most of the soured events of the past twelve or so hours. Explain that away, will you? The cause of all my troubles doesn't exist. Bullshit. It's real as rain.

I'm a fucking wreck, not well, extremely uncomfortable in my skin and in my life. And now, the first thing that happens to me upon arriving at my sanctuary is a guest that is astounded by the fact I have a temporary absence of an arm, and my girlfriend is seemingly assaulting me due to her embarrassment at my level of dishevelment. Apparently, I have a face and a persona that invite abuse.

"How do you get a one-armed man out of a tree?" the same woman asks to the room of other people I don't know.

Marsha turns to her, and burns an imploring look her way. The others smother their giggles.

"Patty!" Marsha scolds her, which is as good an introduction to her name as I could have wanted. She is a "Patty." That is always bad. They started in childhood as a Patty and never progressed to Pat or Patricia. She probably is a troublemaker. She has met her match, that's for sure, so I ponder her question. It's the surest way to impress Marsha, or at least get her to like me more, which right now would be like she might begin to like me again.

I have a mental image of a man without an arm, much like the man from The Fugitive, hanging on a branch of a tall tree. He looks a little desperate and there is no doubt he'd like to come down. My mental imagery muscle is strong now. This will help me solve the riddle.

"I would think a ladder would help," I answer, but Patty just shakes her head. The others keel over now.

"Patty, enough!" Marsha scolds her, and there is a sting in her words. "The rest of you, stop it. John, go take a shower!"

I am back to thinking the ladder is not the answer, but offering him food might get him motivated to descend very carefully.

"Offer him food and drink," I answer, and that must be a very funny answer, as the other friends of Marsha send their own drinks up and out of their noses.

Patty shakes her head again. I'm stumped.

Unless the tree is a metaphor for something. I wish Manning was here. He's good at metaphors. He understands their symbolism. Being in a tree could indicate the man is in trouble, and so I answer, "Get him a lawyer," and now with the crippled-over reactions of Marsha's friends, you'd have thought I was one of the Stooges, slapping my own face and sticking my fingers up my own nostrils while making that peculiar "nyuk nyuking" sound.

"Then how?" I ask Patty, as I have given up, and do need a shower as my nub needs to be cleaned and lightly powdered with salt.

"Wave to him," she tells me.

The others sit with their hands over their stomachs and mouths. She pours herself another glass of "I Can't Believe It's Merlot–Vintage Year 2067," and asks, "How do you get a one-armed Irishman out of a tree?" and this I will not even attempt to figure out, as my knowledge of the eccentricities of the Irish is zero.

"I don't know," I tell her.

"Patty, stop it now!" Marsha says as she snatches the bag from me and heads to the kitchen.

"Wave to him," answers Patty.

Then, before I have a chance to feel duped, she asks, "How do you get a one-armed Polish man out of a tree?" and this, I suspect, is all about the legendary Polish slow-wittedness and I think I might have this one.

"Tell him that to climb the tree, he must descend to the ground!" and I'm proud I came up with an innovative solution. I know it's a fresh approach, based on what I've read as regards the Polish history of doing things counter intuitively. The room is silent, just looking at me, salt tears of laughter now dry on the guest's faces, no doubt imagining the sight of the one-armed Polish man thinking he is climbing the tree by descending from it.

Patty drinks from her glass, shakes her head no, and says, "Wave to him."

I am amazed that there can be so many situations solved by the same answer. Of course, I'm tired. Not exactly thinking sharp. Yes, of course, wave to him. That's assuming he's so polite he is willing to jeopardize his safety for the sake of manners.

"Get changed!" Marsha in full command now.

*****

Quick shower and pat dry the nub. Stick my fingers in the slit and check on my babies. I pop two of my pills in my mouth and pull on a T-shirt. I've hidden a small salt shaker in the drawer and I sprinkle some of it on the nub.

"You're in such trouble, John," Marsha stands at the threshold to the bathroom, arms crossed, looking at me like I was a troubled teen, maybe with some sort of disease I got from being behind closed doors with a girl. "Look at you, sprinkling yourself with salt, taking the salt pills, talking to yourself incessantly…"

Of course I talk to myself. It's a memory retention exercise. Christ, everybody knows that. What Marsha is upset about, what she considers abnormal, is really quite normal from a medical perspective. She's just going to have to live with that until my arm grows back and my emotional memory returns.

"I'm sure my doctors know what's best for me. If helping me grow my arm back will require salt, then salt is what I need. If talking to Lassie or to myself helps restore my emotional memory, than that is what I must do."

She continues to stand at a distance, not breaking the plane of the door, not sure she wants to be in the room with me, which I understand, because mortals tend to stay at least three feet away from potential gods. I feel that way right now. I feel strong. I know I'm an unusual man. I will grow my arm back and prove it. It will be a fine arm, an arm of legend. A game changer. Arms will want to be like mine. They will write about it. I might go on the Devices and give interviews about it. I will encourage whole generations of the limbless to take salt and think hard about growing the limbs back. I will engage The Institute in research to discover the triggering mechanisms of appendage rejuvenation.

"I want to ask you not to talk about your fantasy of your arm growing back, not tonight. Not with my friends. Please, John, not tonight," she asks, and she's got the sad kitten look in her eyes. That gives me pause, but still…

how can she call what I have been going through a fantasy? It shocks my brain. Lassie's at her feet, looking at her, then me, then her again.

"Is my arm growing back a fantasy?" I ask the dog.

"I can't believe you are dismissing my concerns for your mental state, John. It's fucking disrespectful…"

"And how fucking disrespectful is it of you to NOT believe me when I say it is happening. Here, look, let's see if they're secure enough to come out and show you!" and with that I unveil the nub, hold it towards Marsha and try to seduce my babies out of my arm with a finger full of "I Can't Believe It's Not Toothpaste."

This backfires, as all Marsha does is turn away.

"One day, John, I'll be able to look at it. But not yet. And I'm not sure I will be here one day!"

"Look, they are coming out. I feel them moving in there. They want the toothpaste. Watch, they will appear…"

She slaps me. Which means she doesn't consider me her god.

The slap hurts me. It should hurt her for giving it. But she isn't crying. She has no remorse in her violence. She's angry, looking at me like I'm a child she doesn't really like or want but has no idea how to get rid of.

Lassie at her feet, growling, strangely protective of me. Good girl.

Now, I feel something awful. I feel an awful sensation in my face and stomach. I feel an awful sensation in my head. And suddenly, I'm making tears, just like Marsha, just like everyone else who cries. It makes me weak, makes me nauseous, makes me ashamed. But mostly weak. It feels like with each tear, I get weaker. People cry, then they sleep, or are quieter. Because their strength, in the form of tears, flowed out of them.

I must put the tears back in. I wipe my face and lick my hand, full of my own salt. With the toothpaste still on my finger, it tastes like a combination of salt and peppermint. It warms me. It makes me calm. It soothes me. I like it. Maybe I will try mixing Marsha's orgasm tears with some toothpaste. That is a good idea, I think.

Marsha stares, now not like at a child she doesn't like, but like one she doesn't understand at all, one she might drown in the bathtub after having a secret pregnancy and her father is a priest and this would be very bad indeed.

"I'll tell them you're sick. They'll understand. If you're hungry, I'll make you a plate and put it on the bed."

With that, she turns and leaves the bedroom. With that, she sucks the air out of the room. And then, my babies emerge and the index finger caresses my face, wipes what feels like another tear and takes it back into the nub, likely to feed the others.

*****

I sit on the bed, the dog at my feet.

I'm naked. I've arranged my penis and my testicles to lie flat on the mattress, my legs open wide, penis arranged neatly on top of the testicles, splitting them in two down the middle so they rest symmetrically at the base of the penis. The whole gang looks a bit like a Cornish hen, which I have never eaten, but have seen pictures of as one of the alternative birds you could eat during the days when people ate a lot of different types of birds.

Lassie jumps up on the bed and sniffs the nub.

"It's growing. You believe it, don't you?" I ask her. "I've seen them. I'm a witness. And yet when I tell anyone about it, they look at me, roll their eyes, or turn their mouths into some little expression of fucking weirdness and they drift a hundred miles away. I need to prove this, girl." She now has her left eye planted against the nub, like she's a Peeping Tom at a keyhole. I think these Ecuadorian circus dogs are the most unusual dogs in the world.

"I need to either be a man without an arm or a man with an arm. I cannot continue to tell people what's happening to me when apparently, you aren't supposed to grow arms back. And why not! If you have the time and energy, why the hell not!"

Lassie's head snaps back, alerted. Then I see. My babies have emerged for her. They pour out of the nub and pet her nose. She licks them. They let themselves be licked. It feels wonderful, warm and sensitive.

"Marsha!" I call out. I need her to see this!

"Marsha! Come here!" I yell so as to be heard over the laughter in the next room. The new fingers get licked by Lassie, and they turn over to make sure the dog licks their entirety, including the palm, which is the most sensitive of all, and Lassie's tongue is wet but grainy and it both tickles and soothes. There must be a huge amount of nerves developing there. I tingle with each lick.

*****

Dammit, Marsha needs to see this!

I open the bedroom door and run down the hallway into the living room. Her friends sit, wine glasses in hand; the man puts some herbal powders into a vaporizer and inhales.

"Marsha, look!" I scream and turn the nub and my babies to her. "There they are, plain as day. Lassie was licking them. They came out for Lassie! They have to trust you. They trust the dog. You must make them trust you."

"What else you doing back there with the dog?" asks Patty, and when she asks, her eyes lower to between my legs and lock on my crotch. The others are looking also. Marsha is frozen in a look I've never seen before.

I look down to see what the fascination is.

I am naked. I forgot. And my penis is fully erect and looking right back at me. It is huge, anaconda proportions, at least from my vantage point.

"Dinner is served," Marsha says. "Let's sit down. John, get dressed, please."

No use telling them about the arm. It's become sideshow to the erection, which, frankly, right now, fascinates me even more than my babies.

*****

It didn't take long. Fifteen seconds or so. Fifteen seconds of gazing at my unpumped erection, my natural erection, albeit brought on by my dog licking my nub, which is neither natural nor unnatural. My penis is back to its familiar limp state. My babies are back in the nub. The dog sits at my feet. All is as if nothing happened. Nothing learned. But I have to think about this. This needs to be cataloged precisely for review with Manning and Peeples when I go back to work, in two days.

I had an erection. A hard-on. A boner. A rod. A stiffy. A woody. Blue steel. Throbbing gristle. A chubby. A horn. A pan handle. A pork sword. A tallywacker. My little pony pitched a tent. On its own.

This means something. This is a general revitalization of my biological support systems. Perhaps the healing and growth of my nub and new arm has cured my erectile dysfunction. Or perhaps I am just getting over the coma on schedule and this is a normal process.

I will pee. I will see if there is any change there.

I sit on the toilet. I used to stand, but I made such a mess with my vapor hitting the seat and tank that Marsha asked if I would sit, like a woman does. It is more practical, and my manhood isn't threatened, and I can rest and read.

I pee. It's still mist. One cannot expect complete rejuvenation equally across all functions. I can wait on that.

*****

"What were you trying to prove? Were you trying to embarrass me?"

It's Marsha, outside the bathroom door, and she's not waiting for an answer. "Get ready for dinner, it's getting late."

"I'm sorry. I forgot I was naked," I tell her and it's true. I would never knowingly run out into a living room full of guests naked, presenting a fully engorged, vein-bedaubed and shining erection. I'm not that kind of man.

"I'm taking you to an analyst tomorrow. We'll talk about all you have been going through," she tells me, "There might be some light prescription he can give you to take care of the symptoms. You'll have to see him regularly to deal with your delusions. That's the plan. Right now, the guests know you have been going through some difficult times. And they're artists, so nudity doesn't shock them."

I don't want to sit and hobnob with artists. You can't trust them. And I don't want to see what they call analysts. They run electricity through you. They rearrange your genetics. They remove your blood and replace it with what they call less agitated plasma, which isn't blood at all, but a blood substitute made by a medical subsidiary of the I Can't Corp. It's laced with barbiturates and reduces the blood pressure to the point that you nap every other hour for twenty minutes each time. Needless to say, not much gets done, which depresses the patient even more, but which keeps the patient a patient. The motto of the industry is "If my patients had more patience, I'd have more patients."

They do things to you we would never do at the Institute, and there isn't much we wouldn't do in the interest of collecting information. You can wind up sicker than when you went in. I have done many groups testing their impressions of analysts, and most of the respondents were happier before seeing them, if they remember anything about their emotional states at all. Most of the time, they think they had been seeing analysts since childhood, so this was just a way of life.

I can't see an analyst. I know more about human nature than they do. My job as a focus group moderator gives me as much knowledge about the human condition as there is. There's nothing they can tell me. And what if they actually said, "Gadzooks, he is indeed growing his arm back!" What then? I'll tell you what then. Marsha takes me to another analyst, then another, until she gets the answer she wants.

My reality puts a lot of people's belief systems in jeopardy.

"OK," I tell her, as I'm hungry and would like to eat. "But if they see that my arm is growing back, you must see it too. That's only fair."

She slaps me again.

"Stop it, John! I want normal tonight. I want back to normal!"

I stand before her, naked. I take her hand with my good hand. She resists, but I look at her with what is known in some circles as puppy dog eyes. She loosens up and lets me guide her hand to my penis. I put my penis in her hand. She holds it, but she doesn't enjoy holding it, any more than I enjoy having her pasta on the end of my fork.

"It was hard. It was like a sword," I tell her and I'm not boasting, I am merely describing my naturally erect penis.

"Whatever, John. Most men think the world of their cocks. In that you are not unusual," she says in a monotone voice that tells me she has heard men speak glowingly about their "cocks" and it bores her.

"Maybe you can make it hard again, Marsha," I say.

"We have guests, John. Please get dressed."

"Make it hard, Marsha. For both of us."

"John..."

"Please."

She looks at me with her rendition of puppy dog eyes and starts to stroke my penis.

"No, you have to lick my nub," I tell her, "Like Lassie did."

She slaps me, and this one is hardest of all. "You fucking asshole!" and she leaves as if insulted. Right now, women confuse me entirely. The only ones that understand me are my babies and my dog. And I know that, one day, my babies will be grown, will officially mature into my new right arm, and will have to be treated accordingly, with respect, as a practical physical unit, responsible for chores and duties and waving at the annual Thank You Very Much Parade. And I know Lassie, as happens to all dogs, even with extender hormones, only lives to twenty years. After that, I'll be alone again and I need to figure this out. I don't want to die alone and rot before anybody discovers my body. Yes, I believe Manning and Peeples will inquire as to my whereabouts after three days of absenteeism, but then

I will be a rigor-mortised bloat, and that is not very dignified. And how long will Manning and Peeples be around?

*****

Dressed. Presentable. Unpredictable penis locked behind zipper. Troublesome nub in a shirt. Sitting on the couch, flanked by Marsha's friends.

Patty of the One-Armed Men fables sits to my left, my armed side. Brice the man sits to my right. He leaves about a foot between us, keeps checking my nub to make sure he is out of physical contact with it while he prepares the mist inhaler for the herbal dosing.

Another woman, named Mary, sits opposite. She keeps her legs open just enough to let me see up her skirt. She is not wearing any panties. Her feminine folds have an uncanny resemblance to my nub. Fascinating. She smiles as I steal glances. I assume it is not polite to glare overtly, so I offer only quick peeps, to satisfy a curiosity.

*****

Marsha lights another candle on the table to illuminate the dinner, which frankly would be more appetizing in shadows. Shedding light on this pale, greasy mash doesn't up the appetizing quotient.

I look again at Mary's vagina, while Marsha fishes the greasy food out of the cartons and slides it onto our plates. It has been in the bag too long, and has congealed. She can fork one dumpling out and everything comes clinging to it, as if they are trying to escape the dankness of the carton.

It looks horrible, but the smell of Chinese-Somalian food is nice and pungent. Brice the man talks while he grinds up the herbal dose.

"This is extra pure, almost pharmaceutical. A buddy of mine gets it from a Ticketist named Ezra," he says as he lights up the chamber with the herbal dose.

"Ezra, the Ticketist?" I ask, "the one that gives you tickets for just about anything?" Brice nods while he works his potions.

No one really knows what's in these doses, as they are rumored to be dispensed by the CRL as an entertainment. They say it's harmless. I don't know enough about it either way, and Marsha and I have never smoked a dose together. She told me she has a short history of dosing, but she grew tired of the after-affects, which can include irritability; thoughts of suicide; muscle ache; diarrhea; uncontrollable sexual impulsiveness; loss of the sense of taste, smell, or touch; paralysis in the toes; flaking of the skin on the face and neck; shortness of breath; and brittle nails. The risk of after-affects is not attractive.

I am not so keen to alter my consciousness. Maybe when I gather more memories I will be willing to sacrifice a few. But now I must make a decision to engage, to blend in, to be one of the gang.

"Funny thing is the minute he sells it to him, he gives him a ticket for buying it," Brice continues, all the while fixing the dose into the chamber, testing the hose to see if it's clear, and occasionally lighting a small amount to see if the whole operation is working. While he prepares the ritual, Patty, Marsha, and Mary eat and Lassie stares at the whole group, with extra focus on Brice's dosing ritual and Mary's vagina.

"Strange dog," says Patty through a mouthful of dumpling.

"It's the best dog in the world," I say in Lassie's defense. "She saved me from being eaten alive by the coyotes."

"John," Marsha says in a pleading voice, like I'm not supposed to talk. Did she want me to make friends by sitting silent?

"And I know your ticketist, Ezra," I say, now looking defiantly at Marsha. "And I think he is a bit of an asshole."

All ticketists have a side game, a freelance business, because they are in touch with everyone, and have the biggest network in the city, the country, so they all behave the same. Ezra might have written the book on freelance.

"I'd like some more wine. Can someone pour me some more wine?" Marsha asks with her glass thrust out over the table. The new wine box hasn't been opened, and I know those seals they put on them to keep the wine from turning are hard to peel off, and Marsha, though she doesn't drink much, has always had a problem opening them.

She looks out over the table. Patty doesn't seem interested in doing much but drinking her own wine and sucking at the end of the dosing hose. Brice is busy helping Patty dose herself and Mary is content watching them then looking over at me and opening her legs.

She opens them in unison with Patty's inhalations. Patty sucks on the hose, Mary opens her legs. Patty blows out the smoke, Mary closes her legs. These two operate like a single organism.

I look to Marsha, who is already looking at me, almost pleading with her eyes that I am the one who must open the wine box so that her best friends can go on drinking, dosing, and demonstrating their pudenda.

I look at the box, sitting on the table. It's a one-gallon box, a merlot, with a picture on the box of the wine lab it came from, with the head Wine Chemist on the box, wearing his lab coat, holding up a test tube filled with red wine, and saying in quoted type, "Only the finest facsimiles go into an Amgen Winery wine. We make no wine that doesn't meet control. From our labs to your homes, good cheer," and it's signed in his signature, which is impenetrable, like most scientists and doctors.

Marsha thrusts her glass to the box, like a paralyzed mute begging for money. I can't open the fucking box. It is a two-handed deal, one to hold the box steady and the other to peel the patented STAY-VINTAGE seal back. Why doesn't Marsha see that? Why doesn't Mary see that? Why don't they ask Brice to do it? Why not Patty? Why not Mary and Patty, one to hold and one to peel? Why me? Don't they see I have one arm? One good arm to hold or to peel but not both. Even if my babies would come out, they are not strong enough to peel back the seal.

Or are they?

With Marsha practically grunting to the wine box now, Mary flapping her legs open and closed like she's trying to get her vagina to talk, and Brice and Patty deep into the dosing experience, I think maybe I should present the box to my babies, and see if they would help me provide Marsha with some refreshment.

"Yes of course, I think I can manage that," and as I say that I let out a laugh that indicates delight at the endeavor, that says, "Hey! I'm with you, having a good time, let's get on with this! Cheerio!" and I reach with my only good hand to the dosing hose and ask "Might I?" as Patty finishes filling her lungs.

"John, I don't think you should," Marsha tells me, "not in your condition."

"What condition is that?" Patty wisely asks.

"He looks fine to me. I'll reload the chamber," Brice says and does.

"Oh come on, Marsha, it's a party," Mary says, legs closed on "Oh come on" and open on "it's a party."

I'm OK, my expression tells her. Yes, I have some issues right now; the slow growth of my arm is one.

"I met a giant down in the flats. He helped me defeat a gang of Stemmers. He says he grows more each day. He was huge. His name is Alex," I tell the group, as a way of making conversation with them, something they might find interesting. Stories about giants are usually good attention getters, right?

The group looks at me with sympathy. Marsha looks at me like an incorrigible, or like I'm retarded, or have some other condition, like insanity, bipolar this or that, and there is not much they can do about it except listen and humor me, feel sorry for me. Fuck them.

"We have the same doctor," I tell them as a colorful aside, sending out morsels for them to politely pick up on, a momentary "Oh really? How interesting," but no, their looks don't change. They dose, drink, eat, and open and close their legs, without skipping a beat. Because they're artists, and artists mostly want to talk about themselves. The erection was an exception, as they love all things sexual, all things that prove embarrassing to normal, non-artistic types. But giants? So the fuck what.

And here I am. The ultimate artist in their midst. On my way to creating a new arm, fresh as the morning air, new as a skin on a baby's behind. Inspired from suffering and adversity! I will exercise that arm into manhood. I will never take an arm or a body part for granted again. Especially right now, as opening the wine is a huge challenge I am being asked to meet.

But, I'm OK, Marsha. I wish you'd accept the new arm-ness. But I wish I could also give you a baby. And I am, in a way. It will have fingers and a thumb. It will need you to care for it, like any baby. You'll have to shop for lotions and skin moisturizers for it. And isn't shopping for a newborn one of the thrills of having a newborn? The fact that you can actually pull off the shelves of a Bureau Store all the products that tell the world, I AM A GOOD PARENT, which of course in today's world – post Calamities – is a very special position, one that allows you to avoid being issued a ticket for the smaller infractions.

And of course, Marsha, you will want to talk about your baby. That will give you some fodder for conversation for your friends, who, for the most part, as far as I can tell, have nothing much to say. So your conversations will be richer. I can hear them in my head: "John's fingers grew an extra millimeter today," or "The nail on his middle finger is getting harder," or "We're doing holding and pointing exercises at least an hour a day with his thumb and forefinger," or "It's bending at the elbow!"

What delightful conversations those statements will foster! What a gift this will be for you! So, I take it back, I'm not sorry I can't give you the traditional baby, but instead, due to an act of Providence, am giving you my new arm and hand.

Think of the hours you will spend searching for the right gloves. Think of the decisions you'll have to make every day: Long sleeves or short? Rings or none? Bracelet? French cuffs? Yes or no?

Think of the hours of enjoyment it will give you, as you give it little tasks to do, to learn. Picking up a book, a pin, a piece of morning cereal. Perhaps helping you put on your own moisturizer, or working in unison with its older brother to comb the back of your hair. And think of the important training you will do it as you teach it to fumble around your vagina. Though I have never found visceral excitement in touching it, now your baby will learn anew, will seek out your clitoris, and learn to manipulate it in unison with your breathing. Then you must think of how this thing, this appendage, that grew out of me is now deep inside of you, probing, offering pleasure and re-learning while it does.

"John!"

I am holding the hose now. I must have inhaled the dose. I don't remember. My memories, and the fantasies they inspire, are more fun to attend. Marsha taps the sides of her wine glass, waiting, impatient, and also apprehensive, it seems, to some other unpredicted moment of human behavior.

"Get me a glass of wine! Please!" she barks.

"I'll have a refill," says Patty.

"Me too," says Mary, and then Brice raises his glass.

I put the end of the dosing hose to my mouth and inhale, in case I didn't. The vapor tastes like chocolate cherry menthol. Not bad. Not too sweet. I hold it in my mouth to let it absorb into the tender tissue of the inside of my mouth and tongue. I am careful not to inhale it, as that is not advised. It can cause your lungs to go fibrotic.

Many people suicide themselves by inhaling the dose. It takes only two weeks of constant inhaling to create a density of crystals on the lung. And then, it's only about six months before you die, usually by drowning in your own mucus. But if you do it right, many people like the feeling.

I look out over the room. Out over Marsha's friends. They blur in and out of focus. Their voices rise and fall, their words in fast and slow motion. Their skin luminescent. Especially Patty's. She wasn't a bad-looking woman. Her blond hair cascades over her shoulders and stops just above her breasts, which are proud and confident little things, very pleased to have been born as breasts and probably happy with their owner. Her eyes are green, very green, very clear, and her mouth is wide and as down-turned as her breasts are up-turned.

I would like to see her breasts.

"John!" Marsha says in the sternest of voices, taking me off Patty's breasts and over to Marsha's glare.

"It's OK if he wants to see my tits," Patty says.

Did I just say what I was thinking? I hope I didn't say anything about Mary's vagina.

"What's wrong with my vagina?" Mary asks. Shit. I am thinking-talking again, full-on Tourette's. This isn't good. This can get a person in trouble.

Patty unbuttons her shirt and unfastens the front of her bra. Her breasts don't fall out but are simply revealed. She has freckles on her breasts. Her nipples are very pronounced. My nub is active.

Mary slides down on the couch and lifts her skirt and reveals her vagina. "There is nothing wrong with this. Look how perfect it is," she says as she displays her vagina as if she is offering it on one of the shopping channels from my memory, describing it so as to not let the price drop too far, flashing the magic phone number for you to call and get the item, this perfectly proud and pronounced vagina.

Brice giggles and grabs the box of wine to open. I grab it back.

"I can do it."

"Well, I just remembered that you don't have an arm, and how it might be harder. Just trying to help, is all. And I do want some wine, with this floor show going on. Not that it interests me, as I'm gay, but this will be a fun story to tell. I was interested in your cock, earlier. Mind showing us that again, as it seems we've reached the hour of exhibitionism?"

"Yeah, let's see your dick," Patty says as she touches her left nipple.

"Yeah, bring out the cock," says Mary, still slouched on the couch, with her fingers making a gooey mess of her thighs and my god, how my nub looks like a close cousin of her vagina. Act now.

Marsha has lost control of the evening, with all the breasts and vaginas being exposed and manipulated. It's better for her now to make sure nothing of value gets broken, and that someone replenishes her wine glass, as if the alcohol might be the only thing that makes this whole evening tolerable.

"What I'd really like to show you is my nub and my new fingers, but I'm not so sure they will come out" is what I tell them. I am not so keen on showing them my penis. I am more modest, not so much an exhibitionist.

"John!" and now Marsha is clearly angry. "Don't you dare spoil the evening!"

"So you want me to instead show them my penis," I fire back, as that seems the only conclusion I can come to. "It's OK to show them my penis, but not my nub?"

"I pass. I don't want to see your nub," says Brice. "I want to see your cock. It was too fast before. It looked delicious, but I want to make sure."

"I want to see your nub," Patty says, with Mary nodding, "I've seen cocks, plenty of them. But a nub, that's a new one. With fingers? Bring it on."

I sense a perfect opportunity. My nub is stirring. My babies awake, looking for activity. I pull my shirt off my shoulder, and Patty stops touching her nipple. She learns forward to get a closer look.

"Crap! John!" and it's Marsha again. She gets up, grabs the greasy plates and bowls of oily food and goes into the kitchen. "Do what the fuck what you want!"

There is a crash of plates and silverware in the sink and she comes out again.

"You do what the fuck you want, you crazy son-of-a-bitch! That's right, he's crazy! Has been since the accident. But you weren't real normal before that either! We settle, don't we. We fucking settle. I settled for a crazy man. So what? I was told not to be too picky. That imperfect companionship was still miles better than abject loneliness. I guess that's what I have. But, dammit John, I will only go so far!"

She looks at me and her eyes are on fire. She looks to her friends, the now topless Patty and bottomless Mary and gay wine-deprived Brice, and I'm thinking – What the fuck. *I'm* the freak?

"Oh, lets c'mon. How bad could it be. Show us your nub," Patty says as she connects the cups of her bra, houses her cupcakes, just like the pictures I've seen of the types of breads people ate by the ton before The Calamities ruined it for bread making and the I Can't Corp invented their own version of it, which everybody thought was shit. But the formula for that absolute shit bread created a ripe material to make things big and tall and the offshoot of its influence was its use in the construction industry as an efficient applicator of house paints, with the dual use as a clean-up sponge.

"How about you show us your little nub, then show us your cock?" Brice asks, and that seems like a fair deal, though I know that after they see my beautiful babies, he won't care about seeing my cock at all.

"By all means, John, show them your new arm, how it's growing back, with perhaps more than one arm, maybe two, or four, like Vishnu, and how you will start your own sect, gather your followers, and take over the world," Marsha says.

"What's left of it," I say, which I think is fairly witty. I appreciate her changed tone, but I'm pretty sure my babies have no interest in Hinduism, and I definitely have no interest in world domination. Not now. Maybe when there was something to dominate, it might've been interesting. I might've been able to stop some of the stupidity, being a measured man, one not so at the mercy of his emotions. I wouldn't have been able to do anything about the natural disasters, but I might have managed the evacuations better, the aftermath, the food chain, clean water, air quality, along with the help of Manning and Peeples.

We might've been able to interface more effectively with the CRL, which was really in its infancy, and only came into power after the third Calamity – the Chinese attack on the internet and the asteroid explosion over the forests of the Northwest and part of Canada, which essentially meant no more affordable wood or paper to the Western states.

Fuck it, I want wine. Thinking about how I might have been able to save the world has made me desire alcohol. I pull my shirt down to my elbow and expose my nub. I turn it to my audience, like a magician showing the empty insides of his top hat to make the rabbit trick even more astounding.

"Wow, it's like bread dough," says Patty.

"Looks like cheese to me," says Mary. "Mozzarella. At least the pictures of it I've seen. Never really had any. Can't find it. Is it good?"

"Wait till his arm grows out of it!" Marsha chimes in, now sitting in a chair out of the view of anything, refusing to see what she can't accept.

"Bullshit, it looks like a brain," adds Brice, and he is right! It does look exactly like a brain. And it thinks like a brain, and my babies are the ganglia, and they have a purpose, which, right now, is to perform a trick: hold my wine glass while I pour from the wine box.

Glass to nub, wave glass around, get attention of my babies. "C'mon, little ones, Poppa wants some wine." I hold the glass and I press the stem of the glass into the folds, forcing it, pressing it, rubbing it, I want them to know the glass, all glass...what it looks like, what it feels like, what it's good for. They shouldn't fear the glass. They should welcome it and hold it for me, so that I might drink, so that I might change these people's minds.

I wait for them to emerge. The others stare. Marsha stares out the window at the dark nothing of the night beyond our window. I feel my nub moving, I feel my babies responding, I coo at them and wait.

Then I see it. The smart one, the index finger, pokes out of a fold in my nub. I look at the others. I am excited! Proof will be had! This will convince them and Marsha of my extraordinary condition. Now Marsha can proudly say that her boyfriend is growing a new arm. That by itself will start a conversation that could last days.

"There it is! Do you see?" I'm practically out of my skin at this!

And the index finger curls itself around the stem, holds it tight. It's strong; I'm surprised by its strength and its confidence, like it's had wine before.

"Pretty cool," Patty says.

I grab the wine box and slowly pour wine into the glass. The finger holds firm. Good for you. Hold and we will toast.

"Marsha, look!" I scream. "Look now!"

"Yeah, Marsha," says Mary, "Maybe it's a parlor game, and there is something holding his glass." I fucking love artists. They're so accepting.

And Marsha looks. And the glass falls to the table and it shatters and wine sprays the room.

"Everyone, go home. Party's over," Marsha says.

I don't feel well.

*****

Sanctuary. My room. My lair. My prison.

I feel trapped in a world I don't understand any more, just because I am missing an arm, or because it's growing back. I'm trapped in a world where NO ONE believes me.

The Calamities made people scared, terrified when encountered with the unfamiliar. They have become savages, tribal, caring only for their daily – no, hourly – survival. The Devices didn't help. Constant use of the Devices – calling, writing, reading, playing, glimpsing – kept people from people. And they wound up liking it better that way. And they could stomach death and kill more easily with less interaction amongst their own. The living reminded the living of the dead. So the living, and all issues of life, are to be avoided.

I have to keep the babies inside me quiet; I have to disguise them, lie about them, deny them. I hope they are not ruined by all this. I hope they don't come out of me deformed, or pointing in all the wrong directions. I must protect them. I have fears that when my arm does grow back, people will want to tear it out.

I must protect my babies from humanity.

ENTRY 24

THE INSTITUE IS THINKING OF "PULLING THE PLUG."

The Institute, its advisors, affiliates, regulatory agencies, stakeholders, investors, and consultants, are now meeting in earnest to discuss the ending of the research project. This is a high-profile project and the populace is anxious to hear the results and reconnect with the respondents. We are formulating our response and how to put forth our best public face. We are adamant that this isn't a failure, and that we have great insights as to behaviors and habits of importance to our assimilation. But we are worried as to the physical and mental well-being of the respondents, as Subject John has shown higher stress levels and some worrisome physical aberrations as concerns both the emergence of his arm and the recent emergence of his penis. The Institute is meeting on this daily. This is new territory for all of us. It is clear we might have thought it through more thoroughly, but due to budget cuts, weather issues, and lack of office supplies, our efforts were compromised.

—I swallow a handful of pills, the ones Marsha says are just salt tablets. She doesn't know. They could be laced with some healing chemical. They taste good, and I feel better after taking them. They give me a warm feeling, especially in my nub. I can feel my babies rubbing their new fingertips together.

My eyes are yellowed. That's the dosing. It wreaks hell on the liver. With the wine, even more so. I don't like this feeling. I am sweating. My nub is too warm. Hot. Like it has a fever. My fingers, deep inside me, feel like they are shaking. Maybe the pills aren't any good. Maybe the pills and the dosing are a dangerous combination. I must stay out of the bathtub. I remember a singer, decades ago, who died in the bathtub from too much of many things. People slip in the shower. They drown in the bathtub. Safer just to wear cologne.

I look at it in the mirror. I touch the folds of my nub. I take some moisturizer and rub it on the folds. I take a cloth, soak it in cold water and place it over the nub, try to bring the fever down.

I watch as my babies pour out of it. And they keep coming, stretching themselves forward, longer than I have seen before.

I've grown a wrist. My hand is complete!

Oh glorious day!

I run into the living room. Now they'll believe me! I'll give Mary something to open her legs about. I'll give Patty a whole line of jokes and make Brice forget about wanting to see my cock.

Now they can see not just fingers, which they could mistake as being just some sort of errant growth, but a whole hand. I run down the hall. I run and run. It feels like forever. I keep going down the hall, which is only twenty-five feet from the living room, but it keeps going and going. Lassie runs alongside me, barking, yapping.

"I'm going to show them, girl. Going to show them my new hand. Maybe we'll all yank on it and pull out the whole arm."

*****

Ceiling. Dark. I'm in bed. How did I get in bed? Where are the guests? I wonder what they thought of my new hand? I turn over. Marsha sleeps next to me. She looks like an angel, and I have never really felt that before.

I passed out. Must've. That's what happened. I wasn't feeling too good. I was hot. Had a fever. The dosing and the wine. And people I didn't like. The woman with the active vagina. The one with the cupcake breasts. They conspire to make me sleep, to avoid them, to hide in sweet slumber.

My nub. I touch it. It's covered over in a T-shirt sleeve, covered up like Marsha wants it. Out of sight. Out of her mind. A package you put away until a later date. Or one you put away to forget.

I look at Marsha. I pull the covers off her. She wears her sleep T-shirt, with a logo for a since-dissolved sports team called Dodgers. It's hiked up above her waist. She has nothing underneath.

I kiss her forehead. She murmurs, deep in sleep. I slide the covers back over her, put my feet on the floor. Lassie's at the bedroom door, like a sentinel.

Except for the T-shirt, I'm naked. I wonder why. I wonder if Marsha's guests wanted to see more of my penis. I see them in my mind standing around me, lifting my penis with the chopsticks provided by the restaurant.

My penis flops back and forth as I walk. It feels larger than before, thicker, not like Marsha's spaghetti. My testicles feel heavy and they sway as if loaded down with lead pellets. I touch them. They feel dense. The skin is tight. I lift them, feel them for tumor, as people often tumor in the testicles. Nothing. And yet the sensation cannot be ignored.

I stand at the entrance to the living room and survey the damage of the party. From the smell in the room, it must have ended recently. No one is here. The vaporizer sits on the coffee table, next to the now empty box of wine I remember caused a fair amount of commotion. I pick it up, put the vaporizer hose in my mouth, and inhale.

I don't know why I am doing this. I don't like doing this in the first place. Maybe I'm doing it to show them that it is me who'll say when the party is over.

There's nothing in the chamber. Just the residue of the dose. Lassie watches me. She has a low-frequency growl going, like she has a respiratory issue. Like she is quietly snoring.

My testicles ache. I reach into the freezer and pull out some ice, fold it over in a paper towel and put it to the ache.

I don't feel the cold. Odd. I put an ice cube directly on the skin of my sack. Nothing. I turn on the stove and heat up a knife, and place that on the skin.

Nothing. I have two rocks between my legs, dead, nerveless, numb.

"What the hell is the matter?" I ask Lassie. Not that she would know about my sexual plumbing, not having any male parts of her own, and being a dog to boot. But I believe circus dogs to be a different breed. She understands me, *that* I know, and somehow, she senses something is wrong with my balls. My penis is a different story. That actually feels good. But the fact that I feel anything down there at all is new and alien and makes me feel vulnerable and at a loss of control.

I have a memory of an erection, but the circumstances around it are foggy. I know that it must have been impressive as I do remember the guests wanting to see it again. My mind transmits a picture of the erection from my point of view, looking right at me, staring in fact, demanding action.

I sit down on the couch, legs splayed outward, as it's uncomfortable to have them together. Perhaps I have elephantiasis. I have a vague memory of this condition. I remember a picture of a dark man from Asia with his testicles in a wheelbarrow, spilling over the sides. He had a beard down to his toe nails. It was frankly unbelievable as I have never seen a wheelbarrow that big or a beard that long.

The light is coming up. The dank orange-brown light of morning. The light of the densely smogged Los Angeles mornings that have become the norm since the meteor shower that rained on Malibu and destroyed every home on both sides of the PCH from Point Mugu to Santa Monica.

It's a light that smells. Smells of the cremation dust on the beaches and in the hills that kicks up every morning around 3 am and wafts eastward to center city. It stays with us until two o'clock in the afternoon, as by then most of it has settled like powder on the streets and cars. I had gotten used to it, never much remarked about it, but here, with my swollen cast iron balls and delightfully sensitive penis, I am seeing the world anew. The smell of burnt human beings is somewhat reassuring that at one time, there was a past.

I want to wake Marsha up. I want her to touch my penis. I want her to feel my testicles to see if she senses anything abnormal. I cannot examine myself, as I have no memory of what my balls felt like before. In truth, I have never much bothered with the things.

I walk to the bedroom. Marsha sleeps, snoring heavily. She must have just gotten to sleep, finally kicked her worthless friends out, probably just in time for them not to see my new hand.

She rolls over, taking the cover with her, pulling it off half of her body, revealing her ass. I stare at it. I stare at the fleshy plump orb separated down the middle. I hear her breathing harder. My penis becomes more sensitive now and I reach down and touch it, as it seems to be asking me to do, with its increased sensitivity.

It's a joy to touch. The feeling rather exquisite and new. It's becoming harder in my hand. Hard like a real penis.

Maybe I will get out the pump and pump right now and wake Marsha up and make her cry and lick the salt off of her face and apologize. I'll say I'm sorry for unsettling her life, for embarrassing her in front of her friends, and for never giving her a baby. I will ask her forgiveness for the past several…and I can't remember how long it has been since the attack, but it feels like years, and it doesn't matter, as now I'll be a geyser of forgiveness and amends.

My penis feels like it goes on forever. I look down and it extends out from my body with a confidence, no, a braggadocio, I've never experienced before, and to my eyes, it looks like it's a foot long. I should measure it. I should.

Lassie struts in, growling. I don't want her to wake Marsha up. I want to wake Marsha up. I want this to be perfect. A new beginning. I'll agree that my arm isn't growing back, that it was part of the stress of the accident. I'll tell her I asked my doctors why they gave me salt tablets, and will tell her they told me because they knew it was a stress disorder and that it was a placebo and that everyone can use a little extra salt anyway, with the amount of desalinized water we're forced to drink.

I let Lassie follow me out of the bedroom, then I pivot right back in and lock the bedroom door, out-circusing the circus dog.

"Oh my God, John," and I did wake her. She is up now. On her elbows, open-mouthed at my erection. I look to see what she sees and surely it has become the largest single part of my body, even rivaling my leg.

"I didn't pump," I tell her as I stare at the massivity about to use my belly button as a hat. "It's all mine."

It's hard as the kitchen counters put in by the Bureau of Appropriate Furnishings. It is like an ivory tusk. I could only hope my new arm would be this strong. Veins run up and down it like the blue lines in the ancient maps of the defunct interstate highway system. Needless to say, it's an impressive thing. It's like my body has grown a handle, and I could be lifted off the ground if three strong men were to grasp it.

"Let's make love," I tell her, "I am feeling such love for you now."

Marsha opens her legs, revealing her naked vagina. She opens her legs compliantly even though she should be plenty annoyed with me. She opens her legs because this thing, my bold new appendage, my totem, demands that degree of tribute.

"Did you get a new pump?" she asks because there is no way the CCC4.8 – GOBOYGO Ultra-Lite Penis Pump could deliver an erection this big without doing serious tissue damage.

"No, this is me. All me," I tell her. "It just happened, all at once, like it happened at the party. Am I right, did I have an erection at the party? I see an erection in my head, in my memory. Was that at the party?"

"Stick it in!" she commands. My balls feel like they are about to implode. My cock points like a dog to a duck. I crawl on my hand and knees on the mattress to Marsha. She puts her arms around my neck, then puts her hands on my face, then reaches below, takes my erection in her hand, gives me a look that says she is both excited and scared at the same time and she guides me and I enter her.

God. I enter her. I don't seem to stop entering her. She gasps, and she never did that before, and calls me god over and over. And right now, I am god. A god. One of them. Perhaps with my new sexual hammer, I am the Thor god, one of the gods of their invention whose history was captured by the digi's and the picture books.

I thrust into her. No longer on my back allowing her to move on top of me, for the first time I move on top of her. It's better, much more satisfying. Each stroke seems to make it harder, like it is working out the muscle.

No longer attached to a machine, no longer worried about a finite time for Marsha to orgasm, I am focused now on the feelings I am having, right now, this second. Her wetness slides me in and out. She holds me tight, as this is a far bumpier ride than she is used to.

"I am fucking you!" I say, and I know it's crude and vulgar, but that is how I feel. I am fucking her. Fucking her good. Fucking her like the pornographic movies depict fucking, except those men are tiny ponies compared to me.

I'm a stallion. I'm a one-armed stallion.

I thrust, but without the arm, there is a lack of leverage to give her all of me. I thrust, holding myself up with my left arm as it strains, weakens, too much weight for too long a time. But my penis dictates to me. Stay! Hold yourself up! This will be worth it! I keep myself up with the left arm and I think how much more pleasure I will feel when I have my right arm back and can hold myself up with both arms. That's something to look forward to. Two arms and big cock. That's something to live for.

I can feel every inch of me move in and out of her. She opens her mouth again and I look deep down her throat. I think I might see the head of my penis at the bottom of her throat. I think all sorts of pornographic imagery, but mostly, when I close my eyes, I see dots and patterns of color: blue, red, green, all moving around against the dark screens that are the inside of my eyelids.

She scratches me. That is new. Scratches, scratching, gripping, squeezing.

I can no longer hear her. I can no longer feel her scratches or her squeezing. Every part of my brain and every sense in me are focused on the strange sensations I feel between my legs. The weight of my balls, now slapping against her and the continued impossible hardness of my penis, my cock, my master, THIS THING growing out of me. THIS THING that I am now in wonder of, this alien entity between my legs.

I hear only my own breathing, heavy, fast, and I sweat. I sweat. I feel like a salamander, or a frog. All damp. A frog with a huge penis. A Killer frog. King Frog of the pond. Marsha's vagina is the pond, and I am diving deep into it, deep down in the darkness, beyond daylight, endless, infinite bottom.

My forehead sweat drips onto her face. I lick it off. Run my tongue over her eyes, suck in the salty tears which she has now as a constant stream.

I have made her whole face wet. Her forehead, her eyes, her palms. Both of us suction together and when I pull apart from her there is the farting sound of wet skin pulling away from wet skin. I slide on top of her, as if oiled. I don't think of her as a woman, a person, a human; she has become a deep hole to me. I fear she could swallow me. I could disappear inside of her. I don't know how long I would have to wait for my arm to grow so I could pull myself out of her.

Stroke. Thrust. Push. All the way up her belly.

The bed, the sheets, are a wet mess, like we are atop a mound of "I Can't Believe It's Not Liverwurst!"

And now what? What is this feeling? I speed my thrusts, my body speeds my thrusts, and I'm a slave to what it wants and it wants is whatever my cock wants. I sense a pain in my balls. A beautiful strange pain that doesn't want me to stop so the pain will stop, but wants me to keep going, to experience all the pain.

It's a pain that feels like it started in my asshole, and is now traveling through my balls, now it's in my belly, now back to my cock. I push harder inside Marsha and she screams. I hope I'm not hurting her. But if I was I cannot stop. I'm like a murderer who knows he is inflicting pain but cannot stop.

More of the strange, burning pain. Whirling around in my balls, racing up and down in my cock, straining the muscles in my belly. Then it all gathers at the base of my cock. I feel as though I might lose my cock. I feel that my cock might just break off, like my arm, and stay inside of Marsha.

I will rush her to Manning and Peeples. They will extract the cock from her and put it back on me. Or maybe, I'll just grow a new one. But that would be too much. Too much appendage growing. Too much strain on my body to grow both an arm and a new penis.

The pain. It's coming up my cock, like a thick obstruction in a smaller tube. It needs to be expelled. The pain must be honored.

The Pain. Now it is pleasure. What is this feeling?

Tighten. Clench. Squeeze. Push. No control. The burn moves up the length of my cock. It is the only thing I feel in the world right now. The beautiful burn, each thrust making it stronger, making it my friend. I want to see what this feeling looks like.

I'm a slave to the sensation. I am just a bystander. My penis is the parade. I can't contain this any longer. I have no control over my body.

The burn bursts out of me! Relieves me! A beautiful relief.

I hear a scream. I think it's me. It matches hers. And don't know what this is, the swirl of sensations I feel, but one of them is warm, like never before.

I know my penis is gone. This was its death march. It committed suicide inside of Marsha. She has gone limp. Maybe I killed her?

No, she is fine.

I push off the bed like an athlete and run to the bathroom to see the damage. I expect a bloody stump. Maybe my balls have evaporated.

I fall on my knees. My legs are weak, like I've been bedridden for a month. Like I felt after the attack when I awoke a week or so later.

I crawl, on hands and knees, to the cold tile floor of the bathroom.

I grab the counter, lift myself up. I look in the mirror.

My arm has grown back.

*****

What glory. What a beautiful thing it is. Pure white, the skin soft and supple, even slightly more elastic than the skin on my other, older, more used arm. There is a light fuzz on the lower arm. I can see the bluish green veins in the wrist. The fingers on my new hand are slightly longer than the ones on the other, and I am thinking that with wear and tear they will join their left-hand brother in size and skin tone.

I lift my new arm over my head, hold my face in both hands, look at my armpit, flex, and conjure an adult-sized muscle in the bicep. I pick up a toothbrush. I handle a bar of soap. I put my finger in my nose.

I feel the left arm to see if things are all in the same place on the new one. All good, a mirror reflection. Elbow, knuckles, wrist, all operational, all complementary. I have my team back.

I look at my penis, now flaccid, but not like a noodle anymore. Proudly flaccid like a Viking warrior, resting, catching his breath after a raping and a pillaging. And I cry. My eyeballs sweat joy.

*****

"John, what are you doing?" Marsha calls out from the bedroom.

I walk to the side of the bed. She is splayed out on the sheets, a pillow between her legs, and she smiles at me like she has never smiled before. Like I just bought her something she wanted her whole life, and I am her hero.

And I turn my right side to her and raise my arm to show her the miracle. And her expression changes. I have gone from hero to monster.

She screams. The dog barks. I try to calm her. The dog breaks down the door.

Marsha throws a lamp at my head. I duck. It hits the mirror behind me and shatters it into an hundred lethal shards. Lassie nips at my ankles and corrals me to the corner of the room, putting a moat of carpet between Marsha and me. She growls at me – that is not the growl of the best friend to the man.

"Stop it, Lassie!" I yell at her. But now she threatens. I slide along the bedroom wall, hands flat on it and non-threatening. As long as I don't challenge the space between the dog and screaming Marsha, the dog seems OK. I slip out of the bedroom, run to the living room, grab the fireplace poker, run back into the bedroom.

"Lassie, attack!" Marsha yells. The dog bares its teeth and I hit it over the head with the poker. It stops growling.

"You're a fucking monster," Marsha yells.

"Shut up! You don't even like this dog!" I yell back. I hit the dog again. Then again and again. And a slice on its fur opens. And I hit it again. It collapses on the carpet; its eyes flash like little light bulbs. And a strange gray dust pours out of the dog's wounds.

A mist flows out of the split skull. A dark grey mist.

"What the fuck is happening, John?" she screams, watching the mist flow out of every part on the dog where the fur has been opened. "I told you to get a purebred!" Marsha says, "The mutts are always damaged!"

The mist vibrates, undulates on the carpet. The dog's entire body collapses on itself, like a balloon that has run out of air.

I reach down, with my old arm, careful of damaging my new one, to touch the mist. It's made up of little silver balls, no bigger than the head of a pin.

"John, what is happening?" Marsha says, now up on the bed, so she is untouched by the little silver mites.

"I know these things," I tell her, as indeed, I have seen these shapes before. It's nanotechnology. Lassie is a nano-bot. A shape completely comprised of shape/color/texture-shifting nanotechnology. Each "mite" holds a memory and the circuitry to create what appeared to be an Ecuadorian circus dog. Each mite communicates with the other in much the same way our cells do. That certainly explains a lot: lack of appetite, disinterest in playing with other dogs, ability to frighten coyotes, lack of bowel movements and more. Wow.

Then, I hear the door burst open and men in Hazmat suits enter. They grab me and Marsha. All too fast. Too fast to know how to react. Too fast to signal my new arm to strike them. Too fast to stop them from putting a gun to my arm. Too fast to know what the fuck to do. Light and woozy. Nice and warm. This is lovely.

I look at the smiling man in the Hazmat suit. I feel I know him. I feel I know him well. But I don't know from where. But it's his manner that's familiar.

"It's OK, John. It's over. All will be OK from now on," he says in cooing tones that I know. I know the voice. Yes. I do.

Why, it's Doctor Manning. Son of a gun!

*****

Moving. I can feel movement and sway. It feels nice. I feel like I'm being rocked very gently from both sides by two very loving midgets.

I see a different place than Los Angeles. I am looking out a window. I must be on my back. I should be looking at sky, but I'm looking out a window. A small window. This is a vehicle, a truck or a van, as I am flat on my back and comfortable, so there is space.

This might be a dream. Or this could be very real. When I dream, it's always about a different place than where I live. A very vivid place. I wake up happy, but then then I look around and get sad. I have spoken to Manning about these dreams, and he takes notes, but says nothing.

The ground is black and sandy in my dream. There are puddles of shiny, black water everywhere, and walking bridges over the swampy sandy ground. There is a city on the horizon. It's green and made of what looks like mostly taffy. Salt water taffy, or at least the pictures of salt water taffy I have seen on the Devices. Stretchy, twisty, lovely. It doesn't look like "I'm Trying to Believe This is Salt Water Taffy." That doesn't look anything like salt water taffy and tends to completely fall apart in your mouth, much like their "These Can't be Mashed Potatoes!" which broke from the "I Can't" format and was a dismal failure.

The taffy buildings are odd looking, but strangely beautiful. Muscular and tendonal. Sensual. Lascivious. Gooey. This is becoming a dirty dream.

Men and women in heavy work gear affix hoses to the puddles of black water and suck the water into the hose, which is the only explanation I have for their activities. Other better dressed men observe them, and enter information into some sort of very advanced info-recording Device. Different from anything I have seen. But somehow, again, familiar.

I like this place. I like where we're going. It feels like home. Shiny black puddles, pumped out by people that are seemingly engaged in constructive activity, overseen by people who seem to be part of the greater team. The multicolor sexually charged buildings in the background, and a reddish, purply sky, a very fruity, berry-like sky dotted with fluffy, fluffy cotton clouds tinged with yellow. The sky looks like a bowl of fruit. It's all very festive. All very good. All very nice.

Marsha can have the baby here.

ENTRY 25

PULLING THE PLUG, INFORMING
RESPONDENTS, PREPARING TO LEAVE.

T he Institute has decided, collectively, at this point, and with some regret, to end the research project. We have no idea whether Subject John – and we will only speak for SJ at this point, not the other respondents – was affected by his fraternizing out of the approved and vetted circle of native contacts, or his encountering a fellow respondent, or the changes to his physicality. The arm we had been watching, and were fully aware of the regenerative process under certain conditions. We were unprepared for the extreme erection and resulting ejaculate. It is now time to gather all respondents and prepare them for a re-introduction and re-immersion. We are fully confident we can restore all previous memory. The Institute would like at this time to thank all our sponsors and consultants who have aided us – financially and intellectually – with this project. The final report will be issued after your approvals.

—Shit. It was a dream. I'm awake. I wiggle my toes, lift my new hand up to my face and then bring it to my penis and have it do a run of inventory on my newly functioning apparatus. That my new hand can now help me do these routine things makes me insanely happy. *That* was NOT a dream. I have a new arm and it has a new hand. I have a functioning penis. New hand meet rehabilitated penis! Get to know each other. You have a lifetime to become familiar.

I'm alive. I think about Marsha, where she is and if she's all right. But I don't want to get up and look for her. I am happy to lie here, in this dark room, one lit lamp, on what seems to be a bed, or what is a very soft surface.

I'm at peace. For the first time I feel like things that're familiar to me are making cameo appearances in my life: the nanotech of the dog, the dream of a place I know, the voice of Manning in the Hazmat suit, the warm feeling of the injection, my new arm, and, my new erective abilities. My brain cells seem to swarm around these new ideas and images, these new experiences, making sense of them, analyzing them. Good. Go to work. Sort it out. ENGAGE!

When I think of Marsha, I can't help but feel that when last we made love, the last time I fucked her, with my most glorious erection, and the sensation of primal ooze pouring out of it, that it was all for a reason.

Maybe I am going to be a father.

As a father, I promise to teach my child to value his or her limbs. If it's a son, I will teach him about erections. If it's a daughter, I will teach her about orgasms. I know they will make me proud. Can't wait.

*****

The door to my room opens and floods my eyeballs with blinding white light. Burning fucking white hot hell. I can feel my pupils dilate to pinheads. I squint, cover my eyes with my new hand (Yes! Even more uses!), and see…Manning and Peeples. I can tell it's them even though they stand in silhouette against that blaring obnoxious light. Their shadows are long. They look like giants. But it's them. Lab coats, relaxed stance, analytic and pensive tilt of head.

They smile at me, then pull up chairs and sit bedside.

"How are you feeling, John?" Manning asks.

"Fine," I tell him, "And even better…" and I raise my new arm as Exhibit A and sing, "Taaaa Daaaa!" They both smile.

"Yes, it grew back, like we knew it would."

"You knew? Why didn't you tell me? Why did you put it all on me, as if it was a condition I was going through?"

"We have much to tell you," Peeples says, "but first, we assume you would like to see Marsha."

Not really. I'm still in the *Why the Fuck Didn't You Tell Me You Thought My Arm Was Going to Grow Back as It Would Have Made My Life Somewhat Easier* mode. I really wasn't thinking about Marsha at all.

"You're not at all shocked that I grew the arm back?" I ask.

"It's what we do, John. It is our nature," Manning says, and I'll be damned if I'm going to let him speak in platitudes right now. I want answers, and I know that people never ask questions of their doctors as doctors are supposed to be almighty and all-knowing and they never have enough time to answer your questions anyway and when they do, the answers are as indecipherable as their signatures.

"John, we have much to tell you," Manning says while Peeples scans my new arm with an apparatus I have never seen recently but that looks familiar. Things are looking bizarrely familiar. My dreams, the objects in my dreams...

"We'll take you to see Marsha after we do a little decompression and reorientation," Peeples adds.

"Am I going to leave this room?" I ask.

"Yes, why?" Manning asks as he fetches a robe from the small closet at the end of the bed.

"Can you turn the lights down in the hallway?"

*****

I'm in a room, at a table. There's a low hum, monotonous but not unpleasant. There are two other people at the table.

Alex the Giant is one. He looks at me curiously, eyes searching mine, head at a tilt. I feel his stare wants to go beyond my eyes, through the pupils, deeper, pick up some clues, some memory debris along the road to my hippocampus, as he tries to jog his vague memory of me and our night of lousy take-out and nasty little Stemmers.

"Hello, Alex," I volunteer.

"Do I know you?" he answers.

"Yes, we went for take-out, I don't know how many days ago. Are you OK?"

"Yes, but I have been in the hospital. Here, in the hospital, where you dropped me off. I think it was you. Yes, your voice is familiar. I have been unconscious many days. I have had some big dreams. About a place I think I know. It was very real."

"Black sand," I say, "I have had dreams of a black sand place."

"That's it, me too! Black sand and soft stretched buildings."

I knew we had a connection. I feel very close to him.

A button pops off of Alex's shirt.

"Shit! I grow still!"

"It's true, you look larger, but in good spirits. And you're not bleeding anymore." I think my tone might be a calmative to this gentle but agitated giant.

"They fixed me. Manning and Peeples," and his eyes go off into the distance, small memories lost in a giant maze.

At the other end of the table sits a very pretty blonde. She's in a running outfit and obviously very fit. She might be a model for the I Can't Corp. Perhaps a package model, though most of the celebrities and models today are all digitally rendered.

She looks very worried, like she's trapped, failing at something, worried about the consequences.

"That's Buffy," Alex tells me.

"Hello, Buffy." As she raises her eyes to me I can detect a tear of frustration and fear.

"*Toh az sajr kesheedan chee meedoonee?*" Buffy barks, "*Yeh rooz ba doostam Chrissie sohbat meekardam. Bad be man chap chap neegah kard. Be man meegeh man sar az kareh toh dar nayavordam. Nemeefameh man chee meegam.*"

Then, seeing that I have not understood a single word she has said, she whips out a pen and writes it all down on the piece of paper and slides the paper to me.

Alex picks it up in his massive hand and reads: "My name is Buffy. One day, I was speaking to my friend Chrissie, and then she couldn't understand a thing I was saying. All my friends left me. They thought I was making fun of them. And every day, I speak a different language."

"So today," Alex says, "and I know this only because where I worked, at the Big and Tall Man Shops, they spoke Farsi, so it sounds familiar."

"But she writes in English," I say.

Buffy scribbles on the paper and slides it to Alex.

"She says she can't speak English, but she can write it."

Alex crumples up the paper and says something back to her in Farsi. She shakes her head like she can't understand what he is saying, and says so, now in French.

"Now I don't know what she says," Alex says as he throws up his massive hands in linguistic defeat.

"It's French," I tell him. "I know a little," and I turn to her and say, "*Ne t'en fais pas, mon petit,*" which means "Don't worry, little one" and is something I remember from digi's made in the Age of Black and White. My memory tells me I have seen a fair number of French ones, directed by a man whose name was also in an alien digi from the Age of Color. I also learned a bit of French from the back panel of the "I Can't Believe It's Not French" packages of breakfast croissants, which was the first joint venture between the I Can't Corp and *French for Dummies.*

Buffy continues in French…

"She says people don't trust people who can speak more than one language," I explain. And it's true. The Institute had researched language prejudice. It seems that the incidence of terrorism had brittled the population to hating all those who were multi-lingual, as they were considered suspicious. Never mind that it was usually their own less-educated natural-born citizens that committed most of the acts of terror.

She buries her head in her hands and curses in German. I can't help her here. I just know what German sounds like. It sounds like angry people speaking English in reverse.

Alex slumps back in his chair, bends all four metal legs, and winds up on the floor on his formidable ass. "Shit!" he says, and finds another chair.

"Why are you here?" he asks me. "I know that I grow all the time, and my life is difficult because of that. I know Buffy can speak every language in the world, but has no control when, and doesn't understand any more than one at a time. But you, what is your unique curse?"

I lift my new arm for all to see and tell them, "My arm grew back."

"And so? What is the big deal?"

And I have no answer to that. I know I'd prefer to have the problems of convincing others that my arm was growing back more than the problem of everything growing constantly.

"Bullshit!"

Alex didn't say that. It was said in a very high-pitched, helium-affected voice. Buffy didn't say it, as she can't speak English, and that was English with a bit of a street cred, strong on the "Bull" with the "shit" trailing off.

"It's Steve," Alex says, and just then a small man, no more than three feet tall, stands on his chair with his head above the edge of the table. He isn't a midget, or a little person, or a dwarf. He is just a very small adult with a very large beard. He reminds me of the pictures I have in my head of the young Hasidic Jews of years ago. But his beard is more robust than the starter beards of the young Jews. He wears a straw hat. A small red feather is attached to the side of the hat's stove pipe. The hat is too big for his head, and would surely descend over the bridge of his nose if his head was not wrapped in rags. This is not because he is injured, or at least I see no blood on the rags and they are hardly of medical quality. It's to keep the hat on. This is my assessment.

"You're one of them," Steve says, stroking his beard like he's deep in figuring out some new philosophical position for a now defunct synagogue.

"Steve is the opposite of me. He is shrinking," Alex says, rolling his eyes. I sense Steve fatigues Alex. Alex is the big dog, Steve the yapping little runt who stays in Alex's shadow for protection. I don't know how long they have known each other, but they seem to understand each other, though it really wouldn't matter if Steve didn't understand Alex, as Alex could put Steve's head between his thumb and forefinger and pop it like a pimple.

"I was six foot tall when I came out of my coma," Steve says. "Then I started to shrink. A little bit, every week. I thought my co-workers were playing games with me, replacing my hat with larger and larger hats. I thought I had a tumor. But Manning and Peeples didn't care. They just ask, 'Do you think you are shrinking? What do you feel about that,' and 'How do your friends feel about that?' How the fuck do you think I feel? The divide between the floor and the elevator door feels like a canyon. Last week, the cashier at the grocery store pinched my fucking cheek when I tried to buy some "I Can't Believe It's Not Beer." He lowers his small head as if at a funeral for his lost inches.

"You're one of them," he snaps, "There's nothing wrong with you. In a month, I'll be gone completely. Nothing left but a hat and a pair of shoes. You don't have problems, I have problems."

"We were all normal height when we came out of our comas!" Alex shouts and his voice fairly rattles the walls. "Did you have an arm when you came out of a coma?" Alex asks me.

"Yes, but I couldn't get an erection."

"Big fucking deal! Big fucking deal!" says Steve as he jumps up on the table and hops around like an angry Hasidic baby. "Did I mention what part of me shrunk the most?" he asks and chooses to answer his own question by hiking down his tiny pants and revealing his penis, which pretty much resembles a button on a fur coat. He points his finger at me, "You're one of them! You're part of this! You tell us your arm grew back, why should we believe you!"

"Have you all been in a coma?" I ask, as this is too much of a coincidence and I start to wonder whether I am, have been, part of some larger experiment run by The Institute? I was in charge of researching the populace. Was someone researching me? And if that's the case then it's acceptable that someone or something might be researching the ones researching me, and what if it goes higher than that, into infinity, the forever, the unknown and how would that happen and who the fuck is going to put together the final report. Not me! No fucking way.

Ezra enters. This could be a Ticketist paradise. He could ticket Alex for growing, Steve for shrinking, and have a field day with Buffy, printing out tickets every time she switched languages. But he doesn't. He doesn't even have his machine. He has a plate of sandwiches. Not Marsha's. Small ones with the crusts cut off. Dainty.

He places them on a table, smiles and winks at me, then quietly takes his place along the back wall of the room, hands behind his back, eyes at the ceiling. If he tries to give me a ticket, I will punch him with my new fist.

"You shouldn't be angry, John. But we do understand," and it's Dr. Manning – Peeples in tow – and he presses a button on the wall, and a large screen behind a false wall is exposed.

"Well, if it ain't More and Less," Steve blurts out.

"Shut up, Steve, and sit down," Peeples commands him and somehow, that frightens Steve, so he sits, and once again disappears under the edge of the table.

I, for one, am glad to see him disappear from sight. He's unsettling, both in his tiny-ness and shrillness. I look to Ezra, and motion him to give Steve a ticket. Ezra shakes his head "no" and goes back to staring at the ceiling.

"Now, just sit right back, and you'll hear a tale…" says Manning, and then in joins Peeples with, *"A tale of a fateful trip…"* and then back to Manning, *"This is a tale of the castaways, they're here for a long, long time…"* then like perfect ping pong, Peeples sing-songs, *"They'll have to make the best of things…"* then Manning with a flourish, *"It's an uphill climb!"*

Somehow, in my memory, I know these words. There is a boat. A skipper. A goofball and a man with a blazer and an ascot. But that's all I got and why the fuck are they singing the theme song from *Gilligan's Island*.

I have no idea where that name came from.

"Stop it," I say as I pound a fist on the table.

I want an end to the metaphors, the obfuscations, the "I Can't Believe They're Not Fortune Cookies" answers to my questions. "There are four scared people in this room, and we want answers."

"I'm not scared! I'm pissed," says Steve as he leaps up on his chair. Alex lets his forearm topple like a tree onto Steve and then takes Steve's entire face in his hand and slams him down in his seat and holds on while Steve rants into Alex's palm until he tires, then slumps down, defeated, exhausted, and I think he just might have shrunk again, as his hat is now lower on his forehead.

"You have all been part of a very important research project," Manning announces from the front of the room while Peeples nods, and I swear to myself right now that if they start to rhyme again, I'm going to hope that Alex will crush them with his right index finger.

"Not just here, but in several key areas of the globe. Areas where there is still available land and salt," Peeples adds.

"What sort of research?" I ask.

"We didn't know we were being used like laboratory animals," Alex chimes in, "It would have been nice to have our consent, yes?"

"We did," Manning answers.

"Not mine! I wouldn't have given it!" Steve says, and Alex shoots him a glare but then reconsiders, as the comment is a necessary one.

Buffy launches into an angry and resentful diatribe in what I can only surmise is a Hmong dialect, and Manning responds in kind.

I am very impressed. The last Hmong died out over twenty years ago, and like all dying cultures, took their language with them. Buffy seems calmed. She says "thank you" in Italian – *Grazie* – a lovely word.

"We gave it before the coma, didn't we?" I ask as this is really the only conclusion one can have. "And somehow, we were altered to not remember our pasts, but to be provided with the necessary new memories to move about society. Aren't I right, Dr. Manning?"

"As a researcher, that would be the accepted path," he says, still obtuse as hell and that also angers me.

"Doctor, these people have a right to know what happened, what is happening, and why," and I say this in a surprisingly calm tone, but you see, my problems are over. My arm is back and I'm experiencing erections a race horse would envy. The others are either growing or shrinking or incapable of saying more than one thought in the same language. I feel like I must help protect the interests of the group, much like the first one back from a war must support the ones not yet finished with their tours of duty. I am a measured man. I am a focus group moderator.

"You have been put here to gauge the human species' ability to accept that which is unexplainable," Peeples says. Now we're getting somewhere.

"Why?" Alex asks.

"Because you are not from here. You are from a place far, far away," Manning says, and both of them look at each other with what has to be regarded as The Big Look, like all the beans are about to be spilled on something of such profundity that they worry I might not be evolved enough to comprehend the magnitude of their vagaries.

"We're from fucking Oz?" says Steve and I have no idea what he is talking about. "That makes sense, as you fucking turned me into a Munchkin."

Steve swears a lot. I have seen this before in my groups. Little people swear a lot to make up for the lack of size. I don't know anything about this Oz he talks about or what being a "munchkin" would encompass, but apparently in Oz there were small people, and they were not treated well. And Steve has thrown in with them.

"No, you are not from Oz," Manning says, "But the concept of Oz was one that you absorbed in your early orientation. You were all fed reams of data we collected from signals in space, huge amounts of digital data that represented a daily log of what went on during the relatively short life of this planet. It increased exponentially during The Calamities, as the species sought salvation outside themselves. Perhaps for a rescue. Digital data in black and white, in color, musical data, literature, still and moving images, they threw it all up there to be intercepted, seen, and appreciated. Shot out electronically, dumped into the cosmos. Like the message in the bottle, thrown into the vast ocean, hoping it lands on shore, picked up by somebody who cares and can offer rescue. We studied it all, for many years, saw how it grew more desperate over time. Indeed, they needed help. But we couldn't just arrive until we knew we would be accepted or how we could help them or if we could help them at all. You are our volunteers. But you needed to be acculturated, to know about them, know what they've seen, created, so you could be of the culture. So you could have their cultural memories. We needed to find out if this species could accept another species not of their own visualization. We had seen many disturbing interpretations of what they called aliens. Frightening, really. It made us curious about the quality of their nightmares, their dream lives. Often times, their historical digi records showed species from other planets that looked like bugs, or lizards, and often times, the women had large breasts and bad teeth. Sometimes, confusingly, they depicted others from the cosmos as vampires."

195

"The aliens with the large heads and big eyes were common," adds Peeples.

Manning continues: "We have never encountered anything like that in the universe. Any universe. Our former enemy, the Pangs, actually looked much like the Earth's small dogs, with opposable thumbs, of course. But that's about as bad as it gets. That these people had skinned their fears to look like slimy, metal-toothed monsters with tails and saliva that can melt metal or bite their way past bone and ribcage was of great concern to us. Oh, and there were the ones that seemed to always pop out of stomachs. That was one of the most curious expressions of all. But our study of anorexia seemed to explain that obsession," and then Manning pings it over to Peeples. "Isn't that correct Doctor?"

Peeples nods and steps forward.

"So each of you underwent a massive feed of the images and historical data into the memory lobe of your thought centers, what the humans call the brain, which, in many ways, is superior to our own. Except for the right side, which generally screws them up big time," he explains and now he pongs back to Manning...

"But not each of you could retain the same information. We hadn't counted on that. We think it is because some of the information, the images, are so shocking to some of you that it tainted the complete transferral. There is a possibility that we tried to feed too much into your memory centers, and that a natural process of selecting went on, in order to fit what it could."

The respondents at the table hear them, but it's clear much is escaping comprehension.

"*No problemo*," says Peeples, "It made you different anyway. And that was the point. There was a certain level that we expected your intelligence to solve certain issues, which is why we wanted you to think hard, write diaries, and talk to yourselves or to the appointed nano-creatures we set you up with."

"I had fish," says Alex.

"I owned a hamster," says Steve.

"I had a dog," I say.

"Escargot!" says Buffy. Which is French for snail but it wasn't a snail that was her nano-creature. Escargot is the name of her tiny dog, which is a relief as it would suck if she had to talk to a snail all day. At least you can walk a dog.

Ezra dims the lights.

Peeples handles a remote, points it at the far white wall, and gives us a preamble. "Now, get comfortable, and watch this little film. We made it both as a re-immersion piece and as an advance film to the CRL to explain who we are."

"Before we start, understand, you are Valarians. From the planet Valaria," says Manning.

"A what from where?" I ask, as I need to register this a little harder.

"Valaria," Manning says. "Some two hundred light years from Earth."

"Then why was it never discovered by Earth telescope?" I ask, as Earth had some pretty cool space technology, from my memory and readings.

"We like to say that Earthlings are three tugaluffs short of a petricid," Peeples says, and that causes all of us to tilt our heads to one side. "Oh yes, You have not been re-entered. Tugaluffs are a food we eat, and a petricid is a meal many eat together." Peeples explains. "Now, pay attention."

Manning jumps in, "Which means they can't ever put a petricid together because they are three tugaluffs…"

"I got it," I say to save him the embarrassment of stating the obvious.

A black and white digi, very grainy, appears on the wall. Manning and Peeples stand to the side of the room and watch our expressions as we watch it. I look around for a one-way mirror and there's none, so unless there are cameras somewhere, we are not being watched.

A planet appears on the screen. It's blackish for the most part and in certain wide swaths, both reddish and greenish. Not as pretty as Earth, as it is true to an extent, that in the beauty pageants of planets, Earth is a serious front runner, or used to be, at one time, when it was referred to as the Blue Marble.

What can be construed in Earth parlance as a "spaceship" zooms out of the planet and I don't think it's real, as it looks a little fanciful and not unlike some of the science fiction digi's I've seen or remember. In the contrail of the spaceship, a title emerges, white type on the black of space, and it says in a very happy and welcoming Marker Felt font:

HELLO, PEOPLE OF EARTH. FROM YOUR NEIGHBORS – THE VALARIANS.

Then Manning appears on the screen.

"That's me," says the real Manning, almost like an excited child who sees himself in a public digi.

The video shot of Dr. Manning has him sitting behind a shiny metal desk. He wears what looks like a band-leader's uniform…

The real Manning whispers in my ear, *"It starts with a 't' and it ends with an 'e' and that spells trouble, trouble in River City!"* He sings this at whisper force and with great relish, pushing a tremendous amount of his breath on the back of my neck, especially at the "t" and "trouble" and "City." Manning likes sucking on mints, so now the air I breathe is minty fresh.

"I loved that transmission," he mints on, "Most of it wasn't very clear, but this song was, perhaps because it was part of many replays, as if it might have been the most important part of the story. We also received a lot of transmissions of something called *Hello Dolly* but I like this one the best. It was very popular in Valaria for a while. Do you remember it?"

"Shhh!" I say and he answers with a very apologetic, "Yes, of course, sorry."

The promotional digi for Valaria continues. I see a place with black sands. These are the black sands of my visions in the ambulance. There are men working, in protective suits, working equipment, hoses and tanks and meters and gauges. As the camera moves, what looks like oil spurts from the ground. When it does, a small band of men place a heavy cap on the hole and the spurting stops. Hoses travel to a big bus-like vehicle, and it seems like the oil is being poured into the bus. Then the bus takes off, and then the bus flies, and then the bus is in space, and then the bus lets the oil out and the oil catches fire and burns up.

Manning provides the narration for the film:

"As you can see, Valaria is abundant in oil. Too much in fact. We must cart it off to space and let it burn up, heated by our nearest star. Valaria is a friendly planet…" and here the images turn to the taffy-like city I saw in my visions, and we visit with people on the streets, which are clean and well maintained, though there are some puddles of what seems to be oil at the edge of the rounded curbs.

The people, or the Valarians, are all very similar to humans, or at least to the humans I've had contact with. And I don't see any freaks. But they don't have noses. The place on their face where their noses should be is just a clean flat plane. Manning's narrative continues: "As you can see, the biggest difference between a Valarian and an Earthling is the absence of the proboscis. We breathe less than you on Earth, and we tend to breathe mostly from our ears and the pores in our skin, which is very much like yours except more active in both the intake of air and the release of water."

That explains why everyone looks slightly moist.

He continues as I see images of Valarian families playing in a park, and little Valarian children being scolded by their Valarian parents for splashing in an oil puddle. Everyone's clothes are also a little murky, and my assumption is that this is because of the abundant and random oil.

After a bunch of images of the peaceful and playful Valarians, the images go to an animation of the planets and more Manning narrative: "Valaria is located well past your Pluto, past the dark zone and went unnoticed by even your most sophisticated telescopes, which at the time of The Calamities, you were developing at breakneck speed. Of course, they were all destroyed during the many revolutions, riots, and wars as – and we don't mean this as an insult – your fear and ignorance pushed you to destroy most of the technology that might have helped you discover other planets, other peoples, other life, both superior to your own and different in complementary ways. We believe this great destruction was due to the threat felt by your religious institutions. We believe you were, as a species, on the verge of discovering life on other planets – and we're not talking fungus or ice crystals here – and so the concept of one god was threatened."

I'm going to tell Manning and Peeples to take this section out of the film, as there is no advantage in telling fearful and ignorant people that they are fearful and ignorant. In my experience, they are likely to beat you up.

Dr. Peeples joins Manning on the screen: "We have been involved – during the past year – with an outbound fact-finding mission to see if you gentle people of Earth..." – and I will tell them to keep this part in even though it's a total lie. These people are as gentle as overweight two-year-old twins after ten cups of espresso and a big bar of "I Refuse to Accept It's Not Chocolate." The Calamities were not all caused by natural disasters. Man had a big hand in keeping the fires burning. Wars were waged when natural disasters proved too hard to recover from. Wars are a great diversion and can be shrunk or made larger based on how a general wakes up in the morning.

Back to Peeples: "...to see if you gentle people of Earth would accept others not of your planet. Especially if it is a symbiotic relationship. We sent four representatives, not including myself and Dr. Manning, to live amongst you, and to each have a separate affliction..."

And Manning steps in to clear this up, saying, "Not afflictions really, but certain physical differences, unusual for your species, but requiring acceptance nonetheless. Conditions of, let's say, continued physical growth or its opposite; shrinkage..." and Steve jumps up and barks, "That's me!" like he just won an award for having fingers the size of lentils. Alex says, "I was not accepted as I was getting larger. I worked in a Big and Tall Man's shop, but then I became too big and tall and then they fire me. How big and tall do you have to be before you are too big and tall? I thought they would be forgiving. No!" and he slams his hand on the table, nearly causing it to split in two, but popping Steve off his seat, then landing him on his ass back on the chair.

Manning continues, "Or the loss of the use of one's penis or the inability to continue a conversation in one language for more than forty-five seconds," and Buffy swears and Alex groans and I'm wondering if the good doctors rehearsed this speech for the film at all, as Peeples has stammered a couple of times and Manning seems to wander.

They must have thought they had this brilliant way to figure out whether Earth would accept an alien life form without realizing that everyone here has some sort of affliction and is living a shit life, so how can you find out about "alien" acceptance if all you really are is another handicapped human living a shit life. And I have seen some rough afflictions. The Siamese twins come to mind. And they were happy.

Then, on the screen, I see a noseless and hairless Alex come into the frame. He waves and says, "Hello, my name is Tord. On your planet I will call myself Alex, after the husband in *The Donna Reed Show*, which we received many transmissions of. It was one of my favorites, and the man, Carl Betz, had a strong chin. I will be growing at a mysterious rate. But I will not know this. I will be human and I will react as a human and you will react to me as a human, a neighbor, and, I hope, a friend. Thank you."

And then a noseless and hairless Steve – normal size and not bad looking – walks into the digi frame, waves, and says, "Hello, my name is Orst and I will be shrinking at an unprecedented rate. I hope you understand. I look forward to driving many of your smaller cars." And then Buffy walks on and waves, and because her nose is so small anyway, she really doesn't look all that different. It seems like Buffy would be physically comfortable on any planet, which perhaps is common amongst those perceived to be good looking. She just waves and says, "Hello," in perfect English and the Buffy that sits in the room pounds her fist on the table and starts muttering in Thai or something very Asian with an emphatic chop-chop sound.

"Her Valarian name was also Buffy. She was born during an age when the new parents were trying different names for their children," Manning explains.

"Tiffany was also popular," adds Peeples.

Then there is another man on the screen and I think it is me.

I have no nose. I touch my nose on my face as I watch my digi avatar wave at the audience and say, "Hello, my name is Forn. Forn 683. I am the chief philosopher of this mission, responsible for recording my thoughts and conducting interviews with humans of all walks of life. It will be my responsibility, upon return, to gather the information of the four voyagers and compile it into the great new book that we might, as joined civilizations, use to guide our actions and behaviors. With Doctors Manning and Peeples, we will probe the needs and desires, the limitations and abilities of the people of Earth. We will, in exchange for our habitation on your planet, give you all the oil you require. In return, we need salt. You have plenty of that, and as a species, we need it to survive. So, what do you say?"

And then, in unison, all of us put on our fake noses and wave to the gentle peoples of Earth. And I realize that, on Valaria, I am a very important man.

*****

The wall goes black. The lights come back on.

"That's it?" I ask. "That's the extent of the digi?"

"It's as far as we got," Manning says, "We were going to put together a more complete film while we were here, but we got a little sidetracked. There was so much to learn, we were overwhelmed and understaffed."

"But first, we need to tell you about yourselves," says Peeples.

"Yes," Alex – or Tord – says, "You have a lot of explaining to do."

"'Splaining to do," Manning chuckles as he says "'splaining" in a sort of Spanish accent. "The transmissions became the foundation for your cultural education. This feeding was the 'coma' you were put under, so that your minds could absorb the data without stress. Then, of course, we affected your genetics to create the conditions you would experience."

"Valarians are a programmable species. We can alter our genetic codes to achieve whatever condition we want," Manning says. "So, for a defined period, Tord can grow, Orst can shrink, and Buffy's brain has been programmed for periodic linguistic shift."

"And I can grow a limb?" I ask, as this would sure-as-shit solve some stuff for me.

"We didn't intend for you to lose an arm, Forn," says Peeples. "Erectile dysfunction was all we programmed you to suffer. Losing the arm was what they call a...a..." and Peeples searches his brain for some expression to sum up what losing my arm was to them when Manning chimes in, "A Lucky Strike extra!"

"You knew his arm would grow back and you never told him?" Steve – Orst – asks.

"It would ruin the research model," I say, and Manning and Peeples nod.

"The reason I had to talk to both my dog and myself, and occasionally think about events really hard, very specifically and remember the details, is because you've buried a transmitter in my brain, am I not correct? You have buried transmitters in all our brains, yes?"

Manning and Peeples shift uncomfortably, then nod yes. Then shake their head no.

"But we had other ways of recording the experiences of the others. We needed verbals from you. You are most skilled at organizing your thoughts in a linear fashion, as you are rather a celebrity on Valaria for doing just that. In fact, you'll be pleased to know, you transmit every third short cycle and the population looks forward to watching you talk about what you are thinking about. We didn't want to put the same technology in all the subjects." Manning explains.

"And why not?" Alex/Tord asks.

"Well, we did want to actually. But it's very expensive. And our budget for this project was cut," says Peeples, and he's pretty sheepish about it.

As he should be.

It means Valaria is as fucked up as Earth, with budget cuts and money spent wastefully. It means they are not just absent noses, they don't have good money managers either.

"No, Forn, not wastefully," and I realize that they can access my thoughts as I'm having them. They must have receptor chips hooked to mine.

"Yes, that's it. Receptor chips," says Manning and now I think real hard for him to cut it out and stop paying close attention to my thoughts.

"OK," he says as he adjusts a small dial on a band he wears on his wrist as he talks. "Thank you," I respond to his acknowledgment of my request for cerebral privacy.

"We spent a lot of money investigating, first, how to get more salt out of our planet and then, which other planets have enough salt and what would they take in trade for it. Earth, the furthest away, and our last choice due to the general strangeness and randomness of the transmissions, had salt and desperately needed oil. But the mission cost more than we thought it would. Just figuring out the technology to get us here and back in twenty-four Earth hours took three long cycles to develop," and now Manning looks right at me and says, "We put the verbal sound technology chip in your brain as you are more intellectually qualified."

"Hey!" Steve/Orst pipes up, indignant as hell at being considered less qualified than myself. In truth, he is. His observations would surely be all rants and swearing, generally useless as a scientific study. And Buffy, with her affliction of linguistic shift, would be a nightmare to translate and, of course, you could lose a lot in the translation. Tord might have been able, but his affliction would be trouble on any planet I think. Giants might be universally shunned.

"Your memories," Manning says in a way that makes me think my memories are the money shot on this trip, "will be organized, and you shall expand upon them, and it will be called *Book of John*. You are to make it enjoyable to read, much like the authors of Earth when people read. It needs to have some familiarity to it, perhaps in the style of the Elmore Leonard. He was swell."

"Or the James Patterson oeuvre," adds Peeples, "Those are my favorite, and I heard he wrote a book a day, so how hard can it be?"

Manning nibbles on a sandwich corner as he speaks. "Then of course, with your superb intellect, you would be able interpret the events for both Valarians and humans, so a code of conduct could be established."

"Why not *Book of Forn*?" I ask, as that is my Valarian name.

"We think 'John' will resonate with the humans more," Peeples says.

Now that I know I'm a Valarian, these guys don't impress me so much.

ENTRY 26

ISSUES OF CROSS-SPECIES FERTILIZATION.

At this juncture, John has some intuitive beliefs that Marsha might indeed be pregnant with his spawn, but he is not sure. This is a complication we had not planned for, but now must deal with. Marsha did indeed exhibit a window of ovulation right at the time of John's first ejaculation, and though the window for human fertility is small, John sort of "sailed it home," and now, we have a hybrid species dilemma. The Institute must discuss with John the possibility of removing the egg from the host and growing it back in Valaria. The Mother would have a small lobotomy to remove the memories of the incident, and then put back into her apartment. The Institute would pay her rent for the next 10 years, or until Earth's total destruction, whichever comes first. This seems to be the normal estranged paternal-maternal etiquette. We are still not sure how the more multi-offspring–rich sperm of the Valarian male will affect the human female egg. There is some evidence the human egg can hold up to ten embryos, and the human baby is much larger than the Valarian baby, by about three pounds on average. Valarian births resemble more a litter of kittens in both size and number. We can't be sure how the human female will react to giving birth to a litter of hybrid Valarian/Human offspring, especially without noses, though the lack of a proboscis might be welcome in this case, as the human babies' tend to run all the time. But these are the issues we need to deal with immediately, as our departure must commence in the next two hours.

—We walk the long white, bright, humming hallways to see Marsha.

I haven't thought about her for hours. I don't know what I'm going to tell her. *Hello Marsha! By the way, did I tell you I'm from another planet?* or *Hello Marsha! How do you feel about men without noses?* or *Hello Marsha! Listen, pack a bag, we're going on a little trip…to another galaxy! What? Yes. Bring your bathing suit.* What the fuck do you tell a woman you lived with for the past five months or so that it's time to move to another planet?

"Tell her you love her," Manning says.

"I thought you turned the receptor down?" and I'm a little annoyed; for Chrissakes, do what you said you'd do!

"I did, but your thoughts are so strong now, they are getting through even though the receptors are virtually muted. That is why I say it might be that you are feeling love for her."

Peeples stops a few feet in front of me and spins on his heels.

"She is pregnant with your child," Peeples says.

I stop. Lean against the wall. My fantasy now a reality. I had a suspicion that with all the semen that poured out of my new erection, some must have stuck, but I realize it's all very complicated and involves a great deal of luck to impregnate a woman these days. One out of six women is sterile. One out of four men is sterile or has weak sperm. Bad swimmers they call them. Not me. My guys can do the backstroke.

"That is why the dogbot reacted like it did," says Manning. "It sensed the moment of insemination. It was programmed to be attuned to Marsha's biorhythms as well as record both your voice and movements."

"The coyote attack was especially exciting," adds Peeples.

"Oh yes, we watched that over and over. It was quite the struggle. We almost pulled you from the field right then, but we talked about it and thought that the research hadn't really changed its scope and it might have become deeper," Manning says.

"And we had the opportunity to see how enhanced Earth salt would aid in your healing and rejuvenating process," Peeples says, "Big thumbs up!"

"What does she know?" I ask.

"Not much. We left that to you," Manning says.

"No noses, and we breathe and hear from our ears, right?"

"Is there a problem?" Peeples asks, and it's evident he doesn't get the shock Marsha will undergo when she hears that not only am I not human, she is pregnant with an alien baby and we breathe out of our ears. He thinks she'll take it all in stride. "Humans have been educated by worse alternative pregnancies," Manning says. "We have transmissions of hundreds of their stories of alien impregnation…"

"Even some transmissions of demon births…" adds Peeples.

"Can she have a half alien–half human child? Can her body support that?" I ask, as I don't want Marsha to die in some stagecoach pregnancy. Not in outer space.

"Oh, we don't let the females of our species carry their babies to birth. It's barbaric. We extract the fetus and grow it in the growth labs, away from the stresses of the mother's daily life," Peeples says and I don't like it.

I know how she looked at the rare pregnant woman in the street. I know how she watched digi's of birth stories and wondered if she would ever have that experience. It seems that Earth women have two times in their lives to fully experience their sexual identities: menstruation and childbirth. I am Forn. This is my book. So…

"She's going to have the baby herself. No labs. She is going to birth it naturally," and this puts Manning and Peeples on their heels. They look at each other, worried, as this might be beyond their medical pay scale. Of course, when I say naturally, I don't mean squatting in the forest. I mean…and I don't really know what I mean, as I have never seen a baby being born. Nothing in the memory banks, or that Manning and Peeple downloaded into my brain for this research. Just a notion. But whatever it is, perhaps they have no concept of it either.

Doesn't matter. Before we leave Earth, we'll find a copy of *Natural Childbirth for Dummies*. They must have covered this subject.

"We'll consult back on Valaria. We want the same thing as you do: her safety, and the child's safety," Manning reassures me. I'm only somewhat reassured. But suddenly I am feeling strongly paternalistic, very protective, almost what I would imagine the ancient Vikings were like. I have a new feeling in my testicles and penis. Which reminds me…

"What was the reaction I had with the huge erection? Why was I so suddenly potent, and no longer needed the penis pump?"

"We think it might have been the confluence of the arm healing, the cells rejuvenating at a rapid pace, and the addition of the Earth salts, which seem richer in sodium than our own," says Peeples. "We haven't analyzed the chemical makeup, so we are just theorizing now."

"Well, I like it. Do we have more salt?" I ask.

"Yes, we have enough for about a year or so," Manning adds.

"But we'll have to ration," Peeples says.

One year of great sex. I'll take it.

"As a celebrity, do I get more than other Valarians?" I ask and now, right now, I'm ashamed. Six months here and I adopted some of the worst characteristics of my human hosts.

"But on Valaria, we'll reverse the erectile dysfunction. You'll be normal, like you were before you left, and you had quite the reputation," says Manning.

"But…" says Peeples.

"But what?" I ask.

"You preferred the male of our species," Manning gently informs me.

Fine. I'm not just not human, on my own planet I'm a homosexual. *Hello Marsha,* I recite in my mind, *Look I have something to tell you: I'm not of this planet, you're pregnant with an alien baby, I have no nose and breathe out of my ears, and I'm gay, but the good news is, on Valaria, I'm a celebrity.*

Fuck. This is not news I'd want to wake up to.

*****

Marsha's sound asleep in a nanotech recovery room decorated exactly like our bedroom, down to the errant brown sock pushed up into a corner that has been there for over one month.

She has been through a lot of unexplained bullshit, and I suspect her brain, out of self-preservation, has decided to put itself to sleep. It's good she will wake up in her "avatar" bedroom, as I don't want her to go through any more shock, and she should be in a familiar setting when she finds out she's pregnant, the father's from another planet, and she is about to spend her last hour on Earth.

Manning, Peeples, and I stand outside and peer in through a window on the door to her room. I look at her belly and I can swear it is slightly bigger than when we were taken in.

"Will it go the nine months?" I ask.

"We have no idea how long gestation will take for a half-Earthling, half-Valarian birth," Peeples says over the microphones.

"The reason we remove the fetuses from the mother is that a Valarian litter can take over two years," Manning says. And I do have a memory of this. Unlike Earth amnesia patients, our brain cells are more resilient, which is a result of a longer gestation period. One might assume that the human memory, or the brain cells associated with it, might have been

207

weakened by the constant exposure to the Three Stooges, and the Abbott
Costello men.

But for Marsha, holding a baby, or many babies, for two years will be
intolerable. Too much stress on her body and diet, with the requisite need
of the pregnant human female for ice cream.

"Is there ice cream on Valaria?" I ask.

"No, but we have something close. We make it oil based versus dairy
based. I've already called in an order," says Manning.

Great. Millions of miles from home and we get greeted by an "I Can't
Believe" product…Valarian style.

"I'd like to be alone with her for a while," I tell them.

"OK, but hurry, we'll need to shove off before sunrise," Manning
tells me.

Shove off? Is that what an advanced alien culture does with their space
ships when they leave a planet they have been stealthily inhabiting for half
an Earth year? This is no doubt something Manning and Peeples picked
up from the many transmissions, and I can only assume the pirate ones.

"Are we going to show them that film, you know, the CRL or the
localities? Are we coming here for the exchange of oil and salt?" I ask, and
the results of this grand experiment still feel vague.

They stop in their tracks, and turn to face me.

"No…Forn," Manning starts and I hope he explains the whole thing,
as Peeples can't explain his way out of a paper bag. "Earth will cease to
exist in the next eight months."

"Or sooner. Or later," Peeples adds.

"More earthquakes?" I ask.

"No," he answers.

"Nuclear war?"

"No."

"Asteroids from space?"

"No."

"It has already started," says Peeples, "Some of the land collapses of
late, especially the one in the Middle East."

There was a report, unverified, that a two-thousand-square-mile chunk
of desert fell a thousand feet below the planet surface. It killed all who were
on the land, but more importantly, it sent up another devastating plume of
dust that continues to darken the sky eight months later. But the reports
are sketchy, so I assumed they were mostly rumor.

"They have sucked the energy out of it," Manning says. "It's almost all gone, and unfortunately, it was the only thing supporting the exoskeleton. Oil, natural gas, minerals, they were the stuffing and the glue that held the whole 'shebang', nice word that, together. The entire planet is set to collapse on itself in about eight months."

"And then, depending on the force, it will become a black hole..." Peeples adds, "Sucking all that is around it. Perhaps even their sun. In fact, it could be trouble for much of the galaxy..."

"Or just a bad weather day. We don't know," Manning adds.

"So this is a guess?"

"All science is a guess, John. It is only religion that is sure," Manning says.

"You must acclimate your Marsha to her new future," says Peeples. "We fought The Institute's dictate that we take the embryo, and leave her here. So she will be largely your responsibility."

"Yeah, well, tell The Institute I would NOT have stood for that," I tell them, and I wouldn't have. The nerve, deciding the fate of others without asking them! I know I would've punched someone. Just like a cowboy!

"Tell her she is quite safe on Valaria. We have many very good restaurants and there is a whole new area that we've made oil free," adds Manning and they resume their walk down the long white corridor.

"Good schools!" adds Peeples, "I know that is a concern to humans, even though they hardly go anymore."

*****

I sit on the edge of the bed and watch her sleep. Her breathing is heavy and full lunged. She is breathing for two, as they say.

I almost wish I could put my hand to her forehead and fill her in on all the news telepathically, so she would receive it while asleep and process the information in her dreams. When she awoke, and wondered if it was a dream, I would have already removed my nose, so then she would say, "Wow, I had a dream you had a nose. I am so glad it was just a dream. You look strange with a nose," or something like that. But I don't think humans are that malleable.

Marsha stirs. Then her eyes open to slits and her slightly revealed pupils look at me through an ocular glaze of a deeply drugged sleep. But she smiles, so I know she is glad to see me.

"Morning," I say and I hand her some juice. It has an anxiety suppressant in it, which I think appropriate for what she is about to undergo, both information wise and the fact that, apparently, we will soon be hurtling through a black hole shortcut to Valaria. Which in its own way is cause for some small modicum of anxiety, even for me.

"How long have I been asleep?" she asks.

"Hours. The full eight you like to get."

"I had the craziest dream, John. Insane. You lost your arm, and then you believed it was growing back and you kept yapping about it and trying to show me, but there was nothing to see. Then, you got this huge hard-on, we made love, no, actually you fucked me and boy it was good. No pump. You even came. And when you came your arm grew back, like, because you came, or something. Like the release of semen sprouted the arm. The more that poured out of you, the more arm poured out of you. Then the stupid dog went nuts and you hit it and it kind of turned into this black cloud or something, then some men in big hooded suits came in and then I woke up and here I am. Crazy, huh?"

"Sometimes dreams are symbolic," I say and why the fuck did I say that?

Marsha sips the juice, and I wish it was really loaded with tranquillizers. She would drop into a near coma and they could reprogram her memory banks on the trip back to Valaria.

"Marsha, your dream…" and this is hard, "was part true."

"Which part?" she asks, looking at both my arms.

"The arm part was a dream. No problem with the arm. That might have been symbolic for some kind of helplessness, even though we know dreams don't mean anything," I tell her as I don't want to complicate all the news with the part about my arm actually growing back. Let her think that was a dream. I'll cover it all later.

Marsha puts the glass of juice down and puts her hand on her belly and lies back on the bed. She rubs her belly like she knows there is something in there, that intuitive, biological maternal instinct kicking in hard. Maybe I start there.

"Marsha, you're pregnant with my baby."

She looks at the ceiling, and smiles.

"Was it all that semen, John? Is that what did it?"

"Yes, that part you thought was a dream was true. I had a massive erectile disruption, maybe from some medication I was taking, or maybe from the fact that I am just getting better."

She smiles and that all seems to make sense to her. So I decide to dive right in: "But here's more news. I'm an alien, from the planet Valaria. Put here as part of an extensive research project to discover the level of tolerance on the part of the human race to those not like them. We are a species fighting for our survival, and you have salt, which is vital to us. We have oil, which remains vital to you. But it seems that Earth is in too much trouble right now. Your people are some mean ass sons of bitches, to put it in the vernacular. And so you and I will be going back to Valaria so you can have the baby or babies, as Valarian sperm tends to create what you call litters. You could have up to ten or twelve little Valarians. Also, normally, I don't have a nose, but, and you'll be glad to know this, on Valaria, I am a pretty important man, live in a nice house, and my Valarian name is Forn. You mustn't think of me as an alien. Think of me as a person, from another planet. We good?" Nailed it. As clear a download as could be made.

Marsha smiles at me and says, "You're so funny," then turns her head and starts to snore.

*****

Tord carries Marsha down an infinite white corridor. He has grown some more. Apparently, they can't adjust his condition until we get back to Valaria. Orst neither. He now resides in a shoe box that Peeples carries around.

Tord's hand spreads from the top of her head to the middle of her back. He is, in fact, holding an entire human in his hands, not even using his arms.

"Doctors tell me I must go back now," he says in a much-deeper-than-five-hours-ago voice. "They say it's dangerous to grow anymore. Dangerous to internal organs, which don't grow as much," he says as I try to keep up with his big looping strides.

*****

"We had thought of extracting the egg, John, and growing it without the mother. It's still an option," Manning says as Tord slides Marsha from his hand to a couch in the office. We are all here: Tord, Orst, Manning, Peeples, Marsha, myself and Buffy.

Ezra stands guard with a bowl of hot towels should Marsha need one.

211

"That's not going to happen," I tell Manning. "She goes back with me, we run all the tests we need for the feasibility of her keeping the baby, or babies, to term. If not, we'll figure it out then."

The doctors nod. I am big in Valaria. Celebrity has gravitas.

"No one is taking my baby," and it's Marsha.

She struggles up on her elbows, and plants her feet on the floor. She looks around the room, from a smiling big toothed Tord, to the diminutive Orst peeking out of the shoe box, to a befuddled Buffy, speaking quietly to Peeples in six different languages while she files her nails

"I don't know who you people think you are…"

"We're Valarians," says Peeples, abruptly.

"Yeah, well great! Let me tell you something, we human beings, especially the female kind, are not to be trifled with!" she says.

Manning leans forward in his chair, ever the paternal shrink, clasps his hands in front of him, and says, "We know. We actually fear the human race greatly. Though we can do all sorts of what you would consider advanced feats, both technologically and medically, you have spent most of your intellectual capital creating weapons to destroy each other and all other things generally. It is an awesome thing. In fact, one of the things that appealed to us, should it have worked out, is we felt we would be safe from any alien invasion here on Earth. Dr. Peeples and myself were consistently amused and impressed with your history of fear-based digi's, both from The Age of Black and White and The Age of Color, that showed you cowering in the face of alien invasion, and how difficult it was for you to defend yourself. One of our favorites was the one where the aliens seemed to die off from a bad cold."

"*War of Worlds*, by H.G Bradbury, I think," adds Peeples.

"*War of Words?*" Manning asks. They both ponder that title confusion, then…

"*Worlds!*" Peeples asserts. Good. One down.

"Rest assured," Manning continues, "There are no beings out there in the galaxy with your collection of weaponry. A hostile civilization doesn't have a chance against you guys. In fact, you are the aliens we fear. Because of the degree of fear you had for outsiders, those not like yourselves, you evolved to meet the fear, and then some. You guys nailed it. Nice job."

Marsha looks around the room, scans the odd cast of characters. I'd be happier not to have to continue to explain things to her, just to get this going and launch off to Valaria, without more mumbo-jumbo. Let her experience real immersion, in one big splashy moment. We'll explain then. More so, I need all my real memory back, so I can be the one doing the explaining.

"John, let's go home now. This is tiring. I have no idea who these freaks are, but I just want to go home. OK?"

"But more importantly, in about seventy-two hours or so, this planet is toast," adds Manning, and that statement is curious, because it's so assured. "There have been several explosions on the surface of the sun that are indications of another disturbance. We think it is an incidence of several solar flares by other stars. The flares by your own sun and the simultaneous flaring of these other stars plus the huge holes in your ozone will pretty much cook the planet in the next two weeks. It won't be pretty. In the first twenty-four hours, three million people will die. After that, with the fires and smoke, another ten million. Soon, the planet will be pretty much charred. The water will have evaporated. You will all be radiated beyond any curative. So..." and Manning slaps his hands on his knees and says, "...let's get packing!"

"OK, OK, calm down. This is pure speculation," I tell Manning. "The planet isn't going to implode or explode or bake or fall from the galaxy. It's mostly the Earth people that're scary."

"Maybe. Maybe not. We can't chance it," he replies.

"John, this has been sort of interesting, but I'm ready to go home now," Marsha says, now that we're alone and back in the room. She has already busied herself with packing a small suitcase of her belongings. The good doctors have thought of everything. Marsha's closets are full of nano-facsimiles of her wardrobe, down to the weight and feel of the material. I realize I can't rush her into leaving her planet and life this fast. This will take some time. I have five minutes.

I'm going to let her pack these facsimiles. It calms her, but I know I have to level with her completely. Work her through this. I can hear myself talking, but in an out-of-body way, reciting all I know, and that we are indeed in peril if we stay. She looks at me like she did when I told her my arm was growing back. Patient, but beyond skeptical.

I tell her not to pack everything, just a few things and that, "We can buy more when we reach Valaria. And don't forget, soon most of these things won't fit anymore."

Marsha sits on the bed. It's very quiet right now. And I see a tear tumble down her cheek.

"You're not kidding, are you?"

"No. I am what is to you an alien. You are to me what is an alien. So, in that, we have a lot in common." I dab her cheek with a tissue. I can see in her eyes this is more about having someone she can trust on this voyage than any deeply emotional thing. After all, I have been revealed to be an inhabitant of another planet and a same-sex coupler. Not many relationships can survive that. She can't possibly feel that much for me, but I must make her feel secure. "We've been through a great deal together, and I think there is a deep bond between us. You're going to have my baby. You are the mother of my child. I will take care of both of you," I tell her in the most sincere tone I can muster.

"I have a half-alien baby?" she says as she rubs her belly again. "Will it have a nose?" and this is something I hadn't thought about. Will the child carry the genetic makeup for a nose and nostrils? Will it smell with it? If the child has a nose and can smell with it, will it also smell, like we do, with its ears? Will that be too much smell? Or will there be just a half of a nose, like just a bump with one nostril? If we have a litter, will noses be scattered amongst them randomly? Regardless, we can remove the nose, fix the face, and relocate the sense of smell to the ears.

"I don't want our baby to get ostracized," she says. "How do I know they will accept me? What if, wherever I go, the Valarians just stare at my nose?"

I don't really know how to answer that. I have got to get my memory returned to what I know about my planet and its customs. But Marsha needs an answer. I think it's a big step to leave your planet forever to live on another one, with an alien litter in your belly whose father is a gay man with no nose. Thank god I'm famous.

I will miss this place. I will miss the chaos and irrational behavior, the anger and hate, the plants and people. I will miss the struggle. In the struggle, you feel very alive, even though they were all at different stages of dying.

But not for long. They'll wipe out my memory upon return, except the most immediate of Marsha and the pregnancy. They need to make room for the real memories. I might have some traces of the past, maybe a ghosting of the Stooges to keep my memories of Earth on the light side, with some slapstick relief. That's why I have been so ardently recording my thoughts.

"They won't," I tell her, "Valarians are a kind people. And I have a big house in the country, so not many people will see you." I'm not sure about the house part. But what woman doesn't want a big house in the country?

"You'll take care of me, won't you, John? You won't abandon me? It's bad enough moving cross-country for a man who then dumps you. But out of the solar system?"

*****

Manning, Peeples, and Lassie sit at a console flipping switches.

I'm amazed at the dexterity of the dog's paws, and realize she must have been reprogrammed to have an opposable thumb.

We are in the focus group room that I remember. There is no longer a table in the room. It's been transformed. Six wide, well-cushioned and seat-belted chairs – three by three – sit in the middle of the room. The observation room behind the one-way mirror is the control console.

Tord, Orst and Buffy sit in three chairs in front. Marsha and I sit behind. Orst has been buckled in but is buffeted by pillows and sandbags. Tord sits next to him, and will be responsible for placing his hand over Orst during any turbulence.

Buffy sits next to Orst, trying to ignore his leering eyes. Orst seems to be quite attracted to Buffy. This is not reciprocal.

I help Marsha with her seat belt. She's accepting of the adventure now, more compliant, resigned even, and I sense less worry on her part. She realizes, based on what she knows, that she would not survive the last big Calamity, the true Apocalypse, so this is survival. And frankly, was she ever all that happy on Earth?

"Valaria is many millions of your miles from Pluto," Manning informs us. "It would take approximately nine of your Earth years to reach it. But we'll do it in about five and a half hours."

Marsha smiles weakly. "John, I'm not making trouble…" she says, "And God knows, I'm no scientist. But I think that if a human being, you know, like me, travels that fast, we turn into soup, yes?"

With all she knows right now, and since the humans have spent so much time and money in weaponry and ignored solving the intricacies of space travel, due to the Exceptionalism Movement, which convinced the populace that Earth was the best planet in the universe so why should they want to go anywhere else, she's right. But due to the fact that Valarians are true space adventurers and like to vacation on other planets, especially those with more salt, we have spent almost all our intellectual and engineering capital on space travel. I can't reassure her with science. I must try with something she might have some familiarity with. I hark back to a digi memory…

"Marsha. This isn't *Wagon Train*," I say to her and receive a blank look that tells me she has no idea what that means. But it was a western from the Age of Black and White about the way people traveled centuries ago when they named their wagons Chuck.

"Prepare thrusters," Peeples orders, and Lassie quickly flips switches and does a run of all systems.

The room both shakes and vibrates. The flesh of my buttocks tingles. I can hear Steve's little teeth chatter. Marsha holds my hand. Her hand is clammy.

Then, the shaking is no more. The vibrations level out to a slight tingling, not at all unpleasant. A panel in front of the control console opens up, reveals the stars. We have already broken through Earth's atmosphere, and we're surrounded by distant stars. Lassie locks onto one of them. It appears on the screen in front of her. She enters some data, and puts the craft into autopilot, sits back in her chair, puts her paws behind her head and her feet up on the console. Seriously, if I knew she could actually fly a spaceship, I would not have hit her over the head.

"Valaria," Manning notes.

"Home," Peeples counters.

Several white-coated Valarians enter the room. I can tell they are Valarians because they don't have noses. And there's Ezra, now also noseless. He's better off without it. I wonder how many times, as a Ticketist, he was punched in his Earth nose. I bet he's glad he no longer has that target on his face.

They have trays of drinks and little sandwiches and they serve each of us. I look at Marsha. She sights the nose free Valarians, and I think she's OK with it.

"Marsha?"

"Yes, John?"

"You're OK with this? Me? The baby?"

"Give me time," she says, and I understand.

"I'm not the man you wanted to wind up with, am I?"

"No, John. You're the man I wound up with," she says as she toasts my glass. "We can't always get what we want, so we must be happy with what we get," and with that she downs the whole drink.

We pass through the rings of Saturn. It's quite beautiful. I look at her, and feel the romance in the moment. "To Valaria, then," and I kiss her on the lips, and I sense immediately that without a nose, kissing would feel even better.